DARKLAND ELF

THE WORLD OF ELF, BOOK 2

TERRY SPEAR

WILDE INK PUBLISHING

To all my Shadow Elf fans who have been waiting patiently for the second book in the series!

SYNOPSIS

As a motivational inspirer, Eloria's mission is to convince her friend Persephonice to leave the elf world behind. She knows that if she can't, she will be stuck in their world herself. But what she finds in the primitive elf world is magic and a connection she never thought possible.

Viator is a prince of the darkland elves and captures one of those extraordinary creatures like Persephonice to turn over to his father, but his people worry about the prophecy where a girl from another world would take over their kingdom. He's not giving her up as he realizes he needs her to help fulfill his mission to make his wings transparent. And she has to see where his dangerous quests will take them both...if they can survive the trials.

1

As soon as Eloria Cresthaven heard the rumors of what her next mission would entail, she was hopeful it was all true. She was reservedly thrilled—because she couldn't wait to see her best friend, Persephonice, and ensure she was all right and living happily on the elves' planet. But Eloria was also very much concerned she would find that her friend was not okay. Even so, Eloria's job was to return her to the ship, no matter what. The problem was Persephonice might not want to be rescued. This could be one mission where no one won.

Then her wristband communicator beeped, and she glanced at the message: *You're to report to the commander's office immediately.*

She hoped this could only be good news and the rumors that she would seek out Persephonice were true. She straightened and walked at a fast pace down the corridor to the elevator, took it to the ship's fourth floor, and exited.

When she reached the command passage, she inclined her head in the direction of every person she passed in greeting. All of them outranked her by several ranks. She reached the office of the commander and pushed a button. "Sir, Lieutenant Eloria Cresthaven reporting as ordered."

"Enter," the commander said gruffly.

She was trying to keep her excitement contained and look as serious—and professional—as she could. She was a top academy graduate, and she had to prove she had earned the accolades for professionalism and distinguished service—always. It wasn't enough to just graduate with the distinction.

Eloria was known as a motivational inspirer, and her occupation meant she *wasn't* assigned a lifemate—as one was not required for her job. It also meant that personality-wise, she was always over-the-top enthusiastic about her missions and inspiring others in the same way. It was part of who she was. Sometimes she annoyed her fellow shipmates who didn't want to be...inspired.

"Your mission, Lieutenant, is to locate my daughter, Persephonice, and return her to the ship—at once. I want you to see this tape." He pushed a button and the image flashed across a screen on one of the walls.

Eloria observed the tape that showed Persephonice defying her father after he transported her to their spaceship, and she sent herself right back to the elves' world. Only certain important people had been allowed to see the tape—on a need-to-know basis, she knew. She figured he believed she needed to know the frame of mind Persephonice had been in when she disobeyed her father, or he would never have shown a junior officer the tape.

She noticed then a woman standing off to the side, observing her. She was Dr. Becca Truce, the ship's psychologist, blond hair swept up in a bun, blue-eyed, cagey. "Why don't you have a seat?" She motioned to a leather chair in front of the commander's desk.

Eloria took a seat, knowing the ploy. Make her comfortable

so that the good doctor could set her at ease before she wanted something from her—usually something Eloria didn't want to give her. Eloria was an inspirational motivator who helped people find a way to feel good about themselves. She wasn't about to be used to inspire others to do what went against everything they believed in.

"Persephonice has been brainwashed into believing she had to return to the planet," the doctor said, folding her arms.

Which was a defensive posture, as if Dr. Truce believed Eloria wouldn't buy into her statement. Which she didn't. Not exactly. Not that if she learned more of the situation, Eloria might see that what the doctor said was true. But she would determine this on her own.

"By the elves?" Eloria asked, but she didn't see any indication of that on the tape. Persephonice had been frantic to make her escape from the ship before they pulled away from the elves' airspace.

Not only that, but Persephonice had immediately ditched the transporter bracelet as well, so her father couldn't return her in that manner. He'd tried several times, making several passes over the planet where she'd disappeared. The ship's crew hadn't had this much excitement since they'd first dropped Persephonice off on the planet so they could repair the ship, and she could deter anyone from seeing it. But many believed her father hadn't planned to return for her once he'd left her there. So why did he want her back so badly now? To save face? Rumors abounded that many of the ship's crew felt he was wrong in leaving her there in the first place, as punishment for losing her lifemate before they were mated.

Now, Eloria turned her attention to Persephonice's father, Horatio Whitethorn, commander of the Starship Calligraph, a science exploratory vessel. His blue eyes were narrowed, wary, his red hair streaked with gray.

Eloria was unsure if she was supposed to retrieve her friend by force or choice. She suspected nothing less than force would do. Eloria had been trained as a warrior special class with the additional talent of being a gifted motivational inspirer. Which was a fancy way of saying she could persuade some beings on other planets to do things her way without causing any bloodshed.

Not that she could control beings' minds or anything, but she could often use her wit to convince them. But she never used it to promote violence.

For the first time since she'd joined the crew, she had an audience with Persephonice's imperious father when—even though Eloria had been her best friend—he had never spoken once to her in the three years Eloria had been onboard the ship. She'd seen the doctor numerous times, who had quizzed her in depth about her missions and their outcomes. She'd had two really bad cases with two really bad outcomes that had haunted her for all this time, but no way would she have discussed those with the doc. If she had, they would have grounded Eloria on their home world. She had nowhere else to go. Nothing else she could do, but to serve on this ship. She couldn't mess that up, no matter what.

Her room was soundproof like all sleeping quarters were, which meant she could wake up screaming and not scare anyone into thinking they were under alien attack. And she had woken herself while screaming at the top of her lungs. Numerous times.

She held her head high, like a warrior would, and gazed into Colonel Whitethorn's cold blue eyes.

"Eloria Cresthaven, you have been trained in many different forms of warfare, can handle several types of weapons, but most of all, you are able to motivate others when the majority of our kind cannot. Not only that, but you are Persephonice's best friend."

Eloria gave a stiff nod, acknowledging everything he said was true.

"I understand you have some talent for magic."

She felt a wave of cold chills slither up her spine.

"You know it is forbidden for anyone to sign onto a ship who has a natural ability to use magic," he said, yet she thought he hoped she might be able to use them in this instance. Why bring them up, otherwise?

"Yes, Commander."

"Good, because if I learn that you do have those abilities, you will be put off at the first inhabitable, civilized planet."

Which meant she would be on her own to find work or a way to return to her planet on her own. Not that she had anyone there anyway.

How did he know about her abilities? Or maybe he was just guessing. He had said something similar to another crew member a few months ago, and she swore the girl didn't have any abilities at all. Or maybe, he was hoping Eloria did have some abilities and could use them to force Persephonice to leave the planet. She wouldn't put it past him to threaten Eloria just so she'd be forced to do the job, or else...

"You will remain behind on Cador, the primitive elf planet, until you have located Persephonice. You will then alert me at once and bring her back to the ship. She has lost her transporter bracelet and has no way to return to us without your help."

Eloria tried to keep her expression neutral, knowing very well, like everyone else on the ship, that Persephonice had ditched the bracelet after escaping the vessel, with no intention of ever returning. Which intrigued Eloria and the other girls her age, who fantasized about the kind of creatures that existed on the planet. Were they handsome? Kindly? Courteous? So intriguing that they had enticed Persephonice to remain there with them forever?

But then, there was Eloria's magic. Which could get her into a lot of trouble anywhere she went so she'd kept it under wraps. What would a primitive being think of that?

A crewman came in and spoke to the commander in private.

Eloria recalled reading the ancient writings of the human world of courtly romance, which of course was all a fantasy, and wondered if in the elf world they had any kind of romance like that. The real kind. Not just in books. She'd also read how in the human world in ancient times the women were forced to wed men for power or wealth, which, unless they were lucky, had nothing to do with love.

Not that the langolar's mates were chosen for love either. A computer decided their fate, depending upon skills and personality tests. Would she have been pleased if one had been picked for her? She didn't believe so. Her skills were such that she was deemed unmateable. A male warrior would not need a female warrior to protect his back and would resent it, truth be told. Any other male might feel intimidated to mate a warrior female. She certainly didn't need a man who felt intimidated by her, or one who thought he was superior.

Not that she was looking for one, or wanted one, but she couldn't help being swept up by the dreams of the other girls on board the ship, who delighted in talking about having the perfectly matched lifemate. She tried to tell herself they were silly when her job was most important. And it was. She'd been on five rescue missions before. *Five.* Instead of serving as part of a combat force, she always acted alone. That's what made her successful. Blending in, developing rapport with the native people, sometimes fighting her way out of a situation, hostage in tow, or talking the hostage takers into releasing their hostage, convincing them it was for their own good, or even sneaking the individual out like a thief in the night. Each of the ways had worked for her in the past.

This time, she wasn't so sure. In the past, the hostages *wanted* to be freed. In her friend's case?

The commander said, "We will be close enough to the planet to transport you there within the hour."

Eloria had never once had this much of a lofty mission to complete before, and she was both excited and wary. If Persephonice truly didn't want to return to the ship, how could Eloria convince her to do so? Would Eloria even want to convince her if her friend was happy where she was? Yet, Eloria was born for these kinds of operations. She thrived on them, the more of a challenge, the better. She didn't decide which ones she would commit to and which ones she wished to forgo. Though she was aware that should she fail at finding or returning Persephonice, she could very well be stuck forever on the primitive planet too.

Why had the commander truly chosen her? Surely someone else on the ship could force the issue better than she could. Someone who wasn't close to her friend. Someone who did it solely as a job. Like she was supposed to do. No emotions. No muss. No fuss. Just retrieve the fellow langolar.

Maybe the commander thought because she had been close to Persephonice, she might be able to convince her to come home when someone else would have to use force to do it. Convincing the person that it was her choice was always the preferred way.

"The primitive planet is populated mostly by elves, isn't it?" she asked. They had very little real information about the inhabitants as they were deemed too primitive to observe.

"As far as we are aware, yes. None of our scientists have studied their world, but they seem to be the top of the food chain there. You will leave as soon as you have your gear packed."

So, he wasn't giving her any time to plan or prepare or chicken out?

Not that she thought of herself as a chicken in any way, but she never went on a mission before learning all she could about the people and the land she was to traverse. Though she really didn't have a choice.

The doctor finally spoke. "You are friends with Persephonice. Best friends, from what I understand. Can you be objective and do as your commander bids?"

Eloria assumed they'd send someone else who wouldn't be concerned with Persephonice's feelings. "Of course I can do this." Not that she truly thought she could convince Persephonice to return. She could be just as stubborn as Eloria at times.

"You have your orders."

"What if she doesn't want to return?" Eloria asked, biting her tongue afterward. She knew she shouldn't have voiced the question as soon as she let the words slip out. She knew the commander didn't mean to give his daughter any choice. Eloria wondered if he truly did care about her and worried for her safety. Or he believed that she belonged with her own people. Or, was it more a case of his controlling nature and saving face in front of his crew when Persephonice had so boldly defied him?

Eloria never believed Persephonice would do such a thing. She'd been so brokenhearted over losing the lifemate matched to her that Eloria thought it had...broken her.

"She has no choice," the commander said.

Just as Eloria surmised.

"The planet is unobservable. The people are so primitive, no amount of studying them will benefit our archives. She *can't* remain there and must be returned at once. You are trained in tracking and are well-suited to fighting the elves, if need be. You cannot take any advanced weapons though, so as not to upset the order of their primitive lives."

Great. A stun gun was her favorite weapon. It knocked a being on its butt, if the creature threatened her with bodily violence. The weapon set on another setting could put the creature to sleep. Much more civilized and easier to manage than other methods she'd have to employ, if she couldn't convince them through conversation. And using her magic skills was sure to baffle them.

"If you need anything else that may aid you in your quest, ask the quartermaster. He will outfit you."

Eloria wanted to ask if she couldn't leave Persephonice behind if she truly was happy and wanted to remain on the planet. But the commander motioned for her to leave with a quick flick of his wrist.

She bowed her head, then executed a proper military turn and headed out of his office.

What if she couldn't find Persephonice? Then what?

What if she lied and said Persephonice was dead? One of the truth-seekers would be able to pull the truth out of her. So nope, that wasn't an option. She realized she didn't have a whole lot of choices this time.

But she was taking her stun gun anyway. And when no one could see her wearing it, she was taking her focusing crystal.

2

W ith trepidation and excitement filling her veins, Eloria exited the commander's office and the door whooshed shut. She considered that, if the outcome wasn't good when she attempted to conduct her mission, she may never see the commander, or the ship for that matter, again.

Practically bouncing on her toes, Lauriston, a violet-eyed girl whose hair was the most unusual white-blond color, met Eloria in the corridor outside the commander's door, then hurried with her in silence as Eloria took the elevator to her quarters two flights up. Lauriston wanted to know just what had transpired between Eloria and the commander, and then she would spread the word like a fire raced across an oxygen-fed ship.

As soon as they walked the distance to Eloria's quarters, Lauriston asked, "What does he want you to do?" Her eyes sparkled with inquisitiveness, and she could barely stand still.

"Return Persephonice to the ship."

Lauriston gave a haughty, little laugh. "We knew it! It shouldn't be difficult to do. She's probably sitting on the very spot where we dropped her off, wishing she hadn't so foolishly lost her transporter bracelet in the ocean. Though I must say when that vicious redheaded half-fish creature landed in the transporter room wearing Persephonice's bracelet, I don't think I've ever seen the commander's face that red with anger before."

Eloria smiled, loving that Persephonice had the nerve to do such a thing. Eloria wasn't certain if she would have done that to defy her own father had he still been alive. Which was the reason she was here, working on this ship as a warrior, special class. Once she had no other prospects, no credits to support her, she'd needed this job and her friendship with Persephonice had made all the difference in her life.

Many steered clear of Eloria because she was such a gifted motivational inspirer, afraid she could convince them to do what she wanted, and they wouldn't have the ability to thwart her. But that wasn't what she was all about.

"She's probably regretting every moment she's been there," Lauriston continued, acting as though she truly hoped so.

Eloria knew the girl was envious that Persephonice's father was the commander and probably wished she had that role instead. But Eloria didn't think any child of his would be happy. Not as cold and unfeeling as he was, using his position as the reason he had to treat everyone like he did. Now that Persephonice was gone, and if Eloria couldn't convince her to return to the ship, if she could return, Eloria was seriously considering a transfer to another ship. Only this time, if she could get someone to hack into her records, she wanted the note about her being a motivational inspirer erased. And, if the commander had any idea she could use magic, that was not good. She couldn't decide if he was threatening her with the knowledge— bring my daughter home or else—or telling her that was another reason he had chosen her. She might be able to use her natural abilities to work in her favor in this unknown world though.

"When are you going?" Lauriston asked.

Eloria waved her hand in front of a red light. It turned green and her door slid open to her quarters. "Now." She walked into her room.

"Now?" Lauriston joined her.

Suddenly Verona knocked at the doorframe. "Can I come in? I want to hear the news firsthand."

Like Persephonice and her, Verona was a redhead also. Though Eloria was more of a red-red, Persephonice had blonder tones to her red hair, and Verona's hair was browner with a reddish cast to it.

"I want to go the planet's surface," Verona said, peering out Eloria's window. "I would love to view the waters close up. We don't have half the waterways on our planet that we can see from the spaceship, and that creature that was transported to the transporter room was incredibly fascinating."

Verona was an aquamarine biologist, who studied water sources on the various planets, in the event that someday they needed to use them for their own purposes. But like many of the scientists aboard, they didn't study primitive planets unless they had a formal military contingent, and for now, it wasn't authorized for some of the planets—like this one. The overall command didn't want to upset the primitive worlds as much as they could avoid it.

"That creature was beautiful but also looked like she wanted to bite anyone who got within her reach," Lauriston reminded her.

"Still, I would love to see what the male of the species looks like," Verona said.

Smiling, Eloria shook her head. Verona's chosen lifemate was on another ship and in two years' time, they were to meet and bond.

"Do you think Persephonice has taken one of the elves for a

lifemate?" Lauriston asked, attempting to look wide-eyed and innocent, when they knew very well that's exactly what she thought.

"Eloria, you won't really try to take her away from an elf, if she's bonded with one, will you?" Verona asked.

Verona was always bringing out ancient books and reading snippets about courtly romance and then she had all these notions that true love could exist. Which it didn't. It was a waste of time. The computers told them who their perfect mate was. Emotions made people choose the wrong mates. That had been learned and relearned over the centuries.

"I will have to see what I will see when I get there," Eloria said, vaguely.

She crossed her quarters, which consisted of a small room with a couch that folded out into a bed for one. A wash sink and mirror sat in a corner. A desk for correspondence was built into the opposite wall. A computer sat on top. And that was about it for her quarters. Until she held a higher rank or had a lifemate, which she would never have, she would continue to have a room this small with few amenities. She could watch movies, read books, and play games on her computer, the only source of entertainment she had here. She couldn't decorate, couldn't hang pictures or change the color of the gray walls or the bedcover that was the same drab gray, only in a darker color, or anything. Everything that was personal had to be tucked away in drawers that slid into the wall.

She didn't even have a personal bathroom but had to share a communal shower and privy arrangement down the hall with others of her rank. Well, women only. The men's communal unit was on the floor below her. In fact, only women without life-mates lived on this floor. Men were not allowed to visit the floor. Unless in an official capacity.

"How long do you think it'll take? An hour? Less time? I so

want to go to the Barra Fashion Gallery on Laborite, which was where we were headed until her father decided to return for her. It's so irritating that he would make all of us suffer so. Leave her down there, I say. Then we could pick her up afterward." Then Lauriston smiled. "Or, come to think of it, we could go, then return for the two of you in a few days. You don't shop anyway. And it could very well take you that long to locate her and convince her to come home with you."

"I would think your closet, as small as they are on board the ship, could not hold any more clothes for you," Eloria said dryly, grabbing a backpack from her small closet filled with uniforms —no dresses—as she was never required to wear anything that fancy anywhere, and began filling the bag with essentials.

"The airless vacuum bags flatten clothes into virtually nothing at all, and I can fit twenty times as many garments in there. Besides, if I don't wear it in six months, it's out of here." Lauriston studied Eloria as she packed. "What are you going to wear? Something that blends in with the scenery? Or all of your weapons to intimidate the primitive peoples? Or maybe something sexy to sway them to do your bidding?"

Eloria rolled her eyes. In truth, she wasn't sure what to wear. If she had more time, and they had more data about the people and the creatures on the planet, she'd know just what to wear.

She considered the uniform she wore on board the ship. White, sterile. It wouldn't do. She'd wear green to blend in with the forests that they'd seen on their last approach. And a silky material that dried well if it got wet, but was comfortable in both warm and cold weather depending on the temperature. The pants were full and gave the appearance of a skirt, in case the primitives were offended by women wearing men's trousers as they were on some planets. But it also gave her the freedom to fight if she needed to.

She changed clothes. The leafy green blouse with full

sleeves also would help her blend in with a forest. Hidden under her long skirt-like brown pants, she wore knee-high brushed brown leather boots, waterproofed for inclement weather. She sheathed a dagger at her waist, a sword at her back, and planned to slip her stun gun in her blouse, if she could do so without the other girls catching her doing it. She braided her thick red hair and pulled a dark green cloak out of her wardrobe that, when flipped to the other side, was pure white. It would serve to help hide her in the forest or in a snowy environment, if the landscape had snowy environments, and was perfect to wrap herself in to sleep on the ground.

She put on her rose-gold necklace that held an emerald-green stone. She couldn't wear it with her uniform, but she always wore it when she left the ship on leave or on duty when she was on a mission to blend in with the populace. Her father said it had been her mother's and was imbued with magic to protect Eloria and to use to focus her magic. Her mother had passed on her magic genes to Eloria, according to her father, because he didn't have a magical bone in his body.

She shoved packages of dried food and water tablets to purify the elves' water to keep her well- fed and hydrated in the event she couldn't rendezvous with the ship right away.

She covered her drawer with the cloak and wrapped her stun gun in it. Then she returned to the closet and kept the others from seeing what she was doing as she slipped the stun gun in her blouse. The belt she wore would keep it from slipping out of her blouse. She'd move the stun gun to her belt once she was on the planet and the ship was gone from her sight. She was afraid someone might check her bag before she left the ship. But they might wand her clothes too, looking for anything that was forbidden to take down to the surface of the planet.

"You don't think she's fallen madly in love with one of those primitive elves, do you?" Lauriston asked, a devilish gleam in her eye, her hands over her heart, her eyes casting upward, still pushing the issue.

"You ought to be an actress," Verona said.

Lauriston gave her an annoyed look, then said to Eloria, "You know her father will keep her under quarters arrest when you return her here."

Eloria suspected as much. At least until he could reprogram her and attempt to break her will. She looked over her stuff one more time, trying to determine if she'd packed everything she needed.

"I so wish I could go there with you," Verona said.

Eloria frowned at her. "You would not want to have to do what I have to do." She could imagine Verona stopping every few minutes to examine a water source. They'd never get anywhere.

Verona smiled at her, then sighed. "You have all the luck."

Eloria didn't think she did at all. She thought this could be the end of her friendship with Persephonice, and she could break her heart. Or, worse-case scenario, she wouldn't be able to return her, and the commander would punish Eloria by leaving her behind too. If Persephonice had fallen in love with an elf, it didn't mean Eloria would be welcome on the planet to live there until the end of her days.

Satisfied she had all that she would require, Eloria said, "Well, I'm ready." She brushed past Lauriston, ready to transport to the primitive elf world, hoping it wasn't as dangerous a place as others had warned her.

Not that she feared for her own safety. She was a warrior, special class. But for Persephonice, who, as an overseer who only recorded information for the data logs, nothing more, how could she survive? Maybe that's why her father wanted Persephonice back. He truly was worried about her.

INVISIBLY, the ship hovered over the elves' planet and Eloria was set down near where the ship had landed to block the river before, but she was on a white sandy beach only a few feet from the deep aqua ocean. She wondered if her friends could see her now before the ship departed the area.

Seabirds flew over the water, diving in and soaring out, fish wriggling in their beaks as the birds sailed on the breeze to the cliffs nearby. Beautiful clear blue water, clear blue sky, white sandy beach. It looked like a paradise. And Eloria did think it would be a great place for Verona to explore all the water sources. For the moment, Eloria soaked in the beauty of the salty air and fresh sea breeze. It reminded her of her home world of Tazia where some of the ruling class were shapeshifters. They even had a couple aboard the ship. She wondered what the elves would think of the jaguar, Caitlin, or the wolf, Lenora. Maybe they had shapeshifters in this world too. What did she know?

She thought of the mermaid that had landed in their transporter room and wondered if she was again here, swimming around in the ocean's depths after they had quickly returned her to this world. Was she still wearing the transporter bracelet? It wouldn't work now as the commander had ordered a crewman to remotely deactivate the device as soon as the mermaid was returned to her world.

Eloria turned to study the steep cliffs, the red and gray earthy tones. She observed pockets in the rocks that she could use for hand and foot holds. But it was a long way up there. They looked to be climbable and because of her job, she was always physically fit, but still...if the commander wanted her to be quick about it, why hadn't he deposited her at the *top* of the cliffs?

With resolve, she trudged across the silky, white sand toward the cliffs and what looked to be the easiest path up, where more rocks jutted out for her to grab ahold of. Pockets in the rocks should enable her to use them as footholds when she heard someone calling from the direction of the ocean. A watery, intriguing, deep voice.

She turned abruptly, thinking she would see a boat and somebody riding in it. A male somebody.

A head was bobbing in the water, long red hair floating on the surface. Tanned broad shoulders appeared as the man elevated himself a bit, his arms moving to keep his body afloat and... She squinted. She thought his eyes were green, gazing at her, almost with...longing. A sudden frown hinted at confusion.

Did he know Persephonice? The two of them looked similarly, same build, same size, red hair—different shade of red, but still red—and green eyes.

He swam closer and she watched with fascination, but gasped when a shimmering bronze tail rose and fell through the water, propelling the creature toward the beach.

Oh my goddess! It was the male equivalent of the female that had been transported to their ship! A merman! Verona would have loved to have seen him. Not that Eloria wasn't just as fascinated with him.

She had only read of such a creature, until the female landed on their transporter deck, and Eloria had seen one for real. She was intrigued with this male's handsomely rugged appearance, and she was completely spellbound that he could know Persephonice.

"You are not...," he started to say, frowning.

"Persephonice," she said, hopeful that he knew where she might be, although Eloria didn't see how he could know, living in the ocean as he did. But he seemed to know Persephonice and appeared to care for her. Eloria was absolutely amazed that he would have knowledge of her. "Do you know where—"

The sound of footfalls on the sand made her twist around to see what was headed for her.

She'd forgotten the basic rule of survival when visiting any primitive planet. Always, always watch your surroundings for potential hostiles. And the way the elves dressed in blue tunics and britches ran toward her, there hair and eyes just as blue, their expressions dark with anger, she knew they were hostiles. Which reminded her she should have pulled her stun gun from her blouse and attached it to her belt already.

"Get her!" one of the men shouted, his tone of voice threatening.

"She's... she's not the one."

"Get her anyway! We're being invaded. Grab her!"

Eloria quickly cast a bubble shield that protected against lightweight projectiles—arrows, poison darts, hand thrown rocks. Perfect for a primitive people. She was glad the commander wasn't monitoring her progress, or she'd be in deep space without a ship for using her magic if he'd caught her at it. She had her stun gun too, but only because she was defying the commander's orders, and thankfully no one checked to see what she was carrying when she left. There were way too many of the elves racing to reach her to effectively use the stun gun on them though. Still, she pulled it out of her blouse and fastened it to her belt and noticed her amulet was glowing a bright green, something she'd never seen it do, as if the blue elves had triggered its reaction.

She studied the blue-haired creatures ranting and raving as they jumped and rallied around the outside of her protective bubble. The merman was watching her, not saying a word, appearing somewhat stunned. She imagined he was rethinking wanting to befriend her like he must have done with Persephonice, since Eloria had created so much havoc with these elves. Maybe the bubble was a total put-off too.

Then the merman screeched in warning. And a wave bashed against the shore, breaking her concentration, and the bubble protection shielding her vanished. Her heart nearly quit beating, and she quickly pulled out her sword, despite knowing she wasn't supposed to, but a sword was an ancient weapon, so she reasoned it would be fine on a primitive planet. But then she saw men running toward her with long poles, and she guessed what they were. Blow-dart guns. She sheathed her sword and pulled out her stun gun.

She had no intention of attempting to use her motivational inspiring talent on these people. They were too hostile, and she suspected they had every intention of taking her hostage or killing her.

3

The high elf Prince Zorak had been training a new dragon when he heard all the commotion with the blue elves and flew his dragon closer to see what all the fuss was about, thinking he might need to rescue another kind of elf. That's when he saw Persephonice on the beach in the middle of real trouble, the blue elves shooting darts at her, but they bounced off what appeared to be an invisible barrier. And what was more, she didn't look like Persephonice exactly, her red hair darker, though she was about the same build. But her clothes—they were like what Persephonice had worn when she had first arrived in their world.

The king of the merman was having a fit too and sent a wave crashing against the shore in anger, trying to stop the blue elves from harming the woman. But it wouldn't be enough to deter them.

There was only one thing Zorak could do as the spritely young woman wielded a sword, then thinking better of it, switched it out for some other device. Another kind of weapon? He'd never seen one like it before.

What intrigued him most was this woman had to have used

magic to create the barrier. And since he was a magic user, a high elf, and no other elf had claimed this treasure, she was all his.

Then white, blue sparkly light shot out of the weapon, and every elf it hit fell to the ground—instantly.

That made him worry she might try that on him. He smiled. She could try. He would repel the power from the weapon with his own magic.

Then Zorak guided his dragon toward the beach, the shadow it cast, warning the elves they'd better cease and desist before the dragon released a rain of fire upon them.

THE SKY DARKENED above and several of the blue elves looked up. To her astonishment, Eloria saw a golden dragon carrying an elf dressed in blues, his form-fitting tunic trimmed in gold, sparkling in the morning sunlight. But his hair was dark, and his skin was tanned, not blue like the elves who had stopped in their tracks.

"Shoot the high elf!" one of the blue elves shouted. Gold braid trimmed the blue elf's military-looking jacket, and the way he was shouting orders, she thought he probably outranked the other men.

"But the arrows won't penetrate the dragon's scales," one of the men hollered back.

"That's why I said to shoot the high elf! Not the dragon, you slugeal!"

With the chance of making a hasty retreat, Eloria raced for the cliffs, and quickly grabbed for the first finger holds and footholds she could reach. As fast as she was able, she clambered up the rock face. Her speed and agility from all her continual combat training gave her a chance to evade the blue elves if they didn't follow her up the cliffs. Unless they turned to shoot their arrows or blow darts at her. To her shock, the dragon spewed fire down on the elves, and they quit shooting at the dragon's rider and dashed for the safety of the ocean.

The merman screeched to her, "Who are you?"

Thankfully, with their advanced technology, her inner ear translator was able to convert languages into something she could understand, and likewise, she could mimic their language so they could understand her. She considered the cliff's crevices and how she could slip in between the jagged rocks, should the dragon turn his wrath on her next.

"I'm Eloria, a good friend of Persephonice," she shouted to the merman, assuming that since he had swept some of the blue elves off their feet by propelling a wave in their direction, he had to be on her side, and Persephonice's.

Instead of shooting a stream of fire in her direction, the dragon swooped close, and she screamed. She couldn't help it. Screaming wasn't part of her warrior training, and she had always prided herself in not giving into girly reactions in a crisis situation.

Then again, she'd never had a dragon come after her either. He was immense, and his wings swept a rush of wind at her. The creature's golden scales shimmered in the early morning sun's rays, dazzling her, but it was the dragon's green eyes, blue, red, and gold streams of fire, the wicked, tearing teeth, and just as sharp and wicked-looking talons, that sent chills racing up her spine.

"Eloria!" the dragon rider shouted. "I too am a good friend of Persephonice!"

She couldn't believe Persephonice knew this elf too, but were they truly friends?

"Let me help you. You're too close to the rock face for my dragon to reach you. If the elves use their darts on you, you'll fall to your death. Move to a rock where he can swing around and grab you, and he'll carry you to the top of the cliffs and set you down. Then you can ride with me. How did you end up here? I'm sure Persephonice will be thrilled to see you."

She took the chance that he truly was Persephonice's friend. The blue elves definitely weren't.

She climbed onto a part of the rock wall where it jutted out with a narrow ledge to stand on. The dragon made another pass at her. He was huge and his talons deadly looking. She let out her breath and waited for the pain she knew she'd feel as soon as he grabbed her.

He dove for her, wings folded, talons outstretched. She prayed this wasn't the biggest mistake of her life. The great golden beast grabbed her shoulders with his talons. She was surprised to feel how gentle he was. All at once it was both terrifying and exciting to be carried up and over the cliff, hanging free like that, not riding inside a shuttle craft, or a spaceship. Nothing short of amazing.

"Okay, we're out of the elves' range and he'll set you down here, and then you can climb onto the dragon behind me."

The blue elves were yelling from down below, shooting at the dragon rider, but their arrows couldn't reach the elf or the dragon. The arrows fell earthward, forcing the elves to race away to avoid being hit themselves.

But what would happen when the dragon rider learned her mission was to return Persephonice to her father? She hoped she could befriend him and learn where Persephonice was so Eloria could discover for herself if her friend wished to remain here in the elves' world.

"Where is Persephonice?"

"With Dracolin, the shadow elf. They are married."

Eloria's mouth gaped. She couldn't believe it! She was—not

sure how she felt about the news. Happy for her? Afraid for herself? The emotions swamping her were mixed—glad Persephonice had found a lifemate all on her own, but afraid of what her father would do if he learned the truth. Send an army of warriors to return her to the ship? That's what Eloria feared the most. Well, and giving the commander the news would be bad news for Eloria.

VIATOR HAD HEARD of the redheaded mermaid who didn't have a fishtail, but he'd only learned of her from a shadow elf they'd taken prisoner. Of course, they assumed the shadow elf was making up tall tales because no one in the Darkland Forest where his people dwelled had heard of such a thing. The elves had traveled to other realms, had sailed across the seas, and never had they seen anything like it.

He'd been on the most important of missions—to do outstanding feats of heroism to make his wings transparent. For now, he was just out hunting wild boar when he heard the blue elves' shouts below the cliffs, the calling of the merman king, and saw the high elf prince upon his dragon, heading straight for the cliffs. He'd never seen anything like it, as if he'd intended to crash into the rock walls. What in the world was wrong with him? Was he mad?

Yet, Viator had it in mind if he saved the high elf prince, that could be one of his outstanding feats of heroism.

Viator was at the fringe of the dappled forest, racing to the edge of the cliff, bow in hand, hoping to catch sight of what had all the different peoples so riled up. He heard the prince shouting to the woman, Persephonice, the same woman their shadow elf prisoner had said was the redheaded mermaid with legs, but something more. She could communicate with wild beasts and made them work together, something no one had ever been able to manage.

So he had to see if she was truly for real. Just as he reached the cliffs, the dragon swooped again next to them, and lifted, then came in to set the creature down. She truly had red hair and green eyes that nearly knocked him down they were so unbelievably beautiful. She was staring at him as much as he was staring at her.

The dragon set her down on the ground and quickly released her. Then he settled down near her. "Come to me and I'll help you onto my companion—" Prince Zorak said, then paused. "Are you part high elf like Persephonice is? I'm Prince Zorak and pleased to make your acquaintance. And you are her friend?"

"I am," the woman said, her voice as melodic as the sirens of the sea. Just like Persephonice's was purported to be. "I mean, I'm her friend."

Viator just couldn't get over what he was seeing: a red-headed, green-eyed, land-walking mermaid.

No way could he let the woman get away. And he certainly wasn't going to allow the high elf the pleasure of taking her to his mountain castle. Viator had to share this treasure with his rulers right away. She might be real trouble if these unusual creatures kept showing up, since from what the prince said, she was the second one in their territory. This one wasn't Persephonice. But maybe she could be important enough to his people that it would help him on his heroic quest.

Securing his bow and unsheathing his sword, he dashed out of the cover of the forest, attempting to reach them before anyone was aware he was there. Before anyone saw him, he raced to her side through the tall meadow grasses, knowing using his wings would catch the dragon and Zorak's attention. He grabbed hold of the woman before the prince could respond and have his dragon turn him into cinders, or the prince used some of his magic on him, or anything else. His sword drawn, Viator had the woman under his command now. He threatened to kill her with his sword if the high elf dared to try to take her from him. No, that wasn't heroic, but saving her from the high elf could be.

Then he ran back the way he had come through the thick of the Darkland Forest, pulling her with him. He was supposed to be hunting boar for the nooning meal, but he figured what he caught was even more important than that.

"Do you know Persephonice?" the woman asked him, not fighting him, just going along as if she didn't mind that he was taking her prisoner, and that had him a little worried. Was this her plan? To learn where his people were settled and then... unleash her magic upon them? If she had any.

"Are you her kin?" he asked.

"Friend." She was staring at his wings as if she had never seen anything like it. He wished he could make them invisible. Before long, if he had his way, he could.

"She is with the shadow elf Warrior Chief, Dracolin Rossover."

"Who are you?"

"Alroy Aristotelis Viator. And you?"

"Eloria."

"Just plain...Eloria?" He couldn't believe such a beautiful creature would have such a short name.

"Eloria Cresthaven."

"What does it mean, this Eloria?"

"Brave one."

"Are you? Brave?"

"I am."

He glanced down at her and raised his brows in question. He

didn't think she would be so brave when she had to face all of his kind.

"And what does your name mean?"

"Regal, intelligent, traveler."

"Are you?"

He gave her a dark smile. "I am. I took you as my prisoner, didn't I?"

"Maybe I let you."

That's what he was worried about. "Where are you from?"

"From out there." She motioned with her free arm to the sky.

He glanced back, aware now that several of his brethren were watching from the dark woods, not making a sound, just observing the creature with him. "The ocean? You don't have a tail. If I throw you in our lake, will you swim or drown?"

"You would have to try it and see."

"We don't swim. If you didn't, you'd drown, and I'd lose my hostage."

"Why can't we be friends?"

"I don't even know what you are." He had no intention of being friends with the creature. She was a treasure they could use, hopefully, to gain power and could use her abilities for something useful.

"A friend, if you wish it." She glanced back at Prince Zorak, flying near the woods on his indomitable dragon, scowling.

Did she see the few dark elves observing her? They were like the shadow elves, blending in with their surroundings, priding their ability to remain unseen, yet she seemed to look at each of the men and women he'd spied as if they were fully visible.

"So where are you taking me?"

"To Pembrokish."

"Do you know where Persephonice is now?"

"With Dracolin. Last I heard, she was trying to settle the disputes between the snow giants and the ice dragons of the north." His people were impressed with the creature. He wondered if this one would help them in the same way as Persephonice helped the shadow elves. She could be valuable, but he suspected they'd have to keep her under lock and key, just for their protection.

"Persephonice is serving as a mediator?" Eloria asked.

Persephonice was supposed to be an unobtrusive observer of the different worlds, a collector of information for the archives, but Eloria had always suspected she had a talent for mediation because when fighting broke out between crew members on the ship, Persephonice had always been in the middle of it, settling the dispute. She hadn't tested out for the ability though and Eloria wondered why not.

"We are Darkland Forest elves. What manner of creature are you?"

"A langolar from another world." She stared at his wings.

He folded them flat behind his back as if he didn't like her seeing them, but she was fascinated with them. She wished he'd hold them out for her to touch.

"You are from down south?"

She had to remind herself the people inhabiting this place were primitive and probably had no knowledge of space travel. She had hoped Persephonice had passed along the information about their kind and paved the way for Eloria, but it appeared that wasn't the case. She might have had to resort to telling them very little about their world beyond this one.

"You are friends with Dracolin and Persephonice, correct?"

Prince Zorak seemed to be. And the merman too. Persephonice seemed to have made a lot of friends.

"Me? No."

She frowned at him. "I thought you and Prince Zorak were friends of Dracolin and Persephonice." She began to slow her step, and he tried to speed her up, tugging her along.

"Prince Zorak is a high elf, a magic user. I doubt after I took you from him, he will be feeling any...friendship toward me. And Dracolin is a shadow elf." Viator said it as though she was simple-minded not to realize the winged elves of Darkland Forest didn't have anything to do with any of them.

Something snorted in the nearby brush. She studied the dark mist draping the forest but couldn't see what was making the noise. "Climb," Viator whispered, pulling her to the nearest tree. "Just watch out for the pixies."

"The what?"

But Viator was shoving her at the tree, insistent. "If you don't want to be skewered, climb the tree!"

Something sauntered out of the bush, poking at the ground with its nose. It was dark brown, hairy, and wearing enormous tusks on each side of its snout, that looked like it could spear someone. She'd never seen anything like it.

She wanted to run through the woods and back to where Prince Zorak might still be, but she figured Viator was right. She quickly grabbed a sturdy branch and pulled herself into the tree and climbed upward until she was high enough to avoid the creature. His ivory tusks shone in the sunlight filtering through the tops of the trees. He lifted his head and sniffed at the air.

Viator hadn't climbed after her. Immediately, he pulled an arrow from its sheath, nocked it, and readied to kill the beast. Three arrows fired in rapid succession took the beast down.

"Supper," Viator said, considering the huge size of the animal.

"What is it?"

He frowned at her. "Don't tell me you've never seen one before. It's a wild boar."

She was about to scramble down from the tree and run off when something buzzed past her ear. She narrowed her eyes, assuming it was a large, annoying insect, but instead it was a human-like creature with wings, fluttering about her.

"Pixies," he said as one grabbed his hair.

The winged creature caught sight of his pointed ear and dropped his hair. "A Darkland Forest elf," the pixie said. Her voice carried throughout the forest as if the trees could echo the sound. The pixies carried her word all over the woods.

The green-eyed pixie reached for Eloria's hair, but she covered herself in her invisible protective dome. The pixie flew backwards as if she had been swatted away. She hissed, then dove into the branches higher above. After shaking a branch, several leaves showered down over the bubble.

"Not an elf," the pixie whispered.

"I don't wish you any harm, pixie," Eloria said.

Viator was staring at her. "What magic did you use on her?"

"What are you going to do with that?" She pointed at the dead creature, ignoring Viator's question.

"We will eat the boar." He again looked down at it, and she wondered how he thought he could manage to take her and the dead boar with him.

She quickly scrambled down to the ground, and she didn't hesitate to run off, hoping she could reach the edge of the forest and the meadowlands where purple and yellow flowers were blooming in profusion. Maybe Prince Zorak was still in the area, and he could swoop down on his dragon and rescue her from Viator, since he was certainly not taking her to see her friend.

Before she got very far, she realized the elves hidden in the ferns at the base of the trees were still there and had been following them all along.

She was suddenly surrounded by men and women carrying spears pointed at her. No one spoke a word to her. Their fierce expressions said it all. If she moved, she'd get speared, probably several times by several different spears. With them circling her, she couldn't use her stun gun on those in front of her. Too many of them anyway.

Then some of those behind her ran off. She was going to pull out her stun gun when she saw a shadow from above the trees. The golden dragon.

"Prince Zorak!"

But he couldn't reach her for the trees, and someone grabbed her arm, startling a shriek out of her. Viator. "You are going nowhere. My king will want to see his new prize."

A prize? No way was she going to be some elf king's prize.

"The others will carry the meat home for the meal. You will go with me. We'll cut through to the underground river. We'll get there much quicker that way."

Maybe Prince Zorak would come with dragons and other elves to free her. Unless she was alone with Viator and could use her stun gun on him, and free herself. He hadn't seen her use it down below the cliffs on the beach while dealing with the blue elves. And he hadn't removed it or her sword. He must have believed she couldn't fight him and win.

When they reached the opening for the dark cave, Viator pulled something from his pouch. A stick that when he waved it, cast a soft glow that poked rays of light into the darkness. A river ran through the center, a mix of sand and pebble paths on either side, as the sound of the water echoed off the cave walls.

He hurried her along the river. The damp cave smelled like fresh earth, and she loved smelling all the scents of the world, so much richer than the filtered air of the spaceship. The rough, rocky walls glistened with moisture dribbling down the green moss blanketing them. And the river pulsed like the blood coursing through her body in a never-ending stream. The water flowed with a soothing melody cavorting over rounded stones.

He frowned, sniffing the air. What was the matter now?

"The water...it smells odd. We drink from this water that fills a vast underground tunnel system."

The sight of a pale blue object caught her eye. Viator hastened to the spot, pulling her along. "What is it?" she asked as she studied the blue vase. The porcelain object was painted in swirling gold designs, symbols of some foreign culture.

Frowning, he said, "A river elf's vessel." He lifted it to his nose and sniffed. "No odor." He shoved it into his bag.

"Could it have been—"

"If the river elves are encroaching upon our world..." He stopped speaking and shook his head. His long legs strode along the riverbank as he searched for further clues, tugging her along.

He was obviously concerned about the presence of the river elves. "So if this is your territory, why would they have come here now? And for what purpose?" She rushed after him, not that she could do anything else the way he was gripping her arm.

"No telling with the river elves. If they could, they would send all of us elves from our homes."

"Oh, wait. Since this is a river, wouldn't they feel they would have the rights to it?"

"Not when it runs through our territory."

A man's sized footprint was carved into some of the damp sand. On the heel, a symbol was imprinted.

Viator rubbed his chin. "A river elf's footprint. They have a distinctive mark on the bottom of their shoes."

"Looks like an upside-down wing. Why would they have a wing on their shoe? Do they have wings?"

"They have an odd sense of humor. They leave such a mark showing they are a river elf. Any other footprints would indicate outsiders trespassed over their land. Trespassers are easily found, then it's just a matter of getting rid of the outsider. Yet, they are the trespassers here."

"How do they get rid of an outsider?"

"You wouldn't want to know."

She did want to know. It was the only way to be prepared in the event of an emergency. Eloria studied the footprint some more. Then she realized there was another symbol, nearly worn away. "What is this odd horseshoe shape for?" She ran her finger around the new imprint.

"What?" He examined the print more closely. "Rotted toad-stools. It's Lars's mark."

"Lars?"

Viator continued to pull her along. "He told me once how he'd rule over heaven and earth. Of course, he says things like that often. I never pay any attention to him."

Lars sounded like real trouble. "You know him?"

"At one time, all elves schooled together. Since Lars was the crown prince of the river elves and I, crown prince of the Dark-land Forest elves, was often paired with him in trials."

Eloria's mouth gaped. "A prince?" She had been taught to curtsy in front of royalty on other worlds, though for every kind of people, the customs and courtesies were different. She wasn't awed by royalty. She figured most of them "earned" their position from birth and hadn't worked at it. But she was still conscious of extending the proper courtesies as a goodwill gesture. She frowned. "Trials?"

"Games of wit."

"And...I hate to ask, who won?"

Viator turned to face her. A slight smile crept across his face. "It was half and half."

"Oh. What happened to cause the rift between the Darkland Forest elves and the river elves?"

"Greed. The rivers elves wanted more land, more power. We didn't agree."

She saw a new tunnel recently cut into the wall of the cave, no moss along the edges that would indicate the dampness had reached it. "This appears to be a new tunnel."

Viator examined the jagged edges of the newly created tunnel. "They must have come this way then. I will release you because I might need to fight them if they are around. No telling what the river elves would do to a red-haired, tailless mermaid. I'll be back once I learn what I can. You stay right here, and I'll check it out. You would endanger both of us if you came with me." He paused. "Don't think of returning the way you came. You have no protection unless you stay with me."

"I'm your hostage, remember?"

"You could be dead, if they get ahold of you."

In the tunnel, she had no way of reaching the high elf and his dragon. As soon as Viator was out of her sight, she was heading back the way she came, hoping she wouldn't run into more of Viator's kind in the woods. Or the river elves in the tunnels.

He disappeared into the dark tunnel before she could even say a word. But as his elven light faded into the tunnel, she created her own beam of light, using her magic.

Eloria took a deep breath and considered her other options. She could go into the new tunnel where Viator and she could fight off the river elves together. But she opted to run back the way she'd come. A rock suddenly bounced off another near the river the way she'd come. She extinguished her light. A faint light wavered several yards from where she stood, and it grew nearer somewhere close to the river.

Voices hovering over the light filled the cave. She turned her head in that direction to hear the conversation. "It's working," one of the men said. "Several of the Darkland Forest elves are sick."

"That was a brilliant notion of yours to use the Aegean petal's poison to taint the water..." The conversation died away as the light from torches drew closer to her. She walked farther into the shadows of the dark tunnel, her heart pounding, fearful they would see her. If they were poisoning the Darkland Forest elves, she was certain they'd just kill her. Not without a fight, but if there were too many of them, she couldn't hope to win.

"Did you see something over there?"

Footsteps hurried toward the tunnel, and Eloria scampered into the blackness. Filled with panic, she barely breathed. She had no choice but to try to make her way through the new tunnel in the direction Viator had headed.

Eloria stumbled over a lump of rock and fell to her knees. Pain shrieked through her kneecaps. Glancing back, she saw the lights wavering in the darkness as they moved toward her. She jumped to her feet and ran. No telling what the elves would do to her if they found her. They'd poisoned the river and she was certain they wouldn't want her warning the darkland elves who had done it and how.

She grabbed the walls of the tunnel as she tried to find her way. Then a tiny light ahead of her gave her hope, and she hurried toward it. Her heart raced as she scrambled over the uneven terrain to reach what she hoped would be safety.

The light ahead of her silhouetted her figure for the ones behind her. One of the men following her said, "What is that?"

"A ghost?"

"Not a ghost. A woman?"

"A woman would never be down here alone."

They'd seen her. She hurried toward the light that grew with every step. Then she realized the light wasn't coming from outside, but from more handheld torches, and they blinded her vision. Viator wouldn't have had more than the one stick of light.

Terror gripped her as her throat grew dry. She stopped in her steps, squinting her eyes as she held her hand up to shield them from the brilliant glow.

"Grab her." A deep, harsh voice spoke within the light. She turned back to see the men behind her slow their steps.

Before she could do anything, a hand from behind her grabbed her arm. With a jerk, she was yanked farther into the light and was suddenly outside of the tunnel, breathing in the smell of the forest and of wet rain.

She attempted to jerk herself free from the elf, irritated that she'd probably gotten herself into more of a predicament than before. Two more grabbed at her and whisked her through the forest. The leaves still dripped water from a recent rainfall.

"What is it?" the one sneered as he glanced at her.

The river elves? They were as slim featured as the Darkland Forest elves, but these had pale blond hair and light amber eyes, unlike their dark-haired cousins. They were as handsome a creature, noble in their tall build, dressed in greens and browns to camouflage them in their woodland surroundings, no doubt. So far, she didn't feel they were as much of a threat as Viator feared them to be. Except for the business with poisoning the Darkland Forest elves.

"Where is Viator?" she asked, as the elf squeezed her arm tightly. He ignored her, and she took a deep breath. "Lars?"

The elves stopped in place. "What do you know of our prince?"

She didn't say. She'd hoped mentioning his name would put her in better stead, but it didn't seem to make any difference.

The elf shook his head. "Will we get rid of the trespasser in the usual way?"

"No." Eloria tried to squirm free. Whatever they intended to do to her, it didn't sound good. "I'm just a visitor to this world. And I don't mean anyone any harm."

The elf laughed darkly. "And you won't harm any of us." He pulled her to the edge of a cliff where the sun's early afternoon rays glinted off its red glossy surface. "Look long and hard. It will be the last time you will see such a sight."

They couldn't mean to throw her off the cliffs, but she had news for them. Should she act terrified? Make them believe they could kill her in such a way?

Eloria studied the string of a river winding its way through the narrow ravine. The white pebbled beach sandwiched the river in between. Green streaks of crystals covered the red clay cliffs, while trees dotted the top edge of the canyon.

She couldn't pretend to be a frightened little girl. "Can I not speak with Lars—"

"Prince Lars to you, whatever you are." The elf shoved her from the cliff. Laughter filled the air.

Her amulet glowing brightly, Eloria screamed as the pebbled beach hurtled toward her, only because she hadn't really expected the evil elf to shove her off without any warning. And in that instant, she was reminded that she did not scream, ever.

That's what happened on an uncivilized planet. But wasn't the amulet supposed to...protect her?

"ELORIA?" A voice from faraway called to her. "Eloria. Eloria."

There was great urgency in the man's voice, deepened with concern, but still she couldn't shake herself free from the terror she'd experienced when her ability to create a misty pillow on the rocky beach below had only partly materialized in time to properly cushion her impact. She ached all over and was bruised to be sure. But she was alive, and nothing was broken, she didn't think.

"Eloria," the voice said again. This time, a hand shook her shoulder. Fingers touched her cheek, and she opened her eyes.

"Viator." She bolted upright.

He took a deep breath. "I was afraid the fall had killed you."

"I'll live. Where have you been all this time?"

"Looking for Lars, fighting with him, but then I heard you cry out." He made a face at her. "Why did you follow me out of the tunnel?"

"Are you kidding? Lars's men contaminated the water, and they saw me in the tunnel. They grabbed me, and then you can imagine what happened next."

Viator said something that she thought was a curse in their elf language. Her translator couldn't translate it. "We must return to my home and see that no one drinks of the water until we can determine how to make it safe again." Viator helped Eloria up.

She stared at his wings, one torn, and he quickly folded them against his back. "Your wing is torn."

"Cut. Lars struck out with his sword. I only just managed to fly down here to see to you."

"Will it heal, or do you need to have it sewn?"

"I'll need stitches, but we cannot do anything about it here."

"Take me to see Persephonice and—"

"No. They are in the north. I already told you that."

"Then take me to Prince Zorak, and I'll tell you what I learned in the cave."

Viator narrowed his eyes at her. "You will tell us what you know, under torture, if need be. The canyon leads back to the woods that way." He pointed to the mountains in the distance. "Up there is where Prince Zorak resides, and there's no way to get there unless you have a dragon for transportation. Or you're a winged elf."

Eloria gazed at the pointed peaks covered in greenery as the tips were frosted with snow. It looked like the safest place for the high elf kind to live. She imagined the Darkland Forest elves would have a devil of a time reaching them if they attempted such a feat without wings.

"It is not safe for us here. We must hurry." Viator grabbed her hand and hurried her along the edge of the bubbling river. He scratched his forehead. "Tell me what you have learned, and how you learned of it."

She'd been tortured before and still had some of the scars to prove it, which was why she still had nightmares over it. She'd needed to keep important state secrets those times, and until she escaped or was rescued, she'd had to endure. But not this time. In this case, the people needed her help, and she wasn't here to harm them, unless they harmed her. So far, she'd only suffered threats from Viator.

"The one river elf said they'd used Aegean petal's poison to taint the water. Do you know a cure for that?"

"Yes."

"Why would they do something like that?"

"They are always causing mischief of one kind or another. Only this is the first time they've done anything truly harmful."

Eloria heard a strangely, beautiful music and stumbled on an outcropping of rock.

Viator grabbed her arm to keep her from falling. "Is there anything wrong?" he asked her, as she turned her head toward the cliffs.

"I hear music." She'd never heard such a pleasing tune to the ear. She was pulled to it like once she'd been drawn to the crystals in a cave, shimmering in a mystical light, luring her in her dreams. And now Eloria had to reach the music. Just a few steps and she would see what made the alluring sound. Just a few more steps, and she would join the creatures who tantalized her with their tune.

"Just block the sound from your ears, Eloria." Viator released her hand as he stopped to readjust his pack. "The bewitching sounds of the—"

He turned as Eloria walked into the river.

"Eloria!" he yelled. He pulled her from the water, getting his wings lightly wet. The goddess be skewered. Now he couldn't fly at all. Not until his wings dried.

Eloria didn't stop watching the cliffs where the music drifted down to her.

"You cannot resist the meadowland fairies' music," he said under his breath. "I hadn't realized..." He yanked his pack from his back while she stood beside him. Rummaging through the contents, he finally found a soft bread roll. He grasped it, but when he pulled it out of his pack, he heard Eloria splashing through the deepening water.

Turning, he was horror stricken to see that she had walked so far into the river already. His heart thundered with alarm. He couldn't swim. Could she?

4

"Eloria!" Viator shoved the bread roll into his pack and dashed into the river. Goddess's wounds. He'd drenched his wings. Before he could reach her, she walked off the ledge in the river and the water closed in over her head. She quickly resurfaced as she gasped for air, but the current carried her away.

"Eloria!" Viator's frantic voice echoed off the canyon walls. The fairy music from above stopped.

"I can't swim, Eloria! And I can't fly. My wings are wet." Viator splashed back to the shore and grabbed his pack. Running like the zephyr, he tried to catch up to Eloria as her head bobbed up and down in the frothing liquid. His footsteps crunched on the mixed pebble and sandy beach with his frenzied pace. He spied a submerged boulder blanketed in moss poking out of the water directly in her path.

"Catch hold of the rock, Eloria!" Viator shouted. "Catch hold and I will rescue you!"

Eloria managed to barely just seize hold of the rock's soft edge. The water tugged hard at her, threatening to pull her from the ancient stone.

At least the meadowland fairies had stopped singing, thank the gods.

"Hurry, Viator! I can't hold on much longer," Eloria called out.

Viator dug in his bag as he ran. Upon reaching Eloria's location, he pulled his gold rope out. "I'm going to toss this to you." He formed a loop in the rope, then tied a knot. "Grab hold of it and slip it around your waist."

"MY ARMS." The strength of the water drew the strength from Eloria's arms. She could use her magic on dry land, not in the water. She couldn't believe fairies, something she'd thought were only fairy tales, could lure her with their music to her death. No matter how much she'd tried not to listen to them, she couldn't. Half of her had been caught up in the music, the other half, knowing it was a fascination she couldn't afford.

Every tug from the powerful river strained her muscles further. She rested her head against the pillow of moss. "Hurry, Viator," she whispered. She shivered from the icy, cold water. She imagined her lips would be as blue as the blue elves she'd encountered on the ocean shore. She imagined the color had drained from her body. She must have been a sight. One bedraggled, redheaded langolar. She closed her eyes, trying to think of something warm and dry, like the desert region of Kinnar—a desolate place, but full of history, ruins, and an ancient civilization.

"Don't go to sleep, Eloria!" Viator commanded as he tossed the rope to her.

As if she had any intention of going to sleep as she clung to the rock, fighting the pull of the icy river.

The rope tickled her cheek. Her thoughts jumbled as if in a

dream. She was trying as hard as she could to imagine a fire glowing hot, a blanket wrapped around her, the heat of the desert, but all she could think of was ice-cold snow, sleeting rain mixed with snow covering her as she trekked across a mountain pass in Gambia.

She tried to think of Persephonice and how she just had to see her one last time. Of how she had to tell her how proud she was that she'd taken the shadow elf for her lifemate. She hoped she was happy with him. That she hadn't been forced to be with him.

"Eloria! Grab the rope!"

Viator. He wouldn't take her to see her friend. She would never see her again.

"Eloria!"

She would no longer be Viator's hostage either. Persephonice's father would leave her here to perish.

The rope raked across her hair as it flowed with the current.

"Eloria! The rope...grab the rope!"

The water felt warmer now. She took a deep breath, her arms strained. She wanted to let go.

She halfway opened her eyes and watched Viator pull the rope through the water.

Sleep, Eloria, and you can think on it tomorrow.

"I could hear you from miles away," another male voice said on the shore. "What in the world is that?"

"A girl like Persephonice. Not from here. Her friend. I cannot reach her. She has been affected by the cold."

"Why would she be swimming in the cold river? She swims? Like I've heard Persephonice does."

"She swam enough to reach the rock."

"She sleeps?"

"She is possessed by the frigid waters," Viator said, frantic.

"What will I get if I rescue her?"

"My undying gratitude. Just get her, Balen!"

"Very well. I will do this. But if I get my wings wet, you will never hear the end of this."

The flutter of wings beat over Eloria to her annoyance. Warm hands grabbed under her arms and attempted to wrench her from her safe perch. "No," she said under her breath. Sleep is all she wanted. *Let me sleep.*

"Let go of the rock, woman." Balen groaned with the effort.

"Eloria! Let go of the rock!" Viator yelled.

"Prince Viator commands it!" Balen flapped his wings in a desperate attempt to extricate her from the rock. "Let go, woman!"

"Eloria, come to me! I need your help! I think I'm going to die!" He shrugged at Balen who raised his brows at him. "Help me, Eloria!"

"Viator?" Eloria lifted her head from the rock. "Viator?"

Balen pulled her free from the stone and flew her to the riverbank. Viator yanked a cloak from his bag. He quickly wrapped her in it and then Balen lay her on the ground. "Where did she come from?" Balen flapped his wings. "They're wet. I won't be able to fly for close to three hours now."

"Good, you can keep us company. Mine are soaking wet too." Viator studied her expressionless face. "Eloria?" She stared back at him, uncomprehending, then shivered and closed her eyes.

Balen shook his wings again showering them with droplets of water. "If I could have flown, I could have taken you home."

"You couldn't have managed both of us." Somehow Viator had to get her to safety and if he didn't hurry, they'd be in a lot more trouble soon.

"Well, you're right. Not both of you. She doesn't belong here." Balen touched a wet red curl.

"I'm not leaving her alone, Balen. She's my hostage. Fried griffin feathers, she needs me. Call a dragon."

"I haven't come of age yet. I can't call a dragon. You know that."

Sure Viator knew that, but he was so rattled over Eloria's condition he wasn't thinking straight. He studied Balen's wings. "Your wings are more transparent." He frowned. "Why haven't my wings changed further?"

"Uh, I hate to tell you this, but if you recall from our lessons on the subject, if you have strong feelings of attachment for someone, should you help them in their time of need, it doesn't count. You can only get credit if it is done for someone you don't have any feelings for. An unknown person, or one you despise... it matters not." Balen examined his wings. "I didn't know the human girl. Therefore, my rescuing her enabled me to earn a credit."

"A whole credit." Viator rubbed Eloria's cold hands. "And she's unknown to me. She's a hostage, nothing more."

"You didn't rescue her."

"Start a fire," Viator commanded, irritated.

Balen studied Viator's wings. "You've been cut."

"Lars. Balen, the fire?"

Hunting the boar was one of the duties Viator had to accomplish on his own, but bringing in the cold, wet treasure on the beach should have been enough to make his wings completely invisible. She didn't appear to care for his beautiful wings, translucent in color of purples, blues, greens, and bordered in shimmering gold. They attracted more females of his kind, but he would be glad when he could make them transparent. Something that would happen once he accomplished ten great feats, none of which he was privy to. He would discover what they were, one by one. And today on his hunt, he was certain that taking her hostage would be his greatest feat.

"Shouldn't we return to the castle?" Balen asked.

"We need to get her warm and dry."

Balen rubbed his whiskerless chin. "Why do you have strong feelings for this human, sire? Such a thing will surely be frowned on by your father."

"I don't have feelings for her. You were right in that I didn't do anything to save her. Except I pulled her from the water the first time." He cursed again, annoyed that he hadn't gotten any credit for saving her the first time. He wondered how she had managed to fall all the distance from the top of the cliffs to the rocky shore below and not be injured. By the time he'd reached the cliff's edge, she had been lying on the shore, and he'd been afraid she was dead. *Not* because he felt anything for her, but she could be valuable to them. And could help make his wings transparent. He looked up at Balen, who furrowed his brow at him. "Get a fire started, Balen!"

"Sendal won't be happy about this."

"I'm not marrying the girl. I'm only trying to ensure she's warm and dry!" Viator wasn't happy he'd have to marry Lady Sendal, Balen's twin sister. She wasn't fun to be with, and they argued about everything. The fact Sendal was also a winged elf of royalty mattered not to him.

"Uh-huh." Balen gathered wood for the fire.

Eloria stirred and opened her eyes.

"Eloria?" Viator pulled a blanket from his pack. He wrapped it around her, then stuck his bag under her cheek to serve as a pillow.

She took a deep breath. "Sleep is all I need," she whispered.

Balen piled the branches on the ground. "You know a fire will alert others we're in the area."

Viator nodded.

"Two winged elves that cannot fly and one cold, wet...sleepy girl will be easy prey."

"Just start the fire."

Balen pulled a wand from his pack and flicked it at the wood.

A tiny curl of smoke rose, then a small flame tickled the branches.

"What are you going to do with her?" Balen asked.

"Take her to our home...first. I have to heal my wings before I can fly her home. River elves have poisoned our water. I must find a way to cleanse the water and stop the elves from doing it again."

"I'll help you."

"If I keep getting others to aid me in my quests, I will never have transparent wings."

Balen smiled wickedly. "It appears I'm a half a credit ahead of you, and I only just started today. Now let's see, you have been at this how long?"

"Since earlier today, but I was distracted."

"By?"

Viator's gaze drifted to Eloria's red hair. "She is my mission. To get her back to the castle."

Balen laughed. "I'll get more firewood. Sendal will throw a fit. You know all she thinks of is when the two of you will wed. She has never considered marrying anyone else. And being that she is my sister, I have seen her throw some of the worst sort of tantrums nobody should ever have to witness."

"I know." Viator rubbed Eloria's hand. "Eloria."

A deep-throated growl from the canyon upstream made Viator jump to his feet.

"Two, three, maybe more?" Balen pulled his sword from its sheath.

"Red devil wolves." The red shrubs nearly hid the menace several yards away. Viator turned to Balen and said, "Do you have your bow?"

"I always have my bow with me. Always." Balen sheathed his sword, then pulled the bow from his pack and snapped it into shape. "Where is yours, Your Majesty?"

"In my bag as yours was. It would be better for us to use arrows on the wolves." Viator slipped the bow out of his pack carefully so as not to disturb Eloria's pillow. After readying the bow for use, he hurriedly placed two arrows on the string. He pulled it taut as he closed one eye and steadied his breathing. "I have the two on the left, shoulder to shoulder."

"I have the other."

"Now!" Viator shouted.

The wolves lunged and the elves let loose their arrows. The animals collapsed on the ground without a whimper.

"There'll be more." Balen retrieved their arrows.

Eloria rolled onto her side.

"Eloria." Viator hurried to join her. Kneeling before her, he took her hand and warmed it with his own.

The music from the meadowlands began again, and Viator grabbed the bread roll from his bag.

"You think she's hungry?" Balen asked, sounding astounded as he crouched beside them.

"The fairies lured her into the water. Of course, they only wished for her to join them in the meadows at the top of the cliffs on the other side of the river. They didn't realize they would have drowned her in the process."

"Why doesn't she just block their—"

Eloria tried to stand, but Viator grabbed her arm and shook his head. "You stay seated here for the moment." He tore the roll apart, then hurried to stuff the soft, cooked dough into her ears.

She stared at him for a second, then frowned to see her clothes soaking wet. "What happened?"

"Seems the meadowland fairies have quite a pull on you."

"What?"

"Their music...they lure the unsuspecting. For days, even our own elves have been caught up in their chant. Then when the fairies tire of their new-found friends, they release them. Most of us have been trained to fight their influence, but some aren't able to, even so."

Eloria touched her ears. "You will have to speak up. I can barely hear you."

Viator smiled. "That is fine as long as you cannot hear the fairies."

ELORIA LOOKED OVER AT BALEN. His blond hair was darker than Viator's and his blue eyes, paler. She studied his wings. In a showy male display, he rose to his feet, then spread his wings wide and flapped them twice. She smiled and then shivered. "Nice wings. I've never seen anyone with them before. I thought Viator was a fairy."

Viator snorted.

"Well," Balen said, as he knelt beside Eloria, "she's a pretty intelligent woman after all."

Viator frowned at him to see the interest he showed in Eloria. "She is not of royal blood. And not a winged elf like us."

"Not of royal blood?" Balen's brow furrowed. "But you...well, you..." He turned his head in the direction of the castle nestled on top of the mountain peaks surrounded by Darkland Forest. "The king will be furious to learn of this."

"What? The dark elves threw her from the cliffs. I rescued her...that is all. She cannot stay here all alone to fend for herself. She is my hostage and will be a gift to my father."

Balen looked at the green crystal glowing on the gold chain hanging around Eloria's neck. "There is more to this than you say. The king will be peeved." He took a deep breath. "And worse than that, Sendal will be a terror."

Eloria squeezed the water from her hair. "You have not introduced me to your friend, Viator."

"She's a commoner and calls you by your name without using your title?"

Viator watched Eloria as she listened to them, straining to hear their muffled words. "Eloria, this is Lord..." He turned to Balen. "What do you mean there is more to this than I say? I say what I mean. There is nothing more to it than that."

Balen took a deep breath as he observed the emerald shining brightly on its rose-gold chain. "My mother told me once that a strange girl would conquer our kingdom. We would know her when we saw the glowing stone she wore around her neck. I would say this girl might qualify, sire. Would you not agree?"

"I've never heard such a tale. Certainly, our soothsayer has never said such a thing."

"Perhaps my mother was wrong. Perhaps. But my mother is rarely wrong. In fact, never, that I can recall."

Eloria stared up at the meadowlands.

"You cannot still hear them, can you?" Viator asked, concerned.

"What?" She turned to face him.

He let out his breath with relief. "This is Lord Balen, son of Duke Corson, advisor to my father."

Eloria bowed her head to Balen in greeting. "Balen," she said, nodding her head in recognition. "For strong and healthy."

Viator laughed and shook his head. "Balen means brave. Baline means strong and healthy."

Balen studied Eloria. "Well, that red hair of hers is really something. She doesn't know the ancient language though?"

"Sure I do." Eloria shook her garments. "Miss a word or two, now and then, is all."

"Do you think you can walk?" Viator helped her to stand.

"My legs are uninjured." She pulled the cloak tighter.

Balen frowned at her clothes. "Why does this female wear

such things?" He pointed at her pants. "Do they not wear gowns?"

Viator hurried to snuff out the fire. "With traveling, she is wearing what she needs to."

"How did you...find her?" Balen grabbed up Viator's pack for him.

"Prince Zorak had her in hand. I couldn't let him have her."

"Now you've started a war with the high elves?" Balen shook his head.

Viator grabbed Eloria's arm and led her over the pebble beach. The notion rankled him. "They have no claim to her. She's mine. As a gift to my father."

Balen chuckled. "Right. For your father."

"I still can't believe you earned a credit for rescuing her and I did not." Viator glanced at Balen's wings.

"Credits for what?" Eloria asked.

Viator explained what they had to do to come of age as a winged elf. "Do you hear that?" Viator looked heavenward.

"No." Eloria shook her head.

"Aye, Your Majesty," Balen said. "More trouble."

They spied a dark gray speck in the sky. At the same time, they heard growling behind them, and they all turned to see red devil wolves crouching as they readied to lunge at their helpless prey.

BEFORE ELORIA COULD REACT or the elves pull their bows from the pouches, fire streamed in a steady flow from high above, striking at the wolf menace. Eloria's clothes instantly dried while her body warmed at once. Balen and Viator's wings were immediately dried, too, from the heat of the fire while the three of them ran away from the inferno.

Balen grabbed Eloria by the waist and lifted her into the air. "Viator!" she screamed, as a red wolf dodged the burning piles of fur and headed straight for him. In shock, she watched as a dragon swooped down while Viator jumped onto its back. An elf dressed in armor reined the beast in.

The dragon's breath finished off the last of the red wolves before turning and heading for the mountain castle again.

"Is he all right?" Eloria cried out as she couldn't see what had become of Viator.

Balen smiled. "Aye, young lady. The prince is riding with one of the royal guards, but when he returns to the castle, the king will have a say about this."

"About what? The royal guard being used to save his son's life?"

"About you. I suspect you will cause a great controversy in the castle today." Balen shook his head. "As has been foretold," he said under his breath.

"Can I remove these?"

"Yes. The fairies' song cannot touch you this far away."

When Balen landed on the balcony of the west wing, several lords, ladies and servants stood watching them. "Oohs" and "aahs" were exclaimed by most as Balen reached for Eloria's arm and pulled her aside. Viator slipped down from a rope tied to the saddle on the dragon. The royal guard turned the creature away from the balcony as all, but Eloria, showed their respect to Viator. Balen pulled at her arm to force her to curtsy. Belatedly, she did.

Viator took her hand and led her to one of the women standing nearby as gasps were heard from the crowd. "Find her a suitable gown to wear, at once. And...disarm her."

"My liege." The lady curtsied once more. She waved to Eloria to follow her. Eloria turned to Viator. He motioned with his head for her to follow the lady.

Eloria had been lucky that Viator had not disarmed her, maybe thinking she needed to have protection should they fail to protect her on the way here. The stun gun was set to only work for her, so if anyone else tried to use it, they couldn't. But she didn't want to lose it for good.

With reluctance, she hurried after the woman whose shimmering wings barely shown as they were tucked neatly against her back. Her blond hair was braided and hidden under sheer veils. "Are you close to being of age?" Eloria studied the woman's nearly transparent wings.

The lady nodded.

She was curious how the female winged elves came of age. "Do you have to perform ten tasks, too?"

The woman shook her head.

"Do they just turn transparent then?" Eloria frowned as the woman shook her head again. What was her problem? "Can you not speak to me?"

The elf glanced at Eloria's necklace and studied the glowing gem, then quickened her pace, her gaze averting toward the floor. She was afraid of her, Eloria assumed. Whatever for? Eloria had exhibited no malice toward the elves, and even Viator and Balen had showed her the greatest kindness, if she didn't take into account his taking her hostage or threatening to torture her for information about the poisoned river in the tunnel.

So what was the woman's problem anyway?

A guard stopped them, and confiscated Eloria's pack, sword, and stun gun attached to her belt. *Great. Just great.*

Eloria heard muffled laughter and turned to see several children watching her from behind white marble pillars streaked with green. Blue and red feathered birds chirped as they flittered about in flower gardens hanging off the balconies. The brilliant colors of red, purple, yellow, and orange flowers filled the hanging baskets attached to brass hooks on the trellis overhang.

"What are you doing with the creature?" a young woman asked as she stopped the other.

"Prince Viator asked that I find a gown for the lady, Lady Sendal."

Lady Sendal glowered at Eloria. From what Balen had said about his twin sister, Eloria was certain she wouldn't ever become friends with this woman, and she also realized she hadn't been able to use her ability to persuade people to do anything she'd wanted them to. Maybe they were too primitive for her to influence them. At least, she still had some magical tricks up her sleeve.

5

"Viator wants a gown for this creature?" Sendal walked around Eloria. "What *is* it, exactly?"

"The rumor is she's a human," the maid said, "like the other one the shadow elves kept for themselves."

"I am," Eloria said. She figured there was no sense in trying to explain what she was exactly. "You must be Balen's sister." She studied the pale blue eyes of the woman and her dark ash-blond hair. She looked just like Balen, only more feminine.

Sendal turned her head to the side as her mouth dropped open. "Has this human no manners when she is among elven royalty?" She sniffed the air. "What is that sweet fragrance she wears?"

"I'm not sure," the woman said.

Sendal furrowed her brow at Eloria. "If you know what's good for you, you'll address my brother as Lord Balen from now on."

"The king wishes an audience with her, my lady, at once."

"Whatever for?"

"The rumor is he's afraid of her."

"Bah, take her as she is."

"Prince Viator commanded I—"

"Very well. I'll get her a gown," Sendal snapped.

"But he said—" The lady stopped speaking as Sendal glowered at her. "As you wish, my lady."

"Come," Sendal said to Eloria. "I will get you that gown."

One of the worst she could find, Eloria was certain. What was it her father had always said before he died? He didn't get mad; he would just get even. So do your worst, elven lady. She hadn't seen the tricks *this* "human" could do.

"BUT MY LORD FATHER..." Viator paced before the king seated on his throne. "I must complete my quests where my instinct drives me." He couldn't believe his father could be so stubborn about the matter. He'd never heard of any father denying his son the right to accomplish his missions to come of age. It just wasn't done.

"I say again, my son, Lord Balen will return the girl back to the cliffs and Prince Zorak can have her if he wants to take on the trouble she could be. Balen will see to it that our waters are cleansed. You will have no more dealings with the human."

Viator made a last-ditch effort to persuade his father that he was doing what was right. "But, Your Majesty, I was the one to discover that the river elves had poisoned our water supply. And Eloria was the one who learned what poison they'd used on the river. If Balen leaves her at the cliffs, no one might find her for days, weeks. She is simply a human and could perish out there on her own.

"It is my duty to resolve the issue of the water. As for the human, we could use her like the shadow elves use Persephonice."

"Balen will go!" the king commanded as his voice raised and his face reddened. "You won't see this girl any further."

The muscles in Viator's jaw grew taut. His father had hidden the secret of the prophecy from him then. And he was the crown prince. How could his father have done such a thing to him? "Then what Balen spoke of was true. You are afraid a strange girl will conquer the realm."

"Nonsense. As unfounded as the notion your grandmother, on your mother's side, wasn't royalty."

"I've never heard *that* said." Viator frowned at his father. What was *this* all about? Had his father thought he might have heard this unconscionable rumor and was trying to dismiss it as another lie?

"You must journey to the seacoast of Neferon, as you have before mentioned. But, of course, you'll have to wait until your wings heal. Why have you not completed any new tasks of yet?" The king was studying Viator's wings.

Viator folded them behind his back. "I rescued the girl. I should have earned a credit."

His father furrowed his brow.

"If you do not fear she is the one spoken of in the prophecy, why do you treat her thus?" His father's concern was as transparent as a grown elf's wings.

"Humans do not belong here." His father folded his arms across his chest. "Lord Balen told me you did not earn any credit when you pulled the human from the water the first time. Do you not see the trouble in that?"

Viator knew that his father was alluding to the same thing Balen had. That Viator had feelings for her, but they were wrong. She could prove useful to them. He was certain of it. He didn't believe the prophecy or that she had any part in it if it was true.

The king waited for his response anyway, then, when it was

not forthcoming, finally said, "This makes me assume that the female has enchanted you. This is a dangerous business, Viator. Do not take this infatuation lightly."

Infatuation? "You are wrong, my lord father. I feel nothing for the woman."

The king looked beyond Viator, who turned as two castle guards escorted Eloria into the throne room.

His heart skipping a beat as he considered her, Viator studied the white gowns layered in ivory pearls and feathers she wore, her step light as she drew close. She curtsied to his father and him. "I thank you, Your Majesty, for seeing me. Prince Viator was good enough to take care of me when the river elves tried to kill me. He hoped I might aid you in some way, but I've come only to see Persephonice."

The king glanced at Viator. He smiled and shrugged. "Persephonice is negotiating a peace up north."

"Why did you come to see the other like you?" the king asked her.

"Her father wants her returned so he can take her home."

Viator's jaw hung. *That's* why she came? To steal her friend away from the shadow elf? That could cause overwhelming repercussions, as much as Persephonice had brought peace to several warring factions.

Then he figured she'd never convince Persephonice to leave her mate.

Though Eloria was but a commoner, she carried herself like a queen, and he couldn't help but be overwhelmed by her presence. Her red hair had been brushed neatly and rested in curls over her shoulders. He wondered why the elven maids hadn't braided it and tucked it under veils as was their custom. Women's satin tresses were just too enticing for the men to see and were to be tucked away and veiled at all times.

"Lord Balen will return you to the cliffs in the morning. In the meantime..." The king paused when Eloria's gaze shifted to Viator. "You will be fed and given a place to sleep for the evening."

Eloria curtsied deeply once more. "You are most kind, sire."

He waved for his guards to escort her out of the room. Viator's gaze never diverted from her. She moved with charm and elegance just like any other noble winged elf female, but she could climb trees, fall off cliffs and survive, and swim like no other. And her red hair and green eyes distracted him something fierce. Sendal was no match for Eloria's distinctive beauty.

His father cleared his throat, scowling at him.

Viator sighed deeply as Eloria disappeared into the corridor beyond the throne room. He wasn't sure what he was going to do with her, but he wasn't going to leave her cliffside where any danger could befall her if Prince Zorak didn't return for her. And he was going to resolve the water issue, despite what his father dictated. He had to. It was part of his mission. And he wasn't going to let Balen earn all the credits they needed for their wings...first.

"She will be seated at one of the lower tables with the lower lords during the supper, though she is but a commoner," the king said.

"As you wish, sire." He knew his father was making a great concession to allow her to dine with his lower lords, but he wondered then, why? Was she someone to really be concerned with? He couldn't imagine how she could be dangerous to his kingdom.

"My physicians tell me your wings will be well-mended by tomorrow afternoon."

"Yes, sire." It annoyed Viator that it would take that long. He'd wished there was some kind of elven potion to cure them sooner, but after the physician sewed the cuts in his wings, rest was all that would heal them now.

"Then perhaps, as you will be away longer this time, you should visit with your betrothed for a while."

His father had never suggested for him to do such a thing before now. Was he trying to tell him who he truly owed allegiance to? It was assumed he was betrothed to Sendal, but no ceremony had been performed in that regard, nor had he any intention of marrying her.

Viator bowed his head, then hurried out of the chamber. There was no way that he wished to spend the time with Sendal. Once he was beyond his father's hearing, he asked a guard, "Where is the human girl staying?"

"West wing, sire, but only the ladies are permitted to—"

"I know very well who is allowed to go there." Viator charged toward the west wing while Balen tried to catch up to him with a hurried pace.

"So what did the king say?"

Viator frowned. His friend had known about the prophecy. Did everyone know but him? "What else was said about the prophecy?"

"Ahh, so he finally told you." Balen smiled. "I figured he couldn't keep it from you forever."

"No, he denied it, but he is bothered by the notion. So much so, that you are to take my place, Balen, in handling the problem with the water. I won't agree to such a thing, however."

Balen took a deep breath. "And the girl?"

"You are to take Eloria to the cliffs."

Balen arched his brows. "And leave her there with no protection?"

"Yes."

Balen nodded. "It won't work, you know."

"What won't work?"

"Your father trying to change the prophecy, won't work." Balen stared at the hallway as the tapestry hangings featured gardens and female elves clustered together singing or sewing. "What are we doing in the women's quarters?"

"I have no idea what *you* are doing here. My father has told me to have a word with your sister." Though he was crown prince, all were forbidden from the single women's chambers, all but the king himself.

"You have not been told to speak to my sister in the women's chambers, sire."

A maid walked into the hall from one of the rooms and hurried to curtsy to the prince, then to Balen. Viator asked, "Where is the human staying?"

Balen laughed. "My sister you wished to see, you said, my prince. My sister."

The lady motioned to the third door on the right. Viator didn't hesitate to walk to the door. He knocked, then waited. A maid opened the door and quickly curtsied to him.

"The human girl?"

The lady motioned behind her. He entered the room as Balen shuffled his feet outside the door.

"Eloria." Viator found her staring out the window at the cloudless sky.

She turned to face him. "What did your father say about me?"

"That we must leave you at the cliffs."

"Where you took me hostage."

"Yes."

"Good."

"You would have no protection."

"Then show me the way to the shadow elf kingdom and I'll wait there for Persephonice."

He didn't say anything with regard to that but studied her gowns. "I've never liked white on most elven women. If they have blond hair, they fade away in such a gown. But with your red hair, you are like a goddess."

Eloria chuckled. "She thought you wouldn't like it."

"Who?"

"Sendal."

"I should have known." If Sendal thought Viator would have lost interest in the human girl, she was gravely mistaken. Her choice of dress only made Eloria intrigue him even more. Yet, he told himself it was only because she could be valuable to them like Persephonice was to the shadow elves. But maybe she wouldn't be. Maybe she was bad news.

"Why is your father afraid of me?" Eloria asked.

Viator shook his head. "Sometimes as we grow older, we become afraid of things we shouldn't fear. My father says I must go to the seacoast of Neferon. The cliffs are on the way." But he was wracking his brain for another option.

Eloria tilted her chin down as she considered his sincerity.

Viator smiled. She wasn't letting him get away with his phony story at all. "Well, maybe not quite on the way—"

"The truth?"

"Quite out of the way in fact, but that's where you were supposed to go."

She took a deep breath. "And Balen?"

"He'll have to come along also...just for show. Since my father said Balen would take you there, it would seem odd if he returned too soon to the castle."

She frowned. "What about the water?"

"I have the minister of health looking into a solution to counteract the poison. We'll take it with us to the river in the caves."

Outside the chamber, they heard Sendal say, "Why, Balen, my brother, what are you doing in the women's quarters? You *know* it is strictly forbidden." There was silence then she said, "The prince is seeing the—"

Her words broke off as Sendal hurried into the room. "Well, my prince, you've missed me so, you've come to see me here. My room, however, is across the hall, sire." She curtsied deeply, then smiled her most charming smile that was as wicked as any elf's could be who was up to no good.

6

E loria couldn't contain her amusement and smiled broadly at Sendal's comment to Viator about where her room was. "He wished to compliment me on the gowns you selected for me to wear." Eloria twirled around in the shimmering dresses, layered three on one, as her long red curls swirled. "I feel just like a princess... which I will be once I marry my prince." She meant her lifemate, if she could have ever had one.

Sendal glanced down at Eloria's green crystal and frowned. "It's not glowing now."

"Nope. It comes and goes. One minute it does, the next, it's asleep." The green crystal was a source of concern for Eloria since she'd been on the planet. The way it glowed from time to time confounded her. Normally, it only did when she had to call on it to focus certain kinds of her magic. It didn't light up and turn off like a broken light fixture at will.

The sound of melodic bells rippled through the air. "It's time for the meal." Sendal looped her arm through Viator's. "Escort me to supper, my prince, as I'm famished."

Eloria followed after the two as Viator turned back to her

and winked. They walked into the hall and Balen's eyes grew big as he watched his sister holding the prince's arm in hers with a tight grasp. Eloria smiled as Balen hurried to escort her to the great hall for the meal.

"You don't mind walking me to supper, though I'm but a human and a commoner?" she asked him.

Viator turned his head to hear what she was speaking of.

Balen shook his head. "You have turned our world upside down with your presence here. My being with you has elevated my position tenfold. And now, I've been told, I will return you to the cliffs. Lucky me. There are several who have beseeched the king that they be allowed to go in my place."

"Why?"

"We've never seen a red-haired girl before. Never. We've only heard all the talk about Persephonice. You are as rare as the neleron flower on our southern slopes. The others wish to learn if there are more of you in your lands."

"Some." She shrugged.

Sendal scowled. "Father won't like it you speak so kindly to this outsider, Balen. And he is having a fit the king has requested you take this creature back to where Prince Viator found her."

"Then perhaps, I should do the deed as I have promised," Viator said.

Sendal's back stiffened.

Eloria smiled. Sendal wasn't winning any points with Viator if that's what she intended to do.

When the four walked into the great hall, the courtiers grew quiet. Viator looked back at Balen, who led Eloria to one of the lower tables.

"At least she's not being seated with royalty," Sendal said loudly enough for Eloria to hear as she took her seat beside the prince at the head table. But she soon frowned as she saw that Eloria was seated with lower ranking royalty.

Balen joined them at the head table while Eloria sat between two barons.

The king and queen entered the hall as everyone stood and bowed. Before they could take their seats, a stiff wind blew through the open windows of the great room. All at once, the candles shivering on the marble walls were extinguished and the hall was plunged into darkness...all except for Eloria. Her crystal cast a soft green light over her ivory skin and gown. Whispered voices grew in volume as candles were hurriedly relit.

The flickering flames soon lighted the hall in a warm glow, but the voices had silenced as all eyes watched Eloria. She raised her eyebrows and smiled.

Viator turned to his mother, who studied Eloria. "What have you to say about her, my lady mother?"

The queen took a deep breath. "She will make a fine queen someday."

"Not ours, surely."

His mother buttered her roll. "And why would you think she would stay here? Your father is returning her with Lord Balen—"

Viator shook his head. His mother could not keep the secret from him any longer. "I've learned of the prophecy."

"Ahh, wagging tongues abound in court. She is unusual, I must say. I've heard she is but a commoner, and yet, she carries herself like royalty." The queen smiled. "I see she's wearing the gown Sendal told me you despise and still, you cannot keep your eyes off the girl."

"I've never seen red hair like hers. She climbs trees, falls off cliffs without injury, and—"

"Most unusual," the queen said. "I understand you are to go to the seacoast tomorrow."

"I should be taking care of the business with the water first."

Viator frowned as Eloria laughed with Barons Crawford and Tal. He should have been the one to sup with her, not them.

"Lord Balen will take care of that business. Your father knows best."

Viator poked his spoon into his boar soup. "It's not our way to default on our quests.'"

The queen shook her head. "You are good of heart, my son. You will do what is right." She studied the gem at Eloria's throat. "I wonder what power she possesses."

"What? Humans cannot even fly. I would not have thought they could have any powers."

"But this one...she already has quite a power over you."

"Nonsense." His body warmed in embarrassment. Now he knew his feelings must have been totally transparent just like his father's had been earlier.

"I sense there is something else. Something that..." His mother shook her head, then lifted her buttered bread to her lips.

"What?"

"She will be a challenge for all concerned...I predict."

ELORIA COULDN'T KEEP from looking at the head table to study Viator from time to time as she ate the elven food. Her whole body heated as she found him studying her in return. She smiled as he winked at her. Langolars, who were not committed to each other, did no such thing with each other. They were just paired, and that was the end of it. Had the shadow elf treated Persephonice in such a way?

The man who sat next to her pointed to her soup. "Boar, my lady. The prince hunted it for our meal. Do you like it?"

"I haven't tasted anything like it. It's delightful."

He nodded. "I'm Baron Crawford."

"And I'm Baron Tal," the man on the other side of her said.

She was surprised to be seated between two men of the king's court. Women who were unmarried were usually seated together in the castles she'd managed to visit on other worlds, and she could see quite a few sitting in such a manner at one of the long tables on the farthest side in the elven great hall. Was the king afraid of her? Were these men guards in reality?

"So what position do you maintain on the king's staff?" she asked Baron Crawford.

"Chief of Security."

"Ahh." She had assumed right. They were there to protect the courtiers from her. The notion amused her. She turned to the other man and said, "And you?"

"Chief of Information."

"I see." He was a spy to keep an eye on her, she figured. He gazed at her crystal with such intensity, she sighed. "Would you like for me to remove it so that you can see it better?" The crystal was protected so that he couldn't destroy it.

Baron Tal looked over at the king, and Eloria followed his gaze. Had he wanted the king's approval first? "Ask your king if it's all right with him. I have no problem with letting you examine the crystal. I harbor no ill will toward your people."

The baron waved for a page, then spoke to him. The boy's eyes grew round, and the baron motioned for him to get on with the task. Eloria noticed all the courtiers watched the page's actions. In fact, she realized everything that had to do with her was being monitored by the whole court. She hadn't realized what a distraction she could be. Then again, if they had an elf at one of their meals on the ship, the same thing would happen there.

The page spoke to the king as he leaned over to listen to him. Then he sat back in his chair. The page was undoubtedly waiting for the king's response, and so was everyone else as the conversation and eating of the meal had stopped completely.

Viator watched her, his face showing concern. What was he worried about?

Finally, the king nodded, then motioned for the page to carry out his word. The page strode back to Baron Tal as quickly as he could without running.

When he reached the baron, he bowed. "My lord, His Majesty bade you to examine the human's crystal."

Eloria lifted the necklace, but when she attempted to remove it, her curls caught in the rose-gold chain. For several minutes, she struggled to separate her hair from the chain, then took a deep breath of exasperation. She looked over at the head table to see everyone waiting in great anticipation.

"Sorry, Baron Tal." Whenever she left the ship, she never removed it. Not until she was in uniform. Though on occasion, she had worn it under her uniform, if she knew she wasn't going to perform any magic. If it had glowed when she was wearing it on the ship and anyone had seen it, she would have been in big trouble.

He nodded, his forehead peppered with sweat, and she realized he was nervous about touching it. "It is only a necklace." She reached up again and tried to untangle her curls from the fine chain. Then finally separating her hair from the necklace, she pulled the chain over her head.

The room was still quiet. Not a soul stirred in the massive great hall. She gazed at the crystal, dark as usual, shimmering in the reflection of the candle lights flickering gently in the summer breeze. Turning to face the baron, she was surprised his face had turned colorless.

She held the necklace out to him, but he didn't grab for it as she expected. She glanced over at the king who furrowed his brow at his lord. "Please, take it, my lord, and examine it all you want," she said to the baron. "I promise it won't harm you."

He stretched his hand out and grasped the chain as whispered words filled the room all at once. Just as suddenly, the blue sky turned green as storm clouds rolled in with frightening speed. Sparks of light tore through the darkening gloom and thunder boomed overhead as the wind whipped into the hall, extinguishing the lights all at once. Feminine gasps and male chatter circulated as everyone sat still in the dark.

Then the crystal began to glow, and the baron nearly dropped it. The light from the crystal highlighted Eloria and him as they both stared at it, but a new noise caught their attention. Turning to view the southernmost window at their backs, they saw a monster of a dragon appear, his green-silver scales glowing in a supernatural mist.

"The dragon of Benzol," Baron Tal and several others said at once.

Its catlike, emerald eyes narrowed as it peered through the expansive window, while its wings flapped, sending ripples of wind into the hall.

"The Benzolian dragon that won't be tamed," Baron Tal whispered.

7

The dragon raised his head upward and shot a stream of blue flames toward the heavens. As soon as he displayed his threat, several of the elven men quickly herded the women and children out of the hall toward the living quarters for safety. Only Eloria and some of the other men of the court remained with their king and Viator.

Lowering his head, the dragon focused on Baron Tal and then Eloria. In the next instance, the necklace the baron held in his clenched fingers vanished, only to reappear around Eloria's neck.

Then the scaled beast twisted its long body around and flew off, one of his mighty wings knocking about baskets of flowers hanging above the large open-air windows. Eloria took a breath finally, then gasped when Viator grabbed her hand and pulled her from her seat.

"Eloria, are you all right?"

She'd been concentrating on the dragon and hadn't seen Viator rush to join her. She still couldn't believe she'd seen another dragon.

Everyone who was left in the great hall still sat stunned at the sight. Her necklace glowed, but softer now and some of the remaining men hastened to relight the candles.

The king stared at her as if *she'd* turned into a dragon, and she faced Viator. "What happened?"

He led her from the hall and returned her to her chamber before anyone could stop him. "Eloria, what do you know about the necklace?" He closed the door to the bedchamber behind him.

She sat on a blue velvet-cushioned bench, and he joined her. Would her words scare him away? Despite fearing they would, she wanted to tell him.

"I had a dream where a white-bearded man came to me in a dream. A dream within a dream, you see. You know how they can be...totally confusing. I was the one chosen above all else to be given the gift, so he told me."

"What gift?"

She shrugged. "He didn't say and in a dream it's hard to ask about these things."

"Go on."

"He told me I'd find a crystal...a special green gem that would help me to fulfill my dreams and many others' too. I had the most important quest to complete. But you know, Viator, it was only a dream. Why once I dreamed a mermaid tried to drown me."

"And?"

She chuckled. "I'd dreamed it once. Just a dream." She couldn't explain about the one landing in their transporter, which was the reason she had nightmares about it. More than once.

He shook his head. "So the next day, you went to the cave to retrieve the crystal?"

"Not exactly."

"But you said—"

"I didn't go the next day. I mean, I didn't really remember having gone at all. Just like the dream within a dream. It was like I had gone there in a dream. My father said the necklace was from my mother, but still, the dream was clear that I had found the crystal myself and not that my mother had passed it to my father to give to me. My mother died when I was four. I don't remember much about her."

"I'm so sorry to hear this. But it sounds to me like you were... shadow walking."

"What?"

"When someone visits a place but is not fully conscious at the time as if they're accomplishing a mission of high importance but where no one must see them carry out the task. We call it shadow walking."

"Oh."

He held her hand. "Talom is a rogue dragon. No one has ever been able to tame him, though many have died trying. They say he is untamable."

"Why, then, does anyone try to do so?" She believed he should be free to roam their world without having to owe allegiance to anyone.

"They say whosoever does will harness the greatest power in the world." He reached over and touched her necklace, turned dark, and it flickered with light. "You have powers that confound us, Eloria. My father will wish you never to return to our lands of Darkland Forest."

She shook her head. "I am only a commoner, Viator. A wingless human girl." She had to let on that she had no powers, no real magic, that she couldn't harm them. "I know many things... how to heal with herbs, I can recognize storms before anyone else seems to—"

"And tonight?"

"It was different. But everything here for me is different."

"How so?"

Eloria stood, then walked over to the window. No more clouds filled the sky, no more streaks of lightning zigzagging to the earth, only a smattering of twinkling stars hanging against a black velvet night. "I felt a surge of power shimmering through my body. It wasn't like anything I've ever felt before. Like I was soaring high above the ground, my heart lighter than air." It was different. She'd never felt this overwhelming sense of power.

He tapped his fingers on the bench. "You wear a magical amulet with who knows what kind of powers and the ability to summon Talom."

"What?"

"You summoned him, Eloria. That's what my father's advisors will say. You summoned the dragon who cannot be tamed."

"Nonsense. He came here...well, for whatever reason. He flies where he chooses, but I had nothing to do with it."

Viator joined her at the window and ran his hand over her fingers. "He displayed his prowess to show us how powerful he was. With one such effort, he could have killed everyone in the great hall. It was a warning. Baron Tal had your necklace and the next thing we knew, the storm was unleashed and Talom appeared. Why? He has never visited our castle before."

Eloria shook her head. "You give me way too much credit. I never even knew dragons existed before I came here."

He rubbed his chin as he seemed deep in thought. "What did the man look like?"

"What man?"

"The one from your dream."

"He was white-haired, with a beard that curled down to his toes. His eyes were as blue as the cloudless sky, and he had a prominent nose. Clothed in shimmering blue-green robes reaching to his turned-up slippers, he reminded me of a wizard, or at least the ones I've seen from the wizards' realm of Caladan. Oh, and he carried a staff with a glowing—"

"Green crystal at its tip."

"You know of him?"

"Sarazan."

"Who?"

He patted her hand and took a ragged breath. "Sarazan. He sounds like the wizard who heads the wizard guild of Caladan. I can't be certain, but all wizards have a distinctive staff. He is about the most powerful of all sorcerers. I can't understand why he would choose a human girl for the task. And as far as I know, he's dead."

"That someone from your, uhm, part of the world couldn't possibly call on me to do anything. I'm not from here." She was exasperated. No way could a wizard from here give her a crystal in a faraway world. "What task?"

"That, I do not know. You must remember something else about the dream. What did he say about the gift he was to bestow on you?"

"If he said anything about it, I can't remember. Not a thing."

"Has he come to you more than once?"

She didn't want to say anything more about the wizard's visitations. Viator would shun her like the rest of his people did, and she didn't want that. Not from him.

"Eloria?"

She turned to look out the window again. The ebony sky sparkled with life.

"How many times, Eloria?"

"Too many to remember."

His hand touched her shoulder as if to coax the words from her. She knew he was dying to know, but she was afraid to say anymore. She tried to relax, but her back was as stiff as when Talom first appeared.

"What happened during these other visitations?"

The door was thrown open and Sendal, her maid, and Baron Crawford walked into the room. "You're not to be in the women's chambers any longer, Prince Viator," Sendal snarled.

"My liege," Baron Crawford said, using much more caution in addressing the crown prince, "his majesty wishes a word with you."

"At once," Sendal snapped. "Furthermore, you're not to return here again."

Unless he wished to be with Sendal, then Eloria figured the irate woman wouldn't have minded. But of course, Sendal couldn't suggest this. Eloria was surprised she would speak so haughtily to the crown prince in such a way. She must have assumed her position was guaranteed.

Viator hesitated, then kissed Eloria's lips lightly. She smiled as Sendal gasped. "Good night, Viator," Eloria said, then kissed him back. He smiled at her when she returned his kiss. "Pleasant dreams, my prince."

"And you, my love."

He called her his love? She wanted to laugh out loud. As much as Sendal tried to aggravate her, Viator appeared to want to irritate the elf. Eloria hoped she wouldn't get payback for it. Then again, surely Sendal would worry about Eloria's powerful magic and the ability to call a mighty dragon.

But the kiss? That little touch had made her want so much more.

"My liege," Baron Crawford said.

"I will speak with you further, my lady, rest assured." He kissed Eloria's hand with tenderness, then bowed low in total reverence while she quickly curtsied to him in return.

When he hastened out of the room with Baron Crawford shadowing him, Sendal paced across the floor. "You will see no more of my betrothed, human."

"Are you going to stop him?" Eloria sat down on the bench. She imagined only the king had such authority and Sendal was just full of hot air.

"His father has already decreed such a ruling. My prince is to have nothing further to do with you. However, my brother is to return you to the cliffs at first light, though our father tried to talk the king into sending someone else to do the job."

The notion disturbed Eloria. She could see Viator's father locking him in some tower to ensure he had nothing further to do with her.

She wished to scare the woman a little—to ask her if she didn't fear the wrath of Talom, or some such thing for being so mean to her. But she couldn't do it. She realized Sendal was scared enough already. She was afraid of losing her betrothed and with that, the future rule of the kingdom of Darkland Forest at her husband's side.

"You have nothing to fear from me, Sendal. Viator would never marry me, you do realize, despite the fact we love each other deeply." She couldn't believe the words slipped off her tongue without her permission. The woman grated on her. Whatever happened to her ability to be an inspirational motivator? Then again, she guessed she'd inspired the prince to show how he felt about Sendal.

Sendal scoffed at her. "It's Lady Sendal to you. You'll never see him again, but if you'd had the chance, you could have asked him about Lela, the river elf he'd grown attached to. If Balen is inclined to tell you the story, ask him. You see, Viator has done this before. Not once, not twice, but three times, he has fallen in love with a woman he cannot have. Convenient, isn't it? But he will marry only me."

8

Was Sendal lying? Eloria wished it was so, but she suspected Sendal was not. Her father had warned her of men like that. He'd profess his undying love to a woman, whom he could never wed for whatever reason. Then he'd terminate the relationship and start anew. If Lela was a river elf, what were the other women he couldn't have? Eloria was dying to ask, but she couldn't. Then Sendal would know she'd gotten under her skin. Not that this really meant anything to Eloria, but still, it did make her see him in a different light.

"Pleasant dreams," Sendal said, then hurried out of the room with her maid.

Pleasant dreams indeed. More like she wished Eloria would have nightmares. Which she could very well have. But they were of her own making.

VIATOR KNEW what his father was going to say before he even said it. Both Barons Crawford and Tal stood nearby, waiting to be dismissed from the king's throne room, but he motioned for them to stay.

That was a bad sign. It meant his father wished his word to be recorded in stone. Whatever he spoke to Viator about, would be common knowledge by morning meal.

"You won't see the human girl any further, my son. Balen will escort her to the cliffs and cleanse the water. As we speak, our healers are working on a cure from the droplets remaining in the river elves' flask for those who have already been poisoned. You will go to Neferon, where your next mission awaits you, as you have already mentioned you sense this is so."

Viator stiffened his back. He wouldn't let his father, or his advisors know how defeated he felt. "Yes, my lord father."

He had never disobeyed his father in any ruling he'd ever made concerning him before. But this time, he knew his father was wrong. It was every elf's right to come of age on his own terms. That was part of becoming a full-fledged adult, after all. Still, his stomach knotted with annoyance, knowing he would have to disobey him.

"What did she say?"

"My lord father?"

"Come, come, Viator. You do not think I allowed you time alone with the girl to...to...well, I only left her alone with you so you could find out how she summoned the dragon. And I know you desired to know this, as well as you wish to be the one to tame him, when all other quests are completed."

He was surprised his father would have realized this. Most young men had given up the notion anyone would ever tame Talom, but then again, Viator wasn't just any man. He was to be ruler someday, and he had to prove he was worthy above everyone else.

And yet, Eloria had entrusted him with her story. He wasn't about to betray her. "She doesn't know anything about Talom,

Your Majesty. She hadn't even known dragons were real until she saw Prince Zorak riding one."

The barons both chuckled.

His father wasn't treating the situation lightly though. "And the crystal she wears about her neck? Where did it come from and what powers does it possess?"

"A cave possibly. She has no idea what powers it possesses."

His father stroked his gray beard, and Viator knew he was contemplating the matter further. He turned to Baron Tal. "You will speak with the girl. Return to me when you have word."

Viator took a deep breath, trying to calm his anger. He didn't want Tal or anyone else questioning Eloria. They had no right. He had a difficult enough time getting her to speak to him without her being interrogated by the Chief of Information.

"That is all, my son. When your wings are healed, you will go to Neferon."

Viator bowed, then hurried out of the throne room after the barons. Catching up to Baron Tal, he said, "You must be careful with Eloria."

He smiled. "Prince Viator, I believe as you do, you are the only one who can extract the information from the young lady. But the king worries about the powers she possesses and believes, as I do, that she will unduly influence you. Therefore, I will do as the king bids and question the young lady, but I won't threaten her, nor will I force the answers from her. If she doesn't know anything, or doesn't reveal anything to me, I will let the king know this. Nothing more."

"But you won't let me witness your questioning of her?"

"No, Prince Viator. The king doesn't wish you to see the lady any longer, and I will have to ensure this as well."

Viator shook his head. "Very well. I will see how the physician is doing with finding a cure for the water in the meantime."

"As you wish, Your Highness."

It wasn't at all as Viator wished. He stormed off toward the potions room.

BARON TAL SMILED SWEETLY at Eloria as he entered the bedchamber with a maid. "My lady," he said, bowing slightly.

Eloria knew it was time for the questioning. When the meal was interrupted by the appearance of Talom, that pretty much ended any chance Baron Tal had at interrogating her. But now, it was time. He glanced down at her necklace, then over at her open window. Was he dying to know if he touched her necklace again, would Talom return?

Eloria was curious, too. "Did you wish to examine my necklace again, my lord?"

He cleared his throat and ran his hands through his hair. No, she guessed he did not.

"Prince Viator says he has asked you about the crystal and where you got it from."

"Yes."

"He said you found it in a cave."

"In a dream."

Baron Tal motioned for her to take a seat on the bench. This meant he was going to take some time, she assumed. She sat down, then took a deep breath.

"What powers does it possess?"

She smiled. "Did Prince Viator not also tell you I have no idea?"

"He did."

"Ahhh, then I must assume you are asking because you think, between the time I spoke with him earlier and now as I speak with you, I have learned something new. Rest assured, I have not."

"Why would a commoner be chosen as queen?"

He was changing the subject. Why? "I have not been chosen to be a queen, a princess, or any other kind of royalty. I don't intend to marry anyone here, or anyone else in these lands." Or anyone at all, if the computer that decided the issue of lifemates had any say in it.

He nodded, then rubbed his smooth chin. "How did you meet Prince Viator?"

Now this was a different line of questioning. "He was...hunting."

"So you lured him there?"

She raised her brows in surprise. What an odd way of putting it. "He took me hostage. I was going with Prince Zorak to his home, but Prince Viator stole me away."

The man's eyes rounded. "I see."

Was this good or bad? She assumed the worst. She'd lured the prince there to the cliffs and for whatever reason, the elves felt she was evil. Did they think she was going to steal their prince away from them?

"Listen, Baron Tal, I have no intention of doing harm to any of your people."

"You may have no intention, my lady, but you do not truly seem to understand the power you possess. This puts us all at risk."

"Ahh, I see. A lowly human girl is very frightening, to be sure."

He straightened his posture and wrinkled his brow at her. "You possess a formidable power I fear, and you have no knowledge of how to handle it. This alone makes you dangerous...not only to our kind, but I imagine to your own as well."

He stormed out of the room with the maid trailing behind him in a hurry.

"Thank you for your help, Eloria," Eloria said under her

breath. "You have been so very cooperative. We must have another chat like this soon." She rose from the bench, then crossed the room to the window. Leaning out of the sill, she felt the cool breeze swirl around her. It was much cooler and the air lighter in the mountaintops. And then a stream of blue fire shot across the sky. "Talom?"

LATE THAT EVENING, Viator slipped into Eloria's bedchamber as she sat staring out the window in the direction of the place where she'd been dropped off. "Eloria," he whispered. The green gem around her neck flickered with light.

She jumped up from her seat. "Viator, have you heard?"

9

Viator took Eloria's hand and led her to a sofa. They sat down. "Balen and I have been discussing this all evening. Since my father is going to have you leave with Balen before my wings have totally healed, he will take you to the fairyland meadows. It's safe for anyone there, as long as you cannot hear the fairies' music. I will join you as soon as I'm able. Then we will take care of the poisoned water."

"And the seacoast?"

"I'll have to take care of that afterwards."

"I was afraid I wouldn't see you again."

"Nothing doing. Why several of the elves I know who are trying to come of age have besieged me with questions of what you are like. I've always been popular among my people, but with you here, I've never seen anything like it. Whispered conversations in the hallways, fervent discussions in the dining hall, from the king to his lowest servant there is no other word than that which speaks of you."

"And Sendal?"

He laughed. "Sour tangerines. I couldn't even smile at a girl without Sendal turning two shades greener. Now with you here, she really shows what I would have to live with, should I marry her."

"Have you a choice?"

"Certainly. Of course, it was always assumed I would marry her as she is a duke's daughter and very nearly my age but ultimately, it is my choice."

There was no more conversation and she looked over to see him studying her features in the pale moonlight with the soft glow of a candle shimmering against the wall. Was she just like the river elf he was infatuated with? And what were the other creatures who were not winged elves that he'd had fleeting feelings for?

"Sendal said you were interested in Lela, a river elf." She studied his response. Just his hesitation made her believe Sendal hadn't lied about Viator's interest in the elf.

"Yes, well, I did care for Lela. But once the river elves broke away from having any good relations with the winged elves, Lela sided with them. I didn't blame her. She is Lars's sister, and it was expected of her."

"I see."

"But I was only twelve when they moved away. We're not the same people we were then."

Weren't they? If the river elves and winged elves repaired the rift, would Viator once again desire Lela...maybe even for his wife? She was an elf at least and royalty, too, though she did not have wings like his kind.

"Yes, we are different now." Viator sat on the bench next to her. She figured he sensed she wasn't sure he still wasn't fond of Lela and wished to close the distance between them.

She hated asking, but she hated not knowing more. "And the others?"

He smiled. "I was young when I met the other."

She couldn't imagine Viator as an infant, ever. Not as tall and handsome as he was now. "Yes?"

She wasn't letting him off the hook. She wanted to know everything about him...just as he wanted to know everything about her.

"A mermaid."

She frowned at him. "A mermaid? How could you fall in love with a mermaid?"

He chuckled. "They have ways of luring the unexpected, Eloria. And to love one, means ultimate death. They lure the unsuspecting to their deaths...it is their way."

"But you say you loved one."

"When I was eight, my father and mother took me to Neferon. My ability to filter the songs of the siren were not strong enough back then. I had no trouble with the meadow-land fairies and my parents assumed I would be able to block the song of the mermaids, but I wasn't able to. She was a beautiful creature with ebony curls and eyes as azure as the sea. But she would have drowned me if my father hadn't stopped me."

"Oh." Eloria looked up from her hands she'd been wringing absentmindedly to see Viator watching her. "Sendal said there was another."

"None other, unless she means you." He hesitated, then reached over and took her hand in his. "Goodnight, Eloria." He touched his lips to her hand and kissed it. "I will see you again, tomorrow afternoon. You have nothing to fear from the other loves of my life." Then he leaned over to kiss her lips, but the sound of women's voices approaching made him jump from the bench. "Tomorrow, Eloria."

He climbed through the window to her surprise and slipped along the narrow ledge to the end of the row of chambers as she watched him. When he reached the end of the building, he waved to her, then disappeared around the bend. She smiled. Not that anything could exist between them, but she was wondering if this is how Persephonice had ended up with the shadow elf Dracolin.

THAT NIGHT, Eloria woke from her nightmare. She couldn't sleep. She tried to think of anything that was pleasant. Instead, she kept thinking about her nightmare: falling into the pit in a cave. That had really happened to her when she had tried to inspire opposing forces to give up fighting. They did, after they threw her into the pit, and she miraculously survived. Courtesy of her magic. But she continued to have nightmares about it.

Shaking her head, she sat up in bed. The elves had loaned her a long, soft gown for sleeping in, but she exchanged it for the white elven gown. If she couldn't sleep, she'd take a little walk around the castle and do some exploring. Hopefully, everyone had turned in for the night. She assumed it was late enough.

She strode across to the door and peeked out. She hadn't expected a guard, but when she saw his gold uniform, she quickly closed the door. He hadn't seen her as he appeared to be half asleep. She should have figured as dangerous as the elves thought she was, they would post a guard.

She walked across the room to the window and peered out. Could she make the walk along the ledge like Viator had done and reach the other side? Sure. She could do anything he could do...except fly. She considered the jagged rocks below this. Taking a deep breath, she figured her own clothes would be better to wear. She changed into her britches and blouse.

Without hesitation, she climbed out the window this time. With a cautious step, she made her way in the direction Viator had taken. But halfway there, she spied a large, flying creature silhouetted against the full moon. Was it Talom again? She couldn't tell, but she wasn't about to hang around and find out either. She hadn't done anything to summon him as far as she knew, and there was a lot she didn't know about in Viator's elven world: mermaids, dragons, winged elves, and river ones. High elves, blue elves, snow giants, snow dragons? What else lurked unseen in their kingdom? She wasn't certain she wished to find out.

Viator seemed so sure footed when he hurried along the stone ledge, but her own feet slipped several times on the moss-covered path. Her heartbeat pounded in her ears as she tried to hurry. She glanced over at the creature as it grew in size while nearing her location. It was headed straight for her.

And then she finally made out its strange features: an eagle's head and neck crowned with white feathers, and gray feathered wings, the body and legs of a golden lion and a long switching tail with a comb of fur on the end. She'd never seen anything like it, but its sharp beak coming ever closer made her try to move too quickly. Just as he shrieked a spine-jarring noise, her foot slipped, making her heart jump out of her throat in terror. She didn't even have time to scream as she fell off the ledge.

10

Viator paced across the floor of his chambers, consumed with worry their plans wouldn't work on the morrow. What if his father discovered what he planned on doing with Balen and Eloria? His father would confine him to his bedchamber with a guard. That was for certain.

He sat down on his bed. He couldn't get Eloria out of his mind. What was the matter with him anyway? He'd never been so distracted by a woman in his life. And yet, he hated returning her to the cliffs. He didn't want to hand her over to the shadow elves either. He knew they'd keep her. Prince Zorak too. But Viator was thinking of a couple of elves who had defied convention and who remained neutral. Maybe they would take her in until he could convince the king she wasn't dangerous.

Though he had to accomplish his mission, he didn't want to leave her behind. He knew his work could take him all over the various lands he'd never even seen, and he'd have no more time for silly interests in a human girl. The thought sickened him. He didn't want to leave her with anyone. He spread his wings, but they were as opaque as before. He wished she was one of his missions.

And then he heard the cry of the opinicus. He knew very well what that singular screech meant. The winged creature nearly had its prey in its deadly grasp. But what would one be doing so close to the castle?

Viator hurried to his window. He couldn't see a thing. It hadn't come from his southerly room, but the wing where the women's chambers were. He ran his hands through his hair. The archers would take care of him if they were alert on guard duty this eve.

And then the half bird, half lion screeched again. It wasn't usual for the swift moving creature to miss its prey like that. He could tell from the noise; it was still after something. Something close to the castle. Viator pulled on his tunic and rushed out of his chambers. Balen soon joined him.

"Sire, where are the archers who should be guarding the wall walk?"

"Who knows? I've never heard of one of those creatures missing its prey and yet it sounds as if it's targeted it again."

Another screech sent Viator in a panic as they raced to the women's chambers. His first thought was Eloria. None of the elven women would be out of their chambers this time of night. Only Eloria wouldn't know the rules. But when he saw the guard, his heart stilled. She wouldn't have left her room, not with a guard posted.

"Sire." The guard bowed in greeting.

"I wish to see if Eloria is all right."

"Your father forbids you to enter her chambers, Your Majesty."

"Then see if the woman is there, for heaven's sake. Have you not heard the opinicus screeching outside the women's chambers?"

"Yes, sire, but I cannot leave my post, by the strictest orders of the king."

"Knock on her door!"

The guard turned and pounded on the door. When there was no answer, he said, "She must be sound asleep, Your Majesty."

"Check, then."

"I cannot go into the woman's chamber."

Viator grabbed for the door handle, but the guard blocked him. "Your father has said if you return here, I'm to have you returned to your room and have a guard posted. I won't mention this incident if you leave here quietly, Your Majesty."

Viator hurried off with Balen dashing after. "Where are we going, sire?"

"Another way to Eloria's room."

"The ledge." He rubbed his chin. "Without full use of your wings, that is a dangerous venture. Let me go in your stead."

"You may come with me if you so choose, but I won't stay behind. I have to know Eloria is safe."

They soon made it to the ledge but saw no sign of the opinicus. Both looked up, but there were no archers anywhere either.

Viator led the way, easing toward Eloria's room and when he reached the open window, he poked his head inside. He couldn't tell if she was in her bed or not, it was so dark.

Balen bumped into him. "Sire," he whispered, "is she in there?"

"I cannot see her."

Viator climbed in through the window, then crossed the floor to the bed. Pulling the partially opened curtains away from the bed, his heart stopped. She had to have left the room through the window. He dashed to the window and climbed back out. "She's not in her room."

Viator knelt at the edge of the path looking for signs she'd been there.

"Sire, the opinicus never misses—"

"He missed. You heard him screech the second time. He missed."

"But the probability he'd miss a second time is unheard of."

"Either help me to look for her or leave. You are not making the task any easier."

"Yes, sire."

Balen crouched, looking for any signs that Eloria had come this way. "Maybe she got farther along the ledge. Or maybe she went the opposite way than the way we came."

Viator stood and looked in the northerly direction. "All right, we'll see if she went that way."

He hurried toward the north side of the castle. When they reached the end, they walked onto the expansive patio used for royal parties and ceremonies during seasonable weather. He glanced up to see archers surveying the mountains. "Well, there are the archers. But where is Eloria? If they had seen her, they'd have returned her to her room."

He looked back at the ledge. "She couldn't have fallen from the ledge."

As quickly as he was able, he returned to the location of her room, then at intervals along the ledge he crouched down looking for signs of her.

His gut wrenched when he discovered a piece of cloth from her pants. "Balen, she's been here."

"I'll fly down and look, sire. Your wings shouldn't be used any more than necessary."

"Find her, Balen."

"Yes, sire."

Balen dropped over the edge. Viator hated that his friend would be the one searching for her and not him.

After several minutes, Balen called out. "I've found her, but she's unconscious, sire."

"Bring her up at once."

"I'm afraid to move her, Your Majesty."

"What's wrong, Balen?" He could tell from the quaver in his friend's voice, something terrible was the matter and the suspense was killing him. He fought the urge to join him by flight, but knew he'd prolong the healing of his wings and he couldn't afford to do that. Instead, he started the long climb down the jagged rock. "Balen, what's the matter?"

"Your Majesty, I wouldn't recommend you climbing down here."

"Then bring her up."

"I beg your forgiveness, but I can't."

Viator knew Balen had to have good reason for his reluctance to move Eloria, but still he was angered. "What in the world is the matter—"

His words were cut short as he saw the matter. Talom was crouched near Eloria, a smoky green mist cloaking him in part, his eyes sparkling like beacons of emerald light.

11

"Has he killed Eloria?" Viator asked Balen. His head swam with the notion she could be dead because the beast had killed her. He'd silence the breath of the dragon with his bare hands if he could, forget trying to tame him.

Balen pointed down the mountain twenty feet. "I think that black pile of ashes was the opinicus."

"He killed the threat to Eloria?" His words were raised in awe. Talom had never been known to save anyone's life. He wouldn't be tamed, and he was like any other wild beast, who earned the reputation of being a rogue, dangerous and deadly.

"Maybe her red hair is what draws him to her."

"She isn't stirring. How do we know she isn't dead, Balen?"

"He nudged her with that scaly nose of his, and she moaned."

Viator took a step toward Eloria. He didn't want to leave her injured on the ledge where she lay so still any longer. He had to take her to a healer at once.

"Sire," Balen whispered. "I tried moving toward her once, but he raised his head and opened his mouth as if he was going to incinerate me. You know, that's how they do it. Just open up and uh—"

Viator motioned for him to be quiet. Talom watched Viator's movements, but sat still, not moving at all. Viator said, "I only seek to help the human girl, Talom. Please, let me aid her."

He didn't figure the dragon would have understood his language, but he hoped it would take his words spoken in a soothing manner as nonaggression. He'd never gotten that close to a wild dragon either before and the prospect was disconcerting. His father would have thrown a fit if he'd known Viator was facing his potential extermination for a mere human girl.

When Viator was nearly at Eloria's feet, the dragon suddenly lifted off and flew away.

"Jeez, Your Highness. He nearly gave me a heart attack. I can't believe he never once opened his mouth to threaten you."

"Help me get her to her room, Balen."

"Yes, sire."

Viator lifted her into Balen's arms, and she moaned slightly with the effort. He hated to hear her in pain, but he was comforted to know she was alive.

Balen lifted her to the top ledge as Viator made the climb back up. He'd never work so hard in his life. Never again was he going to challenge Lars, not until his wings were invisible. Climbing wasn't meant for winged elves.

When he finally reached the top, Balen joined him. "I've put her in her room, sire, but now what do we do? She spoke your name, then closed her eyes. But if we get the healers, they'll know she was out of her room, and they may learn you were trying to see her and..."

Viator hurried to Eloria's guest chambers and climbed in through the window. "Eloria." He strode to her bed, then touched her forehead.

She opened her eyes and smiled weakly. "Viator. He says he'll give me the gift soon."

"Who? What gift?"

She closed her eyes, and he took her hand and rubbed it. "Eloria, what gift?"

"Sire," Balen whispered, "if we're caught in here, it would not go well for us."

"Balen, sneak some aloverot potion out of the healer's chambers. I must revive Eloria and find out about the gift and who has spoken to her about it. The dragon, possibly?" He shook his head as if in answering his own question. "The dragon could not speak to her. She would only understand him if she were a high elf. Get me the potion and quickly."

"Yes, sire." Balen hurried back out through the window.

Viator sat on the bed next to Eloria and wrapped his hand around hers. "Eloria." His words were spoken in hushed tones so as not to alert the guard standing outside her door.

After a good ten minutes, she reached for his hand with her free one. "Rupert?"

Viator stood up from the down-filled mattress, his wings spreading out in a possessive manner heretofore he'd never before exhibited.

Balen chuckled as he climbed in through the window with a flask in his grasp. "Seems you are coming of age, Your Highness. I've never seen you display your wings in such a manner. But what I don't understand is why you are doing such a thing when there is no other male here for you to threaten, showing you have interest in the female."

Viator grabbed the flask. "Do not repeat this to anyone."

"I wouldn't, sire. But still I'm curious as to what angered you so."

"Maybe you should leave the room, Balen, in case any should find us here."

"If you wish for me to, sire."

Viator didn't want his friend to think he didn't want him to share in the information. On the other hand, he was afraid of what Eloria might reveal. And he did worry that Balen would get into as much trouble as he would for being with her in the chamber in the first place.

"Thank you for retrieving the medicine, Balen."

"Of course, sire."

Viator didn't ask him to leave any further, but instead lifted Eloria's head to have her drink the potion. She drank greedily of the liquid to his surprise and when he pulled it away from her, she grasped at the flask, but he wouldn't let her have any more.

"Perhaps, sire, it doesn't have the same effect on humans as it does on elves."

"Apparently not, though it seems to have revived her."

She licked her lips and stared at the flask.

"Eloria, what happened?"

"I'm still thirsty."

Viator smiled. "You've had plenty."

She frowned at him and when her green eyes narrowed, he was reminded of the catlike eyes of the dragon. He handed the flask to Balen, then took her hand and ran his fingers over it. "Eloria, the creature that came after you, what happened to it?"

"I fell."

"Yes, how are you feeling?"

"Thirsty."

She looked from Viator to the flask.

He smiled as Balen chuckled. "Guess she likes the aloverot," Balen said, holding onto the flask tightly.

"Eloria." Viator touched her cheek, trying to get her attention. "You fell because of the opinicus."

"The opinicus? Never heard of it."

"It's like a griffin only has a slightly different tail."

"Never heard of a...oh...it had an eagle's head, and its sharp beak was poised at my throat, and then he fell to the ground in a pile of ashes."

"Because of Talom."

"Talom?" She rubbed her head. "Never heard of it."

"The dragon...the one that came to the great hall."

"Oh. I don't know. I felt really hot all of a sudden, then didn't remember anything more."

"Are you okay? No injuries or anything? I was worried that you were injured."

"I'm thirsty."

Viator and Balen chuckled. Viator reached up and touched Eloria's head and frowned. "She's bloodied her head. She must have fallen and was knocked out."

"I'll get something to clean her up, sire."

Balen left with the flask and Eloria watched him leave with too much interest. Viator took her hand again. "Who spoke to you?"

"The wizard. You know, he visits me in my dreams. Not all of them. Some of them are nightmares—I was falling into a deep pit. Pushed there. Couldn't get the two opposing parties to listen to me and they got rid of me. Or tried."

Viator frowned. "Eloria, what did the wizard say to you?"

"To sleep, I think. I couldn't sleep."

"He told you he was going to give you the gift soon."

"No, he told me I was to sleep."

"Eloria, when we first brought you to the room, you told us he said he was going to give you the gift and soon."

"I don't remember." She lay back on the bed.

Totally exasperated, he rubbed her arm, trying not to think of it, only to offer her comfort. "Does your head hurt, Eloria?"

She nodded.

Soon Balen was climbing through the window again with a pack over his shoulder.

"I am thirsty."

Balen had purposefully left the flask behind. In its place, he brought a water pouch. "Here, to quench your thirst."

Then he handed Viator the cloth and antiseptic. He cleaned her wound, but the cut was no longer bleeding. "She won't need stitches, thank the heavens."

Eloria choked on the water and Viator patted her back as Balen watched the door, fearing the guard might check to see the matter. Eloria's eyelids drew closed and Viator said, "She should sleep now."

"I didn't think it would ever work on her."

"Humans seem to react differently to the potion." Viator tucked her in, then the two exited through the window and worked their way carefully back to their chambers for the evening, both of them keeping an eye out for anything flying in their direction.

EARLY THE NEXT MORNING, Eloria was served breakfast in her room alone. She assumed the staff didn't want a repeat of the dragon's visit at the great hall when she'd eaten the supper meal with them. The only thing she regretted was not seeing Viator. All night she worried she might not see him ever again; in the event his father did lock him in his chamber.

After the morning meal, she was escorted to the courtyard where they first had arrived the day before. Balen greeted her as several other elves watched the proceeding. Many were curious about her, she figured. Then too, they probably wished to see one of their own off. Who knew if Balen would ever return?

"They didn't return my sword or another thing I use for protection."

"If they didn't, they won't. I have a dagger I can give you for protection."

"I want my sword." And the stun gun. Especially the stun gun.

She climbed onto Balen's back and with a whoosh he flew down from the ring of mountains toward the fairyland's meadow.

"I can feel you twisting to see behind us again. Prince Viator won't follow us until later this afternoon. He has to make arrangements to leave without his father getting wind of it. And it'll give his wings longer to heal. In the meantime, I will show you some of the countryside." Balen cleared his throat. "He was concerned about you this morning. He wondered if you were all right after last night."

"All right?"

"Yes, after your fall."

"Oh, it was a dream. I dreamed I was falling in a pit."

"You don't remember the dragon last night?"

"What dragon?"

"Why had you left your room?"

"Why would I have done that?"

He shook his head. "Prince Viator wished to know this as well."

She looked down to see foxglove blooming in profusion all over the long, green grasses. The purple flowers turned their deep-spotted throats up to the awakening sun as Balen settled among them. "Thank you, Balen, for helping me like this."

He cleared his throat in annoyance.

"Lord Balen, I'm sorry I cannot seem to get used to saying royal titles here in your lands. In mine, we don't have royal titles." Military ranks and governmental ranks, sure. But not royal titles.

He reached out and touched her ear. "Can you hear the fairies' song?"

She shook her head as she touched the cotton stuffed in her ears.

"Good because here comes one now." The fairy darted out of the safety of the tall grasses and floated above his head, her hair dangling in ice-white curls about her small face. Her shimmering pink gowns and filmy wings fluttered in the slight breeze. Silky pink lips mouthed words to lure the two, but Balen just smiled at her. "She wishes for us to stay here with her to watch her dance and to hear her songs."

The fairy flitted near Eloria's head, then lifted a shock of red curl to her face. She ran her nimble fingers through the silky strands, then smiled broadly. Flipping around to Eloria's back, she ran her tiny fingers along her white gown.

"What is she doing?" Eloria's brows rose with concern.

Balen smiled. "She is looking for your wings. She cannot understand that not only have you no wings, but your hair is as red as the red deer who reside in the forest near here."

"The Darkland Forest." Eloria looked at the forest shadowed in darkness across the canyon where they now stood.

"Bad experience with the river elves, Prince Viator has told me."

"Why would they have thrown me off the cliffs like that? What kind of horrible..." Eloria glanced up at the sky to see a gray speck in the distance. Her blood rushed through her veins at a quicker pace. "Is it a dragon? Would Viator ride a dragon to join us early?"

12

"Viator cannot ride one on his own until he is of age," Balen said to Eloria. "Reining in a dragon is the last quest he will have to complete to come of age. The same with me."

"What is it then?"

"I cannot tell with the way the sun is shining off its..." Balen's mouth dropped open. "Run!" he shouted and seized Eloria's wrist. "We do not want to be its meal today or any other day! Run!"

Eloria grabbed at her long skirts as she sprinted alongside Balen.

"I know I shouldn't do this, but I have no choice!" Balen shouted, and he jumped into a hole, dragging Eloria with him. They tumbled down through the moss-cushioned tunnel and landed on objects that rolled with their weight at the bottom.

"What was it?" Eloria asked, as she tried to stand up. Something rolled under her foot, and she hurried to plant her feet on firmer ground. She brushed off her gown, then wiped off her hands of moisture, groundwater soaking the moss-covered walls and floor.

"Griffin. Looked to be a fairly large-sized one...and hungry too."

"Griffin?"

"Winged creature that likes to eat winged elves...river elves too, but we are easier prey since we fly mostly in the open like the griffins do. The river elves hide in the shelter of their forest and—"

"What is this place?" Eloria looked around at the walls of the cave cloaked in darkness. The air was chilly, and she shivered involuntarily.

Balen pulled out his wand and lighted the room. He twisted his mouth. "Uh, we need to get out of here."

Eloria screamed as she slipped on the pile of bones scattered from their fall. She swore she had never screamed so much in her life since she'd come to this planet!

Were the bones from recent victims of some kind of awful predator? Before she could question Balen, they heard a noise from up above.

"Eloria! Balen!" Viator called from the meadowland floor.

"Down here!" Balen yelled up to him.

"What are you doing down there?"

"A griffin came looking for a meal. What are you doing up there?"

"I decided to join you...and let my wings heal the rest of the morning in your company. They're not in real good shape, but..." He paused as he peered into the hole. "Uh, I don't want to alarm anyone, but the two of you need to get out of there at once."

The sound of shrieking from above made Eloria shudder. "What is it?"

"The griffin returning," Balen said.

A whooshing sound followed and Viator tumbled down the tunnel and landed at their feet.

Balen shook his head. "I thought you said we shouldn't be down here."

"The griffin returned. But you're right. We mustn't be down here."

They all looked up and heard the flapping of wings. "But not that way," Eloria said.

Viator unsheathed his sword. "This way is not good, either." He turned to Eloria. "Are you okay, today?"

"Certainly. Why wouldn't I be?"

"Do you not remember about last night?"

"I had some pretty strange dreams last night, but I often have them."

He touched her head, but the elves' medicine had healed her wound perfectly. He breathed a sigh of relief.

Balen handed the light to Eloria, then pulled his sword from its sheath. "Do you hear anything?"

Eloria pulled the cotton cloth from her ears and stuffed the pieces into Viator's backpack. "What?"

Viator shook his head. "When it's this quiet, the atmosphere is deadlier."

Her heart was already beating twice as fast as normal as if she'd been running in a tournament with her shipmates in training. And the humidity in the cave contributed to a trickle of perspiration dripping down her cheek. The caves were not like any she'd ever visited...eerie and filled with the smell of decay and death. What lurked in the darkness? They gave her back her pack, but not her sword or her stun gun. Though they never asked her what it was.

The three headed down the narrow passage. Balen rubbed his temple as it freckled with sweat. "Do you think they know we're here?"

Viator glanced back at Eloria. "That sweet fragrance Eloria wears will be sure to tell them."

"Who?" Eloria asked. She wasn't sure she really wanted to know whoever or whatever had apparently finished off unsuspecting creatures that had entered their lair and eaten them, leaving only scarred bones behind. She hoped they wouldn't encounter the grizzly beasts while they navigated the twisted caverns.

Balen took a deep breath as he held his sword at the ready. "I didn't think solving these quests would be so...challenging."

"Not a walk in the gardens." Viator raised his sword at the ready.

"What is in the cave?" Eloria's hand shook slightly while she held the light up for them to see.

"Don't ask!" Viator and Balen said at the same time, and she knew then they were in trouble.

For some time, they walked in the tunnel, twisting this way, then that. The only sound they heard was the dripping of water, their padded footsteps on the uneven rock, and a rat squealing in the abyss before them. Then a shadow moved across the ceiling and vanished.

"We're almost through the caves to Darkland Forest," Viator said, his voice tinged with relief. "If we can just make it there—"

"You've been there before through this way?" Eloria wondered how they could have moved so swiftly through the maze of tunnels and seemed to know just where they were going, which comforted her some.

"Balen and several of the other boys and I used to go adventuring in here. We mapped all the tunnels in our youth."

"What's in the cave, Viator?" Eloria glimpsed another shadow crawling across the ceiling ahead. Her heart picked up its pace, and then she smelled the odor of rotten meat in the air. Undoubtedly its last meal.

"Trolls!" Viator and Balen yelled as they slashed at the beast rearing its hideous head before them. Brown teeth, crooked and sharp, snarled at them as the elves swung at it with their swords. Its matted shaggy brown hair acted as armor as they attempted to fight his deadly claws. Eloria's crystal grew bright, blinding the creature. For a moment, everyone stared at the light. Then, the troll screamed and like a shadow, slipped to the ceiling and vanished.

"Come on." Viator grabbed Eloria's hand and ran through the remainder of the tunnel. "This is the entrance to where the river is." Viator studied the ground as he looked for the dark elf's shoe print.

"What are you looking for, sire?" Balen examined the ground.

"Lars's footprint."

"Here!" Balen said.

"Here!" another voice said in the distance.

13

Viator, Balen, and Eloria stared in the direction of the voice. "There is no echo in this cave because of the river," Viator said under his breath. He feared they'd have company soon. One simple task was becoming a total nightmare to accomplish and yet, his thoughts weren't totally on the task at hand either. Eloria. What was he going to do with her?

He motioned to the new tunnel. The three hurried for its cover and they turned off their light. The crunching of footsteps against stone followed as several men hurried toward the elf footprint. "I know I saw a light up here and heard a voice."

The river elf turned his face toward the new tunnel. Viator, Balen, and Eloria leaned back against the wall, hidden in the darkness.

"We must close off the tunnel. No telling how many winged elves have slipped in through this opening," the elf said.

Viator grabbed Eloria's arm and hurried her and Balen toward the Darkland Forest. "I cannot believe we were so close to cleansing the water...now this." He was infuriated beyond reason.

They heard the tromping of feet behind them as river elves carried the barrels of explosives deep into the tunnel.

Viator whispered to Balen, "They'll set them far enough from the river so it won't cause a problem with the flow of water." Viator took a deep breath. "This tunnel opens into Darkland Forest. We'll have to tread through it and around to the other opening. Then we'll have to return to the caves again."

Balen shook his head. "I hadn't known this would be so difficult a task."

"Do you regret having come?"

"Your Majesty, I wouldn't have missed it for the world."

They turned to see a spark ignite. "Run!" Viator dashed for the exit of the cave, pulling Eloria with him, as Balen ran after them in a full sprint.

The explosion from the blast threw Viator, Eloria, and Balen out of the tunnel. For a moment, they lay still in the deep shadows of the trees. Viator opened his eyes and saw Eloria and Balen nearby. "Eloria. Balen." He hurried to his feet to rouse his companions.

"Aye, aye, there was an explosion in the new tunnel!" he heard a river elf say.

He helped Eloria to her feet, and she wiped dirt from her clothes.

They would be in trouble soon if they did not make a quick exit from the forest. "Balen." Viator shook his shoulder to wake him.

He opened his eyes and smiled. "She was truly beautiful, sire."

"Shh." Viator helped him to stand with a rush to his efforts. The river elves were nearby and growing closer as they broke twigs and crunched fallen leaves with their hurried footsteps.

"Green eyes glowing as bright as the crystal at Eloria's neck," Balen said.

"Shhh," Viator repeated as he held his hand over Balen's mouth. He hurried him toward the cliffs where the trees thinned, and he could attempt flight. He hoped his wings were healed enough now as they should have been had he let them rest further that morning. And he hoped his friend had come to his senses enough that he would fly when he needed to.

Eloria was running at his side and hadn't seemed to have been affected, though she was still covered in dust and dirt.

They soon reached the clearing and Viator spread his wings. "They've nearly fully healed," he said under his breath with relief.

Balen was still stumbling toward the cliffs. "Green eyes...and pearl-white teeth."

"Shh, Balen, the river elves are nearby. Come, we must fly across to the fairyland meadows."

Eloria quickly stuffed her ears with cotton.

Balen nodded. "The teeth almost smile in the mist."

"Who are you talking about?" Viator lifted Eloria onto his back and grabbed Balen's arm and pulled him over the cliff. He couldn't wait any further.

To Viator's relief, Balen instinctively spread his wings and glided to the other side.

"There!" a river elf shouted. "The winged elves have been here again! This means war, Viator!"

Viator shook his head as he soared with Balen back over the mountains to the other entrance of Darkland Forest. Balen turned to him. "Why are we coming back here?"

"The water needs to be cleansed...remember?"

Balen's brows knitted together as he tried to recall. "The tunnel was blasted."

"Aye. I'm afraid when we try to enter the caves again, we will find more river elves there, unless they have left by now." He studied Balen for a moment, wondering who in the world Balen was rambling on about in Darkland Forest. "Who were you talking about, back there?"

"The dragon I will rein in. She is a beauty to be sure."

"ARE we going to cure the water?" Eloria asked Viator, relieved he had hold of her tightly in his grasp. She sighed deeply and wished he'd hold her always like that, with genuine affection.

He shook his head. "Yes. As soon as we have a chance to pour this into the water." He reached for a flask hanging from his leather belt. "From the elven container and from what you overheard the river elves mention, my people were able to determine what poison was used, just to ensure the type they mentioned was truly the same as the one in the flask."

"Was it?"

"Yes. Though there's some concern that it was all a lie, and the poison was something else. Anyway, it wasn't, then they filled this flask with a drug to counteract it."

"Yes, Balen told me this morning. Your wings...they're fully healed now?"

"Aye."

She studied the landscape as they neared the tunnel entrance. Shaking her head, she pointed east. "We should enter above where the footprint was found, just in case they still look for us." She heard voices in there. "They are still in there."

"All right. East it is."

"There." She pointed to a raised mound in the earth. "That's about a mile upstream from the footprint, and there is an entrance there."

Viator landed, then released her. "You still wear our elven gowns."

"They didn't give me time to change before I left."

Viator looked at the entrance. "Perhaps you should stay outside here—"

"I had another thought, Viator. I will take the flask and empty the contents in the river."

"Sounds like a good plan to me." Balen watched for signs of trouble in the forest surrounding them

"No." Viator released Eloria's hand and motioned for her to stay in back of them while he and Balen led the way. "We will stay together, if you won't stay behind, Eloria."

Viator paused, listening for the sounds of voices, then motioned for the others to follow. Balen pulled out his wand, then lighted the area. Eloria's crystal glowed slightly. Everyone stared at the necklace. "Why does it do that?" Viator whispered.

"I don't know." Eloria glanced behind her. She took a deep breath.

The three headed toward the river.

Viator cleared his throat. "Are you sure the river is this way? I don't hear its roar."

"I smell it. Don't you?" She glanced down at her crystal glowing slightly again. She looked behind her, thinking she heard someone behind her, but saw no one.

The light Balen carried disappeared around the bend and Viator with him, as the crystal grew dark.

14

Eloria stumbled toward the bend in the tunnel, hurrying to rejoin the winged elves. The hair on her arms prickled with fear as her fingers felt the turn in the rock wall, but still there was no light to illuminate her way. She didn't want to use her own magic for fear she'd run into the river elves. She lunged forward but bumped into a warm body. Fingers quickly clamped over her mouth. Eyes wild with fear, she strained to see the figure in the dark. A voice whispered in her ear, sending chills down her body.

"Shh, Eloria." Viator's soft voice tickled her ear. "River elves are still in the tunnels. They are searching for a way out."

"They cannot harm us here. No cliffs to throw us from."

"Shh."

The dark elf spoke near the river. "Winged elves are west of here at least a mile."

"Aye...aye, but we've already walked east, what, two miles? And yet we have found no way back to Darkland Forest."

"We'll have to climb the mountains—"

"It will take us several weeks."

The river elves grew quiet. "What do you see here?" another asked.

"This tunnel leads up to the surface to another forest, sire. There seems to be no way out of this place, except for a long climb through the mountains."

Viator tensed as he stared at the dark-haired elf whose dark eyes darted about searching for signs of life. "Lars," Viator said under his breath.

"Viator and another winged elf you say were sighted near here?" Lars asked.

"Aye, sire."

Lars rubbed his chin. "If we can find them, one of them will fly me home."

"And the rest of us?"

"You will just have to find your own way."

"Aye, sire. What about the human girl?"

"The winged elves took her," Lars said, then sniffed the air. "Still, I smell her scent in the air." He kicked a rock across the floor. "I cannot believe you fools threw her off the cliff."

"Your orders, sire, were to throw any outsider off the—"

"I know very well what my orders say. Can you not think for yourselves just once?"

"Aye, sire. I mean, no, sire."

"The power I will have when I have her in my grasp..." He stomped his foot. "Find the winged elves. When we have them, we can use them to get to the girl."

"Aye, sire."

The dark elves scurried back east while Lars stared into the dark tunnel where Eloria and the winged elves hid. The crystal flickered at her throat. Hurriedly, she covered the necklace with her hands. Viator glanced down at it and pulled her close to block the glow of light.

"She will be mine!" Lars yelled, then stormed after his men.

"Stay here, Eloria, with Balen." Viator squeezed her hand. "I'll empty the contents of the cure into the river, then we'll leave again through this tunnel."

"But...," Eloria said.

"Keep her here, Balen," Viator whispered to him. "She cannot come with me."

"Aye, Your Majesty."

Balen took hold of Eloria's arm as Viator slipped out of the tunnel and dashed for the river.

"Hey!" they heard a man shout. "Grab him! Do not harm him. He'll know where the human girl is!"

Balen released Eloria and ran into the cave as he pulled his sword from his sheath. "Hurry, Your Majesty!" he shouted, as he held his weapon up to keep the river elves at bay.

Viator struggled with the lid to the container, but without success.

"Hurry, sire!"

"Somebody tightened the lid too tight!"

The sound of metal striking metal clashed as Balen wielded his elven sword against two river elves' swords. Sparks of light flew from the contact.

"I will fire the elf who capped this flask!" Viator yelled, as he gripped the lid and twisted.

"Hurry, sire! More are coming."

Eloria walked into the cave. The glow of her emerald washed the whole area in a warm green light. The men stood still.

"The human girl," one of the river elves said, as Viator stared at her.

"The winged elf seeks to cleanse our water. Leave him do his job in peace." Her voice was calm, deep and dark. "In peace."

She turned to Balen. "Help Viator open the flask."

Viator shook his head. "I'll get this open on my own." His

face reddened as the knuckles of his hands whitened while he twisted and turned the cap.

"Your sword," Eloria commanded. She had no time for arguments.

"They'll overwhelm us." Balen walked backward toward her.

Eloria held up the necklace as her eyes glowed in the light. "Hold your men back. Do not come any closer."

"She has the power," one of the river elves whispered to his companions.

"It is true what they say," another said under his breath.

Eloria tilted her head to the side as her eyes slimmed like a cat blinded by the light. She felt invincible. "Hold your men back."

An arrow whizzed past Eloria's shoulder. "Archers!" Balen sheathed his sword, then ran to help Viator. The two twisted the cap loose, then dumped the contents of the flask into the river.

Viator dashed for Eloria with Balen on his heels. The three ran through the tunnel without hesitation as they heard Lars yelling, "After the winged elves and the girl! After them!"

Balen hurried to pull out his wand to light their way as Viator helped Eloria over a mound of rocks. "These gowns are not the best for running in," she said under her breath.

"I must know what power you possess." Viator pulled her into the forest. He grabbed her by the waist and lifted her high into the air. Balen soon joined them as the river elves dashed into the clearing.

"There!" a dozen river elves said.

Viator smiled as they shook their fists at them. "Lars and his men will have some time returning home."

Balen shook his head. He glanced back at his wings and saw them turn slightly transparent.

Viator turned to study Balen's wings and frowned. "I told you I could do it on my own! I didn't need your help to open the container!" He squeezed Eloria tight. "What am I to do with you?"

His brusque tone of voice irritated her. "Why are you so grouchy anyway? Leave me with the shadow elves, and I'll wait for Persephonice."

Viator alighted on one of the mountain peaks overlooking Darkland Forest. He spread his wings in semi-triumph. "You see? They are another half-a-credit transparent."

"Only half?" Eloria asked.

Viator twisted his mouth slightly as Balen spread his wings. She could tell he was perfectly pleased with himself—to Viator's annoyance. "I got the other half, because I helped him to open the lid to the flask. Still half a credit ahead of you, Your Majesty, and I started later in the day."

Eloria smiled as she touched Viator's silky wing. "More beautiful every time I see them."

Balen folded his wings and arms. "You cannot be serious about taking her with us."

"I must know what power you possess, Eloria," Viator said.

"I told you I have no idea."

"It has something to do with your necklace."

Eloria shrugged. She'd been trying to limit her use of power, but without weapons, she had no other way of dealing with these people, or beasts. Using inspirational motivation was futile, so she was going to have to begin using her magic to aid them in any way that she could. Then what would they think? She was a high elf? And they seemed to be at odds with them.

"If Lars wishes to have you, there has to be a good reason. He doesn't like anyone who is not a river elf. He must know something that we don't."

"That kind of limits his number of friends." Eloria studied Viator's wrinkled brow. "You're frowning. What concerns you so?"

"You. I should leave you here, like my father commanded."

"Sire," Balen said with an exasperated tone to his voice. "She won't be safe with us."

"She won't be safe here if Lars comes for her. These humans are no match for..."

Eloria folded her arms. "We are perfectly capable of taking care of ourselves. Especially if your people hadn't taken my weapons."

Viator shook his head. He sat down on a smooth stone seat worn by the summer rains. "A sudden gust of wind blew through the castle, snuffing all of our candles out. Then the only light we saw was the one from your necklace. Why?"

Balen sat down on a grassy area. His brow furrowed as he considered the matter. "It was almost like our people were being warned she has this power...pay heed."

"Nonsense," Eloria said. The notion gave her goose bumps all over her arms though, despite her trying to make light of the power she seemed to possess. There was no way she could have any connection with a dragon from this place.

"Then she summoned Talom."

"No one can do such a thing," Balen said. "He is a rogue dragon, deadlier than any other."

"And in the cave where the trolls reside, she actually rescued us when the glow of her crystal sent the creatures scampering." Viator rubbed his brow.

"Too bad I don't have wings that can turn transparent when I accomplish a quest. Doesn't seem fair that only the two of you..."

Viator stood slowly from his seat. "You don't think the crystal is like our wings, do you, Balen? When she accomplishes a worthy task the crystal..." He shook his head and sat back down. "Nah, doesn't make any sense. And yet, the first time I saw it glow was when the pixie bothered Eloria, the light from the crystal seemed to push her away."

Eloria sat down next to him. "I've never heard anything except what my father used to say. The crystal would protect me when I had need. My aunt would hush him when he said things like that. She said folks would think he was crazy."

"How did the wizard advise you to get the crystal, Eloria?" Viator asked.

"The wizard?" Balen asked. "What wizard?"

"It glowed among all of the rest, and it was already lying on the floor of the cave as if someone had cut it out, just for me to find. I had many such crystals displayed on shelves at my home. But this one..." She fingered the emerald. "The one in the dream called to me."

"And you are the only one who has ever possessed it that you would know of? In the dream, I mean. No one else owned it before you? A family member or...I mean, it was already cut into a gem like that of one formed for a necklace, like maybe it had been worn before."

"It had no chain, nor markings that indicated one had been attached to it. Not in my dream. And I had fetched it, no one else. Yet my father said my mother gifted the necklace to me before I died."

Viator frowned. "We can't let Lars get to her." He stood again, then began to pace. "What about the gift, Eloria?"

"I wish you'd quit asking me, Viator. I have no idea about the gift the wizard spoke of."

"Talom wouldn't let Balen get near you when you were injured. But he let me come to you, why?"

"I don't even remember him being anywhere near me. Had I, I probably would have fainted."

"Like when you were thrown from the cliffs by the river elves."

"Yes."

"Had you summoned Talom?"

She shook her head.

"What would your father say if he found you were in the company of the girl still?" Balen asked. "I know what he would say. In that booming voice, he would shatter half the mirrors in the great hall. 'You will have nothing more to do with the human girl!' he would shout."

Eloria stood and stared down from her lofty position high in the mountains. "I have never climbed as high as this. The view is breathtaking."

"Have you seen the seacoast of Neferon, Eloria? They have the most beautiful sugar-white beaches as soft as cotton underfoot. The blue waters are as clear as my wings will be one day. Wisps of white clouds shade us on a hot afternoon." Viator touched one of Eloria's curls.

"And sea serpents eat the unsuspecting." Balen tapped his foot on the ground. "Not to mention some of the other things dwelling in the sea and on those white sandy beaches."

"I wouldn't want to miss it for the world." Eloria walked over to Viator as he leaned over to allow her to ride. Later, she might have regrets, but for now, she wanted to help Viator with his mission. Until she could see Persephonice. She had nowhere else to go.

"Next stop then, the shores of Neferon." Viator lifted his powerful wings. "Coming, Balen?"

Balen shook his head. "You will never hear the end of this from your father, Your Majesty. Never. And my sister...she will do more than shatter the mirrors in the great hall. Lots more."

Viator raised his hand in victory. "We go to Neferon, my friends...the white sand shores of paradise!"

15

The white sands of the beaches of Neferon loomed before them as Prince Viator soared high above. His elven wings never faltered even with the extra weight he carried as Eloria sat upon his back.

She studied the sights she'd never seen before...milky white beaches, blue waters shimmering over the sand as clear as glass, sea birds soaring, then diving into the ocean for fresh-caught fish, a speck of green in the sea beyond.

Lord Balen was studying the ground as his wings floated up and down...graceful as the swans flying across her sky in her world. To be a winged elf with their silky, filmy wings... She sighed deeply. And to think their mission was to make them transparent so they would be like the glass of her bedroom window back home. She liked them just as they were. Her fingers clutched at Viator's leather backpack as he swooped lower.

He landed on the shifting sand. Eloria hurried to slip off his back. She gazed at the clear blue waters swelling in gentle waves. "I've never seen anything like it." Her stomach rumbled. Balen glanced at her and folded his wings. She smiled. "Does this trip include a meal?"

She turned to look at Viator. His wings folded neatly against his back as his brilliant blue eyes mirrored the water's color. His gaze focused on the sea as it stretched to the horizon.

Balen pulled off his pack. "If you don't mind elven traveling food..." He plucked soft rolls and dried fish from his bag.

Eloria took a deep breath of the fishy, salt-laden air. "I have some food." Not enough for very long, and they would think it most odd, but she was willing to share.

Viator turned his attention from the sea. "The minister of security left most of what was in your pack there. As long as they weren't weapons."

"I could have used the weapons for protection." Eloria looked west. Her stomach tightened with concern. She was always so focused on a mission. But how could she get to where Persephonice was to see if she was happy here? If she was and didn't want to leave, Eloria wouldn't have accomplished her mission anyway.

She reached for the roll Balen offered her. He pulled out his dagger and handed that to her.

"Thanks, Balen."

He tilted his chin down.

"Lord Balen."

She slipped the dagger into the sheath for her sword, and after taking a bite of the roll, she turned her attention to Viator's intense posture as he looked back at the water.

Balen watched him. "What is it that you see, sire?"

"My next quest has something to do with that outcropping of stones." Viator pointed to a group of rocks where water broke over its jagged edges. Frothing foam collected like soapy suds ringing the bright pink and orange coral.

Eloria finished her roll. "Good bread." She took a bite of her fish, the flavor spicy from special elven seasonings.

"What must you do, Your Majesty?" Balen stared at the cluster of rocks.

"I must do this alone this time!"

Eloria laughed. "He is getting grouchy again. Viator, sit here with us and eat. You should rest your wings. You have carried excess baggage for many miles to get here. Sit and rest."

Viator turned to study Eloria in her white elven gowns dotted with pearls while feathers fluttered slightly in the breeze. He smiled. "Excess baggage. Why you are the most beautiful—"

"Ahem," Baden said. "The king expects his only son to marry my sister, Sendal. Remember her? A winged elf like you and me and all the rest of our people. You do remember?"

"I will marry whom I choose." Viator slipped a roll from his pack. He studied Eloria's emerald necklace as the sun's rays sparkled off its surface. "It hasn't glowed once on our journey, has it, Eloria?"

"No, not once."

He nodded.

She sipped water from Balen's flask. "Hmm, this is very good."

"Spring water from our mountains." Balen pointed in the direction of their home in the Darkland Forest.

Eloria lay back on the soft sand and studied the fluffy white clouds drifting overhead. They cast shadows on the sand as they moved across the sky on their casual stroll. "So if Viator doesn't marry your sister, who will she marry, Balen?"

"Lord Balen." Balen wrinkled his brow at her.

Viator chuckled. "Give it up, Balen. If she won't use my title in speaking with me, why should she use yours? I'm crown prince of the winged elves after all, and you...are only a duke's son."

"A duke's son is something to be reckoned with." Balen puffed out his chest.

Eloria smiled. "I apologize to you both."

Balen shook his head. "My sister, Lady Sendal, has never considered anyone else to marry. I can assure you she will be a terror worse than any troll if the prince doesn't choose her for his own."

Eloria's necklace flickered with its own light. Viator and Balen stared at it as they waited to see it light up again.

"There must be a pattern to this." Viator leaned down and touched the stone at Eloria's throat. The stone darkened again. He glanced back at the rock sitting in the water a quarter of a mile from shore.

"What is it about the rock that puzzles you, sire?" Balen studied the prince.

"The mermaid." Viator pointed at the figure in the distance as she pulled herself onto the rock. Her long, wet, golden hair draped over her shoulders.

Eloria sat upright. She stared at the figure, then said under her breath, "A mermaid. I never thought I'd see one in the ocean."

A sweet melody drifted over the sea as the mermaid's lips moved with the words she sang. Eloria stood. Viator glanced over at her. "No." He grabbed her arm as she took a step toward the water. "It's like when the meadowland fairies called to her with their song. She has no power to block their bewitching tunes like we have. Help me, Balen."

Balen jumped to his feet. "I still have the cotton she used the last time she blocked the meadowland fairy music." The two hurried to stuff the soft material into Eloria's ears.

"She is so beautiful." Eloria studied the mermaid's shimmering silver-green tail. The fluke waved up and down enticing her audience to come to her. "So beautiful."

Viator sighed deeply. "Yes, well, she would drown you, if she could."

Eloria walked closer to the water's edge as Viator grabbed one of her arms and Balen held the other.

"Can you hear her melody?" Viator asked.

Eloria shook her head.

"Good."

"What is the quest you must perform here, sire?" Balen folded his arms as he studied the mermaid.

"The mermaid needs help, but I'll have to get closer to find out what kind of assistance she requires. Eloria is right though. I must rest first. We all should before we do much else."

"There were rumors circulating in your father's court that a dark shadow has descended on our world." Balen helped Viator lead Eloria away from the water's edge.

The winged elves pulled their blankets out of their packs, then stretched them across the sand. Viator motioned for Eloria to use his.

"But what will you sleep on?" she asked. "I could use my cloak."

He pulled out his own cloak. She nodded then sat down on his blanket.

"I have heard this said, Balen. Even the caves we explored as boys are now filled with trolls, when before, there were none. No telling where they came from, but poof one day, there they were."

"Yes, and I've never heard tell of the meadowland fairies luring anyone with their music and drowning someone in the river in the process. They love to entertain the elves, then release them after a while."

"They did stop singing when Eloria slipped into the water over her head. But still, after you rescued her, they started singing again. It didn't seem to matter to them that Eloria was pulled to the water once more with their songs." Viator shook his head. "And Lars and his river elves have gotten worse. Only recently have they been throwing outsiders off the cliffs."

"And the pixies in Darkland Forest..." Balen said. "Banished before I was born. Now they are back, for some unknown reason. The river elves making our people sick like they did, is definitely a sign of something more sinister."

"A dark shadow." Viator lay down on his cloak spread out beside Eloria and rested his head on his arm. "Those of us who are trying to come of age, face deadlier challenges than even our fathers had to face, I suspect."

"Yes." Balen lay down on his blanket spread out.

Viator studied Eloria's red hair rippling in the breeze. Her green eyes sparkled as her lips turned up slightly. He smiled back at her, then took a deep breath. Turning his face skyward, he studied a dark cloud slipping past a fluffy white one. "A dark shadow."

16

The three companions closed their eyes as a breeze grew in strength. The sands sprinkled over Eloria's face, and she wrapped the blanket over her head. She sighed deeply as her thoughts drifted away.

Her necklace warmed as the crystal rested at her throat. She opened her eyes to see her blanket-cocoon washed in the soft green light. Her lips parted to speak, but before she could utter a word, her blanket was pulled aside. "Eloria," Viator said as he stared at her. Her gaze met his and he frowned as he looked down at her necklace. "I have to know what power you possess."

She shook her head, sighing deeply. "I can't say, Viator. I have no idea why the necklace glows from time to time." Except when she used it to channel her abilities. But she hadn't been doing any of that all the time it had been glowing on and off since she'd been here. She wondered if it had something to do with the elves' world. Like the magic on the planet was influencing it.

"Very well, it's time." He jumped up from his cloak bed.

"But we have rested no more than a few seconds—"

"Five hours have passed." Viator pointed to the sun's lofty location in the blue sky. "I must accomplish my task."

Eloria stood, then brushed the sands from her gowns.

"I had the most disturbing dream, Eloria. You won't be safe with me, I fear."

"You said I would not be safe while Lars, crown prince of the river elves, wishes to use me for his own dark purposes, should he take me back to Darkland Forest."

"Aye, that's what I said."

Viator strode to the water's edge. He stretched his wings, then rose toward his destination. She studied the rocks. They were barren again.

She folded her arms as Viator swooped down in a pass over the rocks to see the matter.

Before another wave crashed upon the coral-covered rocks, Viator settled down briefly, then reached into the sea. Eloria held her breath.

"What is he doing?" Balen walked up beside her.

She shuddered and glanced over at him. "I didn't hear your approach."

"You were sort of concentrating on the prince."

"I'm not sure what he's doing." She turned her attention back to Viator.

Viator lifted his wings just before a wave smashed into the rocks. Balen sighed deeply. "He mustn't get his wings wet...not if he wants to fly again."

"And he can't swim." She walked into the water. The tips of the waves tugged gently at her feet as the water rolled in and out.

"No, winged elves can't swim. It wouldn't matter anyway. If he were to slip into the water, the mermaid would take him into the deep and drown him."

Viator circled around the rock, then landed again. He

reached into the water and this time his back muscles tightened as he strained to pull something from it.

Eloria frowned. "What in the world is he doing?"

Balen shook his head. "He's concentrating on the task so hard, he isn't paying attention to the waves."

Eloria tugged at Balen's arm. "Shouldn't you aid him?"

"He will have a fit. He threatened to take away my title the last time when I helped him to get the top off the flask to cleanse our water. And me, a duke's son. He's bound and determined to earn a whole credit this time toward making his wings transparent. Except to do so, he cannot have anyone's help."

Viator jumped from the rock, barely missing the water's wrath. Eloria shook her head. "It's too dangerous. You have to help him."

"I cannot, Eloria. You don't understand how important it is for us to come of age. A man has got to do what a man has got to do."

"So do more quests, but aid your prince, now!"

Balen studied Viator's struggles, then nodded. "I will blame my interference on you. After all, half a quest completed, gives me an edge over the prince still."

With wings outstretched, Balen lifted into the air, then flew to where Viator circled once more.

She smiled as Viator motioned to the beach. Balen returned the hand movements as he pointed his finger at her. She waved at the two men. The glow of her necklace caught her eye. The winged elves watched it too. Then the mermaid suddenly popped her head out of the kelp drifting over the top of the water. Floating near the rocks, her green gaze fixed on the elves.

Viator spoke to Balen again, but he just shook his head and pointed at the water next to the rocks. The two dropped to the coral and pulled at the fishnet tangled at the water's edge.

"I CAN'T BELIEVE you have disobeyed me." Viator yanked some of the net free. He grabbed Balen's arm, and they rose before the wave splashed them. "I could have done this on my own."

"Eloria begged me to aid you, sire. What could I do? With tears streaking down her ivory cheeks...you know I never could bear seeing a girl cry."

Viator flapped his wings as he watched Eloria. "She was crying?"

"I guess she kind of likes you."

Glancing down at the water, Viator saw the mermaid floating some distance out. "She's back."

"Yes, well, if she reaches for her rock, we must abandon this quest of yours for the time being."

"We have half of the net up already." Viator took a deep breath as Balen raised a brow. "Well, nearly half. Come on, the seawater has pulled away."

They walked on the slippery coral, then yanked at the net with a coordinated effort. More of the net pulled free and the elves smiled. "Easy as..."

Balen grabbed the prince's arm, and they both rose off the rock as the waves pounded it. "Maybe not so easy as all that."

They observed the mermaid drifting closer to the coral. "We won't finish this task for you, oh mermaid, if you crawl up on your rock home." Viator's voice was dark with warning as he folded his arms.

They watched the mermaid as she glanced back at the shore. The elves turned to see Eloria wading knee-deep in the water. Her emerald glowed steadily now in the sunlight. Viator frowned. "What is she doing?"

"Trying to distract the mermaid, I think."

"Come on." Viator landed on the rock again and tugged at the woven ropes.

Balen pointed toward the horizon. "Look at the strange green mist rising on the water's surface."

Viator glanced up at it, then shook his head. "Hurry, help me."

The two concentrated so hard on the task before them they didn't see the mermaid grasp the edge of the coral. Eloria's voice cried out to them. Blocking the sound of the mermaid's song, the elves also blocked Eloria's voice as her words were shouted from so far away. They heard only their heartbeats pounding hard as they struggled with the net and the sound of the water swelling for an encore performance.

Viator turned to see the mermaid's hand outstretched, reaching for his ankle. Before she grabbed hold, she turned her head in the direction of the shore. Viator and Balen lifted off the rock. They turned as Eloria swam into the surf.

"She can swim." Balen rubbed his smooth chin.

"Not for long." Viator watched the mermaid slip back into the sea. "We can't reach her either. Swimming too close to the water, we would drown in the waves ourselves." He grabbed Balen's arm. "Come, we must finish our task."

"But Eloria—"

"Hurry, I hadn't planned to drown the mermaid, only to help her in her quest, but to stop her from reaching Eloria...if I must drown the sea creature, then...well, the net is our only hope."

Balen tugged with Viator with all his might. "I suppose we won't earn a credit with our effort then."

"Half a credit," Viator reminded him.

"Half a credit then."

"No, and since you have some fondness for the human girl now too, rescuing her won't give you any credit either."

"Well, at least the one time, it did."

With a last tug, they pulled the net free only to be swallowed up in the green mist. "Keep hold of the net," Viator shouted.

"I can't see a thing! I can't even see the water!"

"Eloria!" Viator shouted.

"Eloria!" Balen repeated as if he were an echo.

Then the mist receded slowly toward the horizon. Viator pointed at the figure of the mermaid floundering in the water. Her eyes focused on the mist.

"Sire, should we drop the net on her?"

"Eloria's gone." Viator flew with the net to the shore, then dropped it on the sand. "She's gone when I vowed to keep her safe."

Balen dropped his end of the net, then studied Viator's wings. "They're another half-a-credit transparent, sire."

Viator walked to the water's edge. The mist slipped back across the sea. Squinting his eyes, he surveyed the horizon, then frowned. "There's an island of green out there. I saw it when we first set sight on the shores of this land."

Balen shuffled his feet, then grabbed his blanket and shook the sand loose. Viator turned to watch him. "Next, quest, sire? Even if we don't get credit?"

Viator's eyes drifted back to the island speck in the distance. "She has to be there, Balen. She just has to be there."

"The king won't be happy that you have lost your heart to the human girl, Your Majesty. She is the one our soothsayers have spoken of...she will conquer our realm." He hurried to hand Viator his packed bag. "Will we go?"

"They say the island only appears once every sixty-six years. I have seen my great, grandfather's diary about this place. Not good...and no telling how long the island has been floating on the sea. Once its time is up, it just vanishes."

"How long does it appear for?"

"No one knows."

"Then, if we don't make this trip quickly—"

"We could all just vanish forever."

Viator slipped his pack onto his back and unfolded his wings, his heart pounding with concern. "We take her to the shadow elves after this. The path we must follow is way too dangerous for the likes of a human girl."

He and Balen flew off for the island.

"She will be upset—"

"Better upset and alive then..." Viator shook his head as he took a deep breath. He couldn't think of the other consequences of their actions. "You say she cried when she was concerned for my safety? I have never seen a human cry. What were her tears like? Are they like elven girls'?"

"Sire, the island grows close. I fear the gray specks in the sky may be..."

"Griffins!"

17

"Uh, hello!" Eloria hollered from the window of the tower. She leaned out of the windowsill to feel the rock facing covered in green moss. The plants tickled her fingers as she studied the rough stone surface. Indents... footholds? Seventy feet below, water dashed upon the jagged rocks ringing the tower. "It appears to be a corner tower of a castle at the water's edge." She stared at the green mist sifting over the rocks in spurts.

Taking a deep breath, she studied the green-velvet dress covering her slight figure. She ran her hand over the fabric of her sleeve watching as the threads turned dark. Turning her attention to the bedchamber, she observed the room cloaked entirely in green from the bed curtains and bedspread to the marble floors and walls. She pounded on the door. "Hey! Is anyone out there?"

For the seventh time, she twisted the doorknob...and found it still locked. "I know, I know, I've already tried that before, but..." She collapsed on a soft-cushioned, green-velvet chair. Rubbing her temple, she closed her eyes. She envisioned Viator's face as his brow knit deeply in the green mist. She saw the net he carried with Balen as they hovered in the fog. She was glad they had accomplished their task.

She sighed deeply, then stood up from the chair. "Can you free me from this tower now? Will you even be able to find me?" She turned to study the room again. Who had pulled her from the sea and where was she now?

She struck the door with her fist and the walls echoed the banging throughout the hall outside her room. "Hello!" She stormed across the floor and stared out the window at the drop from the tower. "Way too long a drop...but, perhaps if I were to tie the bed curtains, drop them out the window, then climb the rest of the way down the tower using the footholds in the stone...it might work."

She hurried back to the bed and ripped the bed curtains from their frame. Heart pounding, she hurried to knot the fabric together. She tied the end of the curtain to the bed, then pulled the rest to the window. Leaning over the windowsill, she watched as the fabric cascaded to thirty feet above the ground. She could try to use her magic for the rest of the drop. It would have to do. She took a deep breath and climbed into the window frame. With her fingers clutching the curtain with a fierce grip, she began her descent.

Halfway down, a griffin pursuing food, screeched nearby. Then the sound of ripping fabric made her grab hold of the next windowsill she could reach in a hurry. "Whoever you are, you make lousy, flimsy bed curtains." She climbed into the window with the greatest of difficulty as her long skirts hampered her movements.

Once inside the room, she ran for the door. The doorknob turned before her fingers touched it. She ducked into a tiny room she assumed was a wardrobe as the clothes hung about her. Peering out of the dark closet, she watched a cloaked figure search through a drawer in a chest. Green bony fingers picked through the contents, then closed the drawer. The hooded face turned in her direction, but Eloria could only see shadows. She drew back into the garments. The creature turned and headed out of the room. The door clicked shut. Eloria finally took a breath.

She glanced down to see her emerald glowing brightly. "Shoot, you could have gotten me caught!" The screeching cry of the griffin neared the window. She grabbed a cloak from the closet, then pulled it over her shoulders. Raising the hood, she peered out of the room.

A shadow drew into the chamber, then frantic wings flapped at the air. Suddenly, too figures burst into the room. "That was close!" Balen shook his head as he folded his wings. He turned to see Viator staring at the cloaked figure.

Balen unsheathed his sword.

"Viator." Eloria's voice was barely a whisper.

"Eloria!" Viator ran toward her, but she reached him first. With a crushing grip, she hugged him. He pushed aside her hood and turned his head slightly to see the tears on her cheeks.

"You're not of age." Balen shuffled in place. "You can't touch a woman like that, Your Majesty." He pointed at the prince's wings. "You're not of age."

Viator brushed away Eloria's tears and kissed her forehead. He held her close briefly, then turned to Balen as they felt a rumbling under foot. "We must leave at once. I fear the island is descending into the sea."

They looked over at the window where the shadow of the griffin was joined by another. "They won't let us leave this place through yonder window, sire."

Viator hurried for the door, then stopped as bells rang out in the castle. "Warning bells...do you think? Maybe someone saw us?"

"Or perhaps they have discovered my escape."

He stared at Eloria. "Your escape?"

"I was six stories higher, a few minutes ago."

He shook his head. "I should have known these people wouldn't hang curtains out of their windows for decorations."

Viator pulled the door open, but hearing footsteps running down the hall, he closed the door tight.

"Here, sire." Balen pulled up a rug revealing a trapdoor.

"Leading to where?" Viator stared at the slatted door.

Balen studied the door as he pressed his ear against it. "Do you hear the voices calling out?"

Viator glanced at Eloria and frowned to see her emerald glowing brightly. "All right, we'll check it out, but perhaps you should stay here, Eloria."

"Not on your life." She motioned for Balen to open the door.

Balen opened it and pulled his wand from his pouch. He lighted their way as he held his sword at the ready. Eloria followed next as she gripped the railing along the narrow staircase. Bringing up the rear, Viator closed the door with a clunk behind him, then unsheathed his sword.

"What voices did you hear?" Eloria whispered.

"Cries for help."

"I didn't hear anything."

"Shhh."

"Over here!" a voice said in the dark.

"Here," another said a little farther away.

Eloria gasped to see the elves in chains locked in a cell. A winged elf wrestled with his manacles to one side. The other's wingless features made Eloria say under her breath, "A river elf."

Viator slashed away at the chain locking the cell door in place as Eloria spied a mermaid in a tank a few feet away. "I'll get her," Balen said, as he sheathed his sword. "How will we leave the island in time though?"

"Through there." The winged elf motioned his head toward a door as Viator struck the chain binding the manacles.

He hurried to free the river elf and Eloria ran to the door and opened it. Light from outside streamed inside. She squinted her eyes in the bright sunlight.

"Sire, if you take the river elf, I've got the mermaid, our cousin here can carry Eloria..."

The winged elf hurried after Eloria. "We must make haste. The island is sinking into the sea."

They lost their balance as the island grumbled and shook. Viator reached for Eloria's hand and darted into the open. Spying griffins nearby searching for food as their gray bodies cast shadows across the landscape, Viator leaned over and said to Eloria, "Get on."

"But you won't earn a credit if you rescue me, though I'm still puzzled as to why. I can ride on the other..."

"Eloria, the griffins are headed this way. They've surely picked up our scent. Quit arguing with me and get on."

She climbed onto his back as the river elf climbed onto the other winged elf's. Before she could take a deep breath, Viator and the other lifted in the air and swung over the sea to join Balen. He lowered himself to the sea as close as he could get without getting his wings wet from the choppiness of the water. He released the mermaid, and she splashed back into the sea. Eloria frowned to see the mermaid surface. Her sweet luring voice soon filled the air.

Viator's voice was harsh when he spoke to Eloria. "Why must you be so stubborn?"

"Me stubborn?" She shook her head. "I only thought you might earn another credit..."

"You should have carried the river elf, sire," Balen said.

Viator wrinkled his brow as Balen showed off his wings. Eloria squirmed as she leaned over Viator's shoulder.

"Sit up, Eloria," Viator warned. "What in the world are you doing?"

She swung her leg over his back and held onto his backpack as she dangled precariously over the water.

"Eloria!" Balen hollered as Viator reached his hand back to grab her. His fingers touched her waist, but he couldn't reach her arm.

"Hold on, Eloria!" Viator attempted to fly higher out of the range of the taunting melody of the mermaid.

"She's not going to make it!" Balen readied himself beneath her to try to break her fall.

Her left hand slipped from the pack. "I'm coming," she said softly under her breath.

"No, Eloria!" Viator tilted sharply to the right causing her to roll over his waist. He reached for her arm again. Then she released her hold on his pack.

18

"Eloria!" both Viator and Balen shouted as she fell toward the sea.

Viator swooped down and grabbed her wrist, then pulled her back from the foam-capped waves. "Shadow elf territory after this, Eloria." His brow knit tightly as he flew her onto the beach.

The mermaid's songs no longer touched Eloria's ears, and she took a deep breath as she sat down on the shore. "Did you say something to me, Viator?"

He glanced over to see Balen waiting to hear his words. "We'll discuss the matter later." He turned to the winged elf he'd freed. "I don't recognize you. Are you from Darkland Forest?"

"Torrance from Rangoon, Your Majesty."

"What were you doing on the island?"

"The Isle of Green Mists. I've heard it talked about for years. I had a wager with several of my friends I could visit the island and return home again. I've been locked up there for sixty days."

"And you?" Viator handed a roll to the river elf.

"Similar circumstances. Prince Lars bet me the place didn't exist. I knew it did. I was to bring proof of my claim. My only

evidence is my winged-elf friend, Torrance, and the rest of you."
He stared at Eloria's gem as it flickered.

"I don't have any plans to visit the Darkland Forest soon."
Viator handed a roll to Torrance. "And Lars wants to keep Eloria
for himself."

Eloria finished her roll, then untied the tie to her green cloak
and pulled it off. "You can have this." She handed it to the dark
elf. "I found it in one of the creature's closets."

"Thank you, princess."

"Just Eloria."

The river elf shook his head. "If Lars wishes for you to join
him, you cannot be a commoner."

Eloria's brows arched in amusement. "He wished for me to
join him, before or after his people threw me from the cliffs?"

The elf's jaw dropped. "You cannot be serious."

Eloria shook her head. "Prince Viator rescued me." She saw
Viator's mouth drop open slightly. She smiled. "What, sire?
When addressing others while speaking of a royal person, I
must use his or her title."

Torrance pointed at her. "You are the one they spoke of. The
islanders grew frenzied when they sensed you were nearby.
They said you were the greatest prize they'd ever have the
chance to capture. That's why they locked you in the tower, not
in the dungeon with us."

"They did save me from the mermaid. Her fingers
grabbed my ankle. She tried to pull me under. And then I
heard the lapping of water against the wooden hull of a boat.
No paddles moved it. No sails. It slipped like the mist toward
me. Long spindly fingers plucked me from the sea. I looked
up to see you, Viator, holding onto the net as you searched
for me. I tried to cry out to you, but the mist overcame me.
No sight, nor voice had I. Then I woke to find myself dressed
in gowns of green." She poked her finger in the sand. Her

necklace glowed brightly as she drew three symbols on the beach.

"What are they?" Viator asked, as he touched her hand.

The emerald darkened. Eloria stared at the shapes and shook her head.

Balen drew closer. "They are ancient symbols of a dead language, sire. The first is the symbol of Sarazan, the green wizard, long thought dead."

"The one I told you about, Eloria. The one in your dreams," Viator said.

"The second symbol..." Balen pursed his lips. "I'm not sure." He ran his hand around the circles within a circle like the inner coil of a seashell. "I don't know." Turning his attention to the last, he said, "Hmmm, the dragon of Benzol."

"The Benzolian dragon who won't be tamed," Viator said.

"Yes, sire. Many have lost their lives in such a foolish venture. The final quest for coming of age...tame a dragon...call him or her your own. Why would anyone seek to tame *that* dragon?"

"Whosoever will tame the dragon of Benzol will be all powerful, so the soothsayers say."

"Only because no one can tame it...no one." Balen sat down on the ground. He turned his attention to Eloria. "Why would you draw these symbols?"

Eloria shook her head. "I don't know. I suddenly had the urge to draw in the sand. My teacher was always upset with me for...doodling on paper in class, she said."

"You've written more of these symbols, yet don't know what they mean?" Viator asked.

"I doodled."

The river elf jumped to his feet. He smiled as he ran his hand over the green cloak's soft cloth. "Thank you, young lady, for your gift to me. And thank you, Torrance, for being a friend to me all those long days in the dungeon of the isle. And to you,

Prince Viator, and your companion for helping to free me from exile under the sea." He pulled a ring from his pouch and handed it to Viator. "Should you or your friends ever need help, just use this. Twist it three times, and I will come to your aid."

"But one of us can take you home," Viator said.

"Yes, sire, if you should carry the river elf...," Balen said, but was interrupted.

"Leigh."

"Leigh, then. You could carry him to the forest, and you could earn a whole credit."

"No," the river elf said. "I have other business I must attend to before I return home." The elf brushed the sand from his clothes. "Again, many thanks." He hurried away.

"I must return home as well." Torrance stood. "I have been away for too long. I thank you for your aid. Take good care of the princess, Your Majesty, and she will take good care of you." He bowed, then lifted his wings and flew inland.

They watched as Leigh disappeared over a sand dune and Torrance diminished in size. Balen cleared his throat. "Where to now, sire? Will we take Eloria back?"

Viator studied the symbols in the sand. "What does the coiled one mean?"

"There's a book in our library on the subject, sire. I used to read it when I was bored with other schoolwork. There were thousands of symbols in the book. I vaguely remember having seen this one, but can't recall..."

Viator shook his head as he faced Eloria. "What other symbols did you draw?"

"Perhaps if I saw the book, I could remember and identify them."

"You've been drawing them for years?"

"Yes."

He rubbed his chin.

"You were going to take her to see the shadow elves, sire. You said—"

"She should see this book."

"But, Your Majesty, your father has forbidden you to see any more of the human girl. If we take her home with us—"

"Perhaps you could bring the book to us in the fairies' meadowlands."

"The book cannot leave the library, sire. Reference book, you know. All kinds of alarms will sound if it goes beyond the library doors."

Viator sighed deeply. "Then she will have to return with us. Somehow, we'll sneak her in."

"And then?"

"After she tells us all the symbols she has seen, we'll record them and then we'll take her to see the shadow elves."

Eloria climbed onto Viator's back.

Viator glanced at Balen who nodded to him in wordless agreement, though Balen didn't look happy about the prospect. Flapping their wings as if in a choreographed dance, the two headed toward Darkland Forest Castle.

WHEN THEY ARRIVED at the castle in the Darkland Forest, they found the winged elves dressed in masquerade costumes as they attended the ball. The great hall, now decorated in honey-scented jasmine and baskets of flowers, was filled to capacity. Harp-like music with a strange drumbeat filled the air and exuberant elves danced to the music.

"Even better than we could have planned. I had forgotten all about the ball that would be held while we were off trying to complete our quests." Viator led them to his chamber. "Balen, you go to your chamber and get your disguise for the dance. I'll find something for Eloria."

He rummaged through a chest while Balen hurried out of the room. Then Viator pulled out a royal purple cloak and mask for her. "These were mine from some years past...when I was a bit shorter. They should fit you well. The mask should hide your face and the hood of the cloak your red hair and your rounded human ears."

She pulled the hooded cloak on and pulled the hood up over her hair. She stared at her image in a gold gilt mirror. Sure enough, the cloak hid her features, and when she attached the sequined mask, no one could tell who she was, she was certain.

The length of the garment was perfect too. She attached the gold chain that held the cloak in place. Viator had disappeared into another room, and when he returned, she smiled. He wore a cloak covered in feather-weight shells and spread out the garment for her to see. "I've been making this for a year, since the last annual ball. I'd forgotten it was today, but none will know me in this cloak."

"It's really different, Viator."

"Yes, well, that's the rule. The ones whose identity cannot be guessed at the ball, win an award. I like to win."

Balen soon joined them, and Eloria couldn't help herself this time. She laughed out loud, and he frowned at her.

"What is your problem?" he asked, his voice tinged with annoyance.

"Nothing, Balen, your flower petal-covered cloak is the perfect disguise."

"Lord Balen. And true," Balen said. "I'm not fond of flowers, and so no one will know it is me."

"Lovely."

"Yes, well it is our custom."

Viator's cloak clinked as the seashells knocked together

while they walked to the library. They turned down several different corridors, their boots moving quietly as they made their way to the library. Except for the notes of the wind instruments drifting overhead from time to time, the castle was deadly quiet.

When they reached the room where leather-bound books stretched up to the ten-foot-high ceiling, Eloria whispered, "Do you know where the book of symbols is?"

"I do." Balen hurried to the second row of books, but voices stopped them in their tracks.

"What I don't understand is why she would have come here when she did," a man said as he and another walked through the library.

"Yes, well the king was correct in his ruling to send her away at once."

Balen grabbed Eloria's arm to her surprise and pulled her between the row of books, but Viator darted in a different direction to keep the men from finding Eloria. His robe made a racket and the two men gasped in surprise. "What are you doing in here? Everyone in the kingdom is to participate in the ceremony."

"I was on my way, only I got a bit distracted."

The two men and Viator headed to the great hall as Eloria and Balen peeked through the books and watched their departure. Balen sighed a ragged breath. "I hope he knows what he's doing."

"Okay, Balen, hurry. Find the book."

"*Lord* Balen, and females do not order me about, unless of course it is the queen."

He pulled a rolling ladder over to midway down the aisle but stopped when they heard his sister's voice approach as she spoke to someone else.

Just great.

19

"Griffin feathers. Stay here, Eloria," Balen whispered. "I will get rid of them and come back for you and the book as soon as I can."

Her arms prickled with chill bumps. If she got caught now...

He hurried down the aisle and out the other side. Then he met up with Sendal and her friend. "What are you doing here?" he asked her, as Eloria's heart pounded with fear of being caught. What would they do with her then? Lock her in a tower? Throw her off the cliffs like their cousins the river elves had done?

She had to find the book and quickly. Having no knowledge of the elven written language, she climbed the ladder, hoping something would give her a clue. She grabbed the first book she could reach and pulled it open. There were no symbols in it that she recognized from her dreams. After trying three more books, she grabbed the next and her crystal began to glow.

Was it a sign? She certainly hoped so. She opened the book and nearly fell off the ladder. The first symbol etched in her memory was illustrated on the page. And to her amazement, the drawing glowed green. In fact, her crystal glowed too. But the words explaining the meaning of the symbols were foreign to her.

She flipped through three more pages, then turned to another symbol. Again, her crystal and the symbol on the page glowed. If only Balen were here to decipher the words.

Then to her horror, footsteps approached. She hurried down the ladder, then shoved the book under the table.

"What are you doing in here?" A man dressed in a cloak of dragon scales approached her. Seeing her gaze shift to his costume, he added, "Oh, and for your information, these were shredded scales. I did not kill some poor dragon. I've heard that enough tonight in jest. I'm Lord Ren by the way in case you didn't recognize me. And you are?"

She shook her head. She assumed their masked balls were like the ones given in the books she'd read about. Only the wearer could identify his or herself unless someone recognized them beforehand. But they were under no obligation to reveal their identity otherwise.

The man never gave her a chance to speak, and she was much relieved. If he heard her Langolar accent, he would know at once she was not a winged elf.

"Unless you have business elsewhere, as I had a moment ago, you are not to be beyond the walls of the great hall. King's rules." He smiled broadly at her. "I know these to be Prince Viator's garments from a ball some years past. You must be a lady friend of his for him to allow you to wear his things. That means I will be envied by all to get to dance with you first."

Not knowing the first thing about how elves danced, she was certain her lack of knowledge would soon give her away.

He extended his arm to her, and she rested her hand on it. He smiled. "Prince Viator won't be happy I received the first dance from you, my lady. But he should not have left you alone without an escort."

The winged elf was so talkative, she assumed he never noticed she'd never said a word. But when he led her into the great hall, the room grew hushed. Wearing Viator's cloak and mask hadn't been a good idea, she could see now. Everyone undoubtedly wondered who the female was who wore the crown prince's garment for the evening's festivities. And she figured the way the courtiers reacted, he had never loaned his clothes to anyone before.

Ren led her to the center of the dance floor. Viator stood watching, his mouth agape. And Balen standing nearby wore the same kind of incredulous expression.

"Seems His Majesty is surprised to see you here with me." Ren pulled her close and the music began again.

So Ren recognized the prince right away. Did everyone else then? She was dying to ask him how he knew the prince so easily but realized she could say nothing or she'd give herself away.

She followed his moves instead with precision as he walked one way, then another. The maneuvers were easy to mimic, long flowing, and with simple repetitive steps. Soon he had swept her across the entire floor. For several minutes, the courtiers stood watching them, hushed voices spoken as the elves tried to determine who she was.

When she turned once, Sendal glared back at her, and she knew if Sendal could she would have torn Eloria's cloak from her head. But masked balls were sacred, fun-filled affairs, as far as she had read, so it seemed Sendal could seethe all she wanted, but she could do nothing more than that where Eloria was concerned.

"You do not wish to reveal who you are to me? I can hear the muffled conversations around us, and you are as much a total mystery to the others as you are to me. But before the night is out, I will know who it is that the prince favors over Lady

Sendal."

The thought took her breath away. The winged elves were afraid of her. She shuddered to think what they might do if they knew who she was.

"Griffin feathers. Here comes the prince. I should have known he would take you away from me soon." Ren released his hold on her. "Sire," he said nodding his head in a bow. "The lady is most precious, but she would reveal nothing of who she is."

As soon as the prince held Eloria's hand, he pulled her close, closer than Ren had done, and she wondered if his actions were sanctioned or not. She noted too, his cloak seemed to billow out slightly as if he spread his wings. Why would he open his wings underneath a cloak?

He leaned close and whispered in her ear, "Everyone watches us. We must be careful not to give your identity away."

She whispered back. "I found the book and when I saw some of the symbols therein, they glowed at the same time my crystal did. It's beneath the large table in one of the rows."

He straightened his back and stared at her. "Balen will have to tell us what it means."

"Yes, but...but what if I get caught here?"

He pulled her close again. "I'm afraid I won't win the contest this year. Somehow, some of the courtiers have concluded that I have returned from the seacoast. Though I thought the disguise very clever."

"It is your bearing and handsome features that cannot be hidden. I would have known you anywhere."

The corners of his mouth rose. "You are the greatest mystery here, whether you wear a disguise or not."

"Your people will be terribly frightened if they learn I have returned."

"You dance our steps as well as our own ladies who have had

lessons for years. No one could tell from the way you dance that you are not one of ours."

"I'm afraid Sendal will attempt to rip the hood from my head to reveal who I am. She has been glowering at me ever since Lord Ren walked me into the great hall, wearing your clothes."

"Yes, well I wouldn't have thought so many would remember my costume from so long ago. I guess more pay attention to me than I realize."

"Now they are paying this unwanted attention to me. Do you not think they are suspicious? First, you and Balen return. And now this strange woman arrives, wearing your cloak?"

He took a deep breath. "Luckily, my father is not here at the moment. Seems he is seeing a cousin who lives east of here. Otherwise, I would worry that he'd do away with protocol and ask you to reveal yourself. Still, my mother has been keeping a close eye on you since your arrival. I have never disobeyed my father, so she may not believe I would return you here. On the other hand, you are thought to have cast a spell over me, so she might believe you made me bring you here again."

Eloria smiled. "You are saying she thinks I am a bad influence over you."

"You are. I have never danced this close with a woman before, and in reality, should not unless I am married to her."

Eloria's whole body heated with the notion. She tried to distance herself from him, but he wouldn't allow it.

"Your crystal is glowing. I am trying to keep anyone from seeing it as the light is filtering through the cloak."

"I think the light is glowing because you are so close to me."

He chuckled under his breath. "Well, we cannot be sure. If I move away from you, and you are incorrect, others may see the light and then everyone will guess who you are."

She smiled. "And here I thought you only wished to hold me close."

He smiled.

She glanced down to see if the amulet really glowed or if he only said so to keep her close.

"Troll's dung," he said as he looked over at his mother. "My mother just spoke to Lord Tor, and he's on his way over here to either dance with you or speak with me."

"Can you not tell him to get lost?"

"No. I'm afraid it's just not a viable option."

"He won't be like Lord Ren who spoke nonstop and never gave me a chance to speak. As your Minister of Information, Lord Tor will question me as before."

"Yes, unless he wishes to speak with me instead." Viator stiffened and nodded at the gentleman as he approached.

The man bowed to Eloria, then said to Viator, "Prince Viator, your mother wishes to know how your mission went in Neferon."

Viator walked away from Eloria. She quickly glanced down to see her cloak dark, and the amulet not glowing, to her relief.

Lord Tor motioned for the prince to leave the dance floor, but Viator shook his head. "Lord Tor, you know at a dance like this, everyone is to participate. Business can be discussed later."

Eloria noticed Lord Ren had headed in her direction while the prince was occupied, but before he reached her, Balen grabbed her hand and swirled her on the dance floor. He winked at the prince as he turned to watch them, then continued in his steps with her.

She frowned at Balen. "What is going on?"

"The queen is trying to separate you from her son. I must get you out of here as soon as I can. Everyone is talking. They cannot understand who the prince could have fallen in love with. It's the only thing they can surmise with the way you two danced so closely on the floor."

"My amulet was glowing. He tried to keep it hidden."

Balen looked down at her cloak, then smiled as his gaze shifted to hers. "So that's the excuse he used, eh?"

Her cheeks burned with embarrassment. "We must return to the library. I found the right book. The symbols that I have seen before glowed at the same time as my crystal."

"Somehow, I must get you out of here, but everyone is watching us. Before long they will attempt to separate me from you as they have done with the prince."

Her breathing quickened. "I must get out of here then. But how? Your people fear me."

"You cannot wander off alone. And yet I cannot have a woman escort you out of here. A man cannot do this either as men are not to be left alone with a single female, though in your case it has often been done." He glanced at the prince who watched them as Lord Tor stood next to him, his arms crossed. "I've been trying to figure out what to do since I saw Lord Ren escort you into the hall."

"A diversion? Can you think of something to distract your people?"

"Other than you calling your dragon friend, no."

"What about if I just removed the cloak? Maybe everyone will run from the room."

"I'm afraid you will be arrested."

"That wouldn't do." She considered the prince and his long face and furrowed brow. "Take me back to Viator. Maybe he will think of something while we dance."

"You will dance too closely."

"Take me back there."

"Lord Ren is heading this way."

"Quickly, before he gets too close."

Balen did as he was told, his turned-down mouth showing his displeasure. Before they even reached the prince's side, Eloria extended her hand to the prince.

The conversation and music ceased at once.

Viator smiled at her and took her hand, then pulled her close. "Thank you for taking care of the lady for me, Lord Balen."

"Yes, Your Majesty," Balen said, bowing.

Viator again pulled Eloria close.

She shook her head. "It is not glowing."

He laughed. "You have stirred up the elf-kind, my lady. A lady never offers her hand to a gentleman unless she wishes him to accept it forever."

"Oh. Well, had I known..."

"Then you do not have the same custom in your world?"

"No."

"You offered. I accepted. The first part of our engagement is done."

20

E loria smiled at Viator, thinking he was funny for telling her that offering her hand to him, meant they were engaged. "Ah, for elven kind. They won't believe anything would come of this so-called first part of an engagement when they know who I am."

"The ritual is not taken lightly." He kissed her cheek.

She smiled again at him, then sighed and frowned. "I must get out of here. I thought maybe there could be a distraction."

"I've been trying to figure out what to do. We cannot take the book from the library without setting off alarms. And somehow I must get you out of here safely too."

Eloria knew this was going to be bad. But other than both she and Viator rushing for the nearest window so they could jump out of it, what else could they do? If she had to, she'd use her magic, but for now, she would do what she usually excelled at—being a motivational inspirer. Or at least, she was most of the time.

"Let me talk to your mother."

Viator whispered to her, "Are you sure?"

"Yes."

He escorted her to see his mother, and she curtsied to the queen.

"Come with me. I'd tell my son to stay, but I doubt he'd obey me. We'll talk in my solar." The queen motioned for Balen to join them.

When they arrived at her sitting room, the queen took her seat on a chair, then motioned to them to take separate chairs. But Viator led Eloria to a couch and sat next to her as if to give physical and emotional support. Balen sat on one of the other chairs.

"You can remove the mask and cloak—or not—but I do know who you are," the queen said to Eloria.

They all removed their cloaks and masks.

"It's a good thing your father isn't here." The queen looked at Viator's wings. "At least you've made some progress. Slowly, but surely."

Viator inclined his head to his mother. "She recognizes certain ancient symbols, my lady mother."

"Which is why you've risked our wrath to bring her back here? To learn what they mean from a book in our library?" His mother was scowling.

Eloria didn't think this was going over too well, but part of being a motivational inspirer was to wait and observe and then direct the proceedings again.

Viator cleared his throat. "Yes."

"Okay." The queen smoothed out her red gown. "So what do the symbols mean?" She directed the question to Eloria.

"I don't know. I couldn't read the language. But they were symbols I've seen in my dreams. When I looked at the book in the library, my crystal glowed and so did the symbol in the book," Eloria said.

The queen frowned. "In our prophecy, it states a human took a young girl to a world none of us know. If you were gone, far away, it wouldn't come to pass. If you are the one. We worried the other one—"

"Persephonice?" Eloria asked.

"Yes. That she was the one. But she's brought peace to many who have squabbled among themselves forever. And she has done nothing to change anything with how we live. Now here you come. And you have changed much here already for our people. Both of you are like the sirens of the sea, only in land form. You have used your magic to ensnare the unsuspecting."

"My lady mother—"

The queen held her hand up to Viator, ordering him to remain silent. "The woman from the prophecy comes from a long line of dragon keepers. Their babies sleep in the nests with the dragonlings. They treat one another as dragon mates. To them, the elf baby is a litter mate, and they will protect her. I'm wondering if Eloria was one of the dragons' litter mates. Others raised in the same cave are also considered litter mates. Cousins, as well. The elves who protect the dragonlings have magic. Just like the dragons do."

"Like high elves," Eloria said.

"Exactly. And they train the dragons and make companions of them like we do. Except it's different for us because we can fly too. And we don't have inherent magic." She turned to Eloria. "In your belongings, you had a sword and something else our guards believe could be a weapon. What was it?"

"From the world I'm from, it's called a stun gun. It can put someone to sleep or give them an electric charge that takes them down temporarily. I'm not an elf, as you very well know. I'm not from this world."

"Your mother was human? Your father?" the queen asked.

"I don't remember much about my mother, only that she had blond hair and blue eyes. My father had red hair and green eyes like me. He was human. My mother died when I was only four. I

was on my home world with my father until he died, and I
ended up working for a commander of a...uh, ship." She didn't
tell the queen about the spaceship. She was sure that even
talking about another planet would be too much for these primitive elves to understand.

"You know too much of our world not to be from here. Your
mother, maybe, was an elf like us. A high elf, maybe, with
powers?"

"Uhm, my father did say my mother was the one with
magical abilities. I never knew where she was from."

Then the queen changed the subject. "Can you replicate
this...stun gun for us?"

"No. I wouldn't know the first thing about making one."

"But you know how to use it."

"Yes."

"Viator, bring the book here, won't you?"

"It will sound an alarm."

His mother gave him a key. "Now, go and bring it. We'll figure
out which symbols seem important to Eloria."

Eloria hoped they'd finally know something about all of this,
but she couldn't believe her mother was an elf from this world.
How would her father have met her? Had he been on the planet
at some point, fallen in love with the elf, her mother, and stayed
with her until she died? He'd been an ambassador to different
planets, but she knew they didn't have an ambassador for primitive worlds that couldn't understand about other planets or
space travel. If he had been here with her mother, then had he
taken Eloria to their home world after her mother died?

She tried to think of everything that her father had told her
before he'd died, but not once had he said her mother had been
an elf from this world. Nor had he said where her mother had
actually been from, she realized.

"Then I must speak with the high elves and learn if they

know anything about whether my mother was one of them, had a baby girl by a human, and when she died, he left with the young girl," Eloria said.

"Yes," the queen said, sounding eager to get rid of her one way or another. "My very thought. Maybe the problem you bring is to their kingdom, not ours." She appeared hopeful.

Viator returned with the large, leather-bound book, but Balen said, "Let me find the symbols that she drew in the sand. I know where they are." Viator handed him the book.

Balen opened it and began to flip through the pages. He first came to the symbol of the green wizard, Sarandan. Eloria's amulet glowed and so did the symbol on the page. Everyone looked on in astonishment, even Eloria, who just couldn't believe her mother might have been from this world. But why else would Eloria have an amulet that reacted to a book in the library of the darkland elves? And why would it seem to call on a dragon?

Balen slowly flipped pages and before Eloria could even identify the others she knew from memory, they would glow. Viator was writing all the symbols down. "That symbol is for poison," Viator said.

Balen turned some more pages and two symbols glowed. "A fishing net." And on the opposite page, he pointed to the other symbol. "It's the symbol for water."

Frowning, the queen turned her attention to Eloria. "Who taught you these symbols?"

"No one did. I just...doodled when I was in school. No one who saw them thought they were anything more than—doodles, nonsense drawings that had no meaning and they knew I'd just made them up."

"An elf taught you these symbols. It's an ancient elf language, no longer used." Viator was frowning at Eloria too, and she wondered if he was disappointed in her.

The queen rubbed her forehead. "Would your mother have taught you them before she died? Or someone else in the family? When you were between the ages of three and four, she could have shown them to you though."

"I...I don't know."

"Okay, I don't know about the rest of you, but I see a pattern here," Viator said, sounding both worried and excited. "There seems to be too much of a coincidence that some of the tasks I've fulfilled appear to be aligned with the symbols Eloria knows and that her amulet reacts to."

"Nonsense," the queen quickly said. "Anyone could draw conclusions that are just utter nonsense."

Balen and Viator exchanged glances, and Eloria thought they didn't believe the queen, knowing that she had her own agenda—sending Eloria far away from their kingdom. Eloria was thinking that Viator was right.

"Taming the dragon is part of my quests because it is something I must do," Viator said, ignoring his mother's comment. "The poison in the river, the fishing net—we've all encountered those. I'm not sure about the green wizard, though."

"See? What did I tell you?" his mother said. "You can find reasons for all of this, which truly have nothing to do with anything."

"Okay," Balen said, "The shadow symbol could be that of the shadow elves. Maybe they need us to help them with a quest."

"Me." Viator gave Balen a look that told him this was his quest and not Balen's!

But both had been involved in all of it, so Eloria was thinking it meant they all had to do it together. She was eager to help if she could.

"Maybe I'm supposed to see Persephonice, and you're supposed to help me," Eloria suggested, hoping they'd take her up on her suggestion.

"I agree," Viator said and Balen nodded. "So we don't know about the wizard, except that Eloria is dreaming about him."

"About the wizard?" the queen asked, looking a little alarmed. "He is dead."

Viator rubbed his chin thoughtfully. "She shadow walks, my lady mother. Maybe she also has some...familial connection with him. Family. An uncle or grandfather."

"He is ancient. And dead."

"Maybe his spirt is connected to her for some reason." Viator didn't seem to be ready to give up on the notion.

Eloria wondered if the wizard had come to her in an effort to help her fulfill the prophecy. And leading her to locate the crystal had been the beginning.

"How would that be connected to you and your quests?" his mother asked. Then she dismissed her question. "Forget it. I know what you will say. What are the other symbols?"

They were getting near the end of the book. Eloria only remembered drawing ten symbols. Would there be only ten in the book that would glow for her?

"A dragon's lair," Viator said. "That's two references to a dragon. The dragon itself and its lair."

"An amulet," Baden said, turning to the next page.

Everyone looked at Eloria's glowing amulet.

That should have been the last of the symbols she had drawn, but when they turned to the last page of the book, a new symbol she didn't recall glowed.

"It's mist," Balen said.

Viator snapped his fingers. "Like the island that disappeared into the mist."

"What? That is no more than folktales and legends. There is no truth to it," the queen said.

Eloria ran her hand over the green gown she was wearing. "This gown came from the castle on the island cloaked in mist."

Frowning, the queen touched the fabric. Then she snapped at her son. "What were you doing on that island? You could have been lost forever!"

"Rescuing Eloria! And some other elves."

"Green wizard, dragon, dragon's lair, coiled-up rope, amulet, poison, water, fishing net, fire, shadow, mist. Eleven ancient elven symbols." Balen closed up the book.

Eloria stared at the book. "The mist symbol was the only one that I hadn't remembered seeing."

"Seeing?" the queen asked.

"In my dreams. Maybe my mother didn't teach me the symbols, but the green wizard did."

The queen scoffed. "Nonsense. He's been dead for years. This girl is leaving to see Prince Zorak and his people to learn if her mother was one of them *now*." The queen gave Viator a look like he better not even think of going there with her. "Lord Balen will take her there. If that is unacceptable to you, I'll send Lord Ren to do the task. If she leaves, discreetly, I won't have to tell your father how you disobeyed him."

VIATOR COULDN'T BELIEVE that he was going to lose Eloria again. He needed to accomplish his quests, but he felt that *she* was the key to his success. Which should have irked him. He should have handled this all on his own.

He rose from the couch and pulled Eloria to stand. "Go with Balen and learn what you can about the high elves and how you might be one of them." He smiled at her then, pulled her into a hug and kissed her. "If you are, you will be close by. The high elves live in the mountains beyond Darkland Forest where our mountain range is located, called Darkland Mountains. Theirs are the High Mountains where most high elves live." He had every intention of visiting her while she lived with them.

"You will complete your quest, Prince Viator. I know in my heart that you will," she said.

His mother scoffed again. "Of course he will. He is the crown prince of the darkland elves. Balen, take the girl now, before I change my mind and send Ren with her instead."

"Yes, Your Majesty." Balen quickly took Eloria's hand. "We will go the back way while everyone is still enjoying the celebration."

"Eloria, be safe." Viator squeezed her free hand.

"And you too, Viator, uh, Prince." Eloria smiled at him, but she looked sad to go. He was certain she wanted to stay with him to help him with his quests, though he needed to do this on his own.

Yet, in the worst way, he wanted her with him, whether he made his wings transparent or not.

The music from the great hall flowed throughout the castle, and all he wanted was to dance with the mystery woman the rest of the night through. Though he tried not to worry about it, what if she wasn't related in any way to Prince Zorak, which Viator considered she might be, and Zorak wanted to court her instead?

21

Before Lord Balen flew Eloria to Prince Zorak's high castle in the mountains, he retrieved the rest of her things, including her stun gun, which she so appreciated. She might not need it, but she was glad to have it for backup, just in case. She was also glad she got to go with Balen because she couldn't talk about any of this to Lord Ren.

Balen carried her off the wall surrounding his castle, soaring across Darkland Forest. She didn't think she'd ever get used to flying like this. They flew high above a snaking river, and she spied what looked like a giant beehive way down below, perched on a massive rock in the middle of the widest part of the river. She thought it looked remarkably like a coiled rope. "Wait, Balen."

He snorted.

"*Lord* Balen. Look down there."

He glanced down at the thing she was pointing to.

"A memorial."

"Doesn't it look like a coiled rope from way up above?"

Balen hovered over the monument from about hundred and fifty feet high, staring at the object.

"Goddess, yeah. Uh, oh." Balen glanced back at the darkland elves' castle.

"You can't check it out without telling Viator."

"If I return too soon, the queen will know I didn't take you to see the high elves right away."

"Leave me down there. I'll explore it. You wait until it is safe enough for you to return to your castle, and Viator can join me down there."

"Are you kidding? You are the one who is always getting into trouble, and we have to keep rescuing you. And we don't even get any credit for it. There's no way I'm leaving you down there alone."

"You have to tell Viator."

"I will. I'll drop you off with the high elves, return for Viator, and he'll probably tell me to stay behind while he checks the monument out." Balen continued to hover in place as if he was waiting for her agreement, which surprised her.

"You know I have something to do with the prophecy."

"You *are* the prophecy, and it only means trouble for my kind."

"Okay, so you know also that somehow the three of us are tied together in this...conundrum."

He looked blankly at her.

"Mystery, challenge."

"The queen will have my head. She can be quite vocal and physical, well, using her guards' muscle, if she learns I didn't take you to see the high elves and leave you there."

They heard wings flapping behind them from some distance and he immediately whipped around to see who, or what, was flying toward them. She'd hoped it was Viator, but feared it was a griffin or another flying creature that ate elves. Instead, she saw it was Lord Ren.

"The queen had to have told him to follow us and make sure

I did what she told me to do." Balen flew off, not waiting for Ren to catch up. "He's already going to suspect something's going on because I didn't go straight to the high elves' castle."

"Say that I was arguing with you because I decided I wanted to see the shadow elves first. So who is the memorial dedicated to?"

"The...the green wizard. He was a high elf, but a friend to all elves, no matter their origin. It is said that he was not that way in the beginning. He had a strong dislike for any elf that wasn't one of his kind. But then something profound happened in his life and he changed his ways. He is the only elf I know of that could be called a friend of the blue elves when he wasn't of their kind."

"You don't know what changed him?"

"No. No one does. Scholars have tried to figure it out for centuries, thinking if they could determine what helped him to change, maybe all of us could."

She saw a tower of white sitting high on cliffs and thought it reached toward the sky as if they were heavenly beings. Two dragons flew off the wall walk and swooped down, turning well before they were more than specks in the sky. She'd wondered if they were attracted to her or her amulet, but they didn't seem to take any notice of her.

Balen finally reached the wall walk and landed on their stone patio, surrounded by the high, crenelated walls. Archers sat atop the wall walk, watching for any dangers. A couple of dragons sitting in the courtyard watched Balen and Eloria as he released her.

"I'll wait with you until I'm sure that Prince Zorak is taking you in," Balen said.

She appreciated that he hadn't just flown off.

"Viator hasn't given up on seeing you again, but once his father returns home—"

"He has to finish his quests. So do you. I'm sure we will see each other again." She had it in mind to ask Prince Zorak to take her to the green wizard's monument. Then she could join Balen and Viator there.

"I'm not so sure. If Prince Zorak has his way, you may be staying here. If you're family."

"I'll have him take me to see the shadow elves so I can speak with Persephonice, which is *my* quest." Eloria sure hoped the high elves wouldn't confine her here. She couldn't allow it, but they had their own magic skills too.

Balen inclined his head to her when two royal guards rushed out to join them.

"This is Eloria. Prince Zorak saved her from the blue elves. Prince Viator took her home with him, but I've brought her here to speak with Prince Zorak about her friend Persephonice."

She wondered why Balen hadn't said she might belong here, but maybe he was leaving it to her to explain who she was to Prince Zorak.

"We'll escort her to see Prince Zorak, Lord Balen," one of the guards said.

Lord Ren landed right after that and said to Balen, "I thought you had changed your mind about bringing the lady here."

"I tried to convince him to take me to see the shadow elves," Eloria said to Ren.

Balen agreed, then he took a deep breath, looking uneasy about leaving her with the high elves.

"I'm fine. Tell Viator, Prince Viator, I'm fine." Then she headed to the hallway leading into the castle and prayed she would be fine. But when she met with Prince Zorak, he was scowling at her.

She assumed then he was angry that she'd been with Viator for so long, but she hadn't offered herself as a hostage to the darkland elf!

"Why have you come here?" Prince Zorak asked. Before she could say anything, he answered for her. "You've come here to force Persephonice to return with you to rejoin her father?"

"He's concerned she's lost her bracelet, which means her way back. And she's had no way to communicate with him."

"And if I tell you she has no intention of returning with you? That she has married the shadow elf warrior Dracolin, then what do you say to that?" the prince asked.

She folded her arms. "I would say I'd have to hear it from Persephonice." No way could she take the word of this prince or anyone else.

"And when you hear it from her? Then what? Will her father accept this coming from you? Or will he want to hear it from his daughter as well?"

"If you want to know the truth, he will accept no answer other than the one he wants to hear. Namely that she is eager to return to the ship."

"I'm surprised you're being so honest with me. I cannot imagine her father will be happy when you return to give him the news."

"I only want Persephonice to be happy. If she loves Dracolin and wants to stay here, I have no intention of trying to tell her she's wrong and needs to reconsider."

"From what we've heard of her father, I don't imagine he will welcome the news. What will happen if you tell her father she isn't returning?"

"I will be set off at the next world they come to. In other words, it won't go well for me. I had no choice but to come here and try to persuade Persephonice to do what her father bids."

"So you do plan to try and convince her to leave."

"No. It has to be her choice."

PRINCE ZORAK DIDN'T TRUST the woman. She was as beautiful as Persephonice. But what he didn't trust was that she would leave Persephonice here and risk her own safety when she left here. Which meant he had no intention of letting her see her friend. *Ever.*

He grabbed her wrist and before she could jerk her arm away, two guards rushed forth and held her still, while Zorak removed the wristband. Now she couldn't communicate with her commander, nor could she leave, unless the prince said so. He removed her sword and the strange holstered weapon.

"I would be extremely careful with that if I were you."

"What is it?"

"A stun gun. It stuns the enemy or puts them to sleep, depending on the setting."

He took her pack and dumped the contents on the stone floor. When he found another wristband like the one Persephonice had worn, he took that also.

Then he had one of his men repack the bag. He handed it to Zorak, who said, "We will have your accommodations ready now. You can take this with you." He handed her the bag. "You'll have plenty of opportunity to eat, so you don't need to worry about that."

She opened her mouth to mention that she might be half high elf, but her guards hauled her away and she decided right then and there she didn't care if she was related to any of them or not. She was leaving this place and either rejoining Viator, or heading straight to the shadow elves' kingdom, hoping she wouldn't get herself into any more trouble. Getting off the high mountain could be a problem though.

She started walking down one opulent corridor to another where tapestries hung on the walls and the doors were trimmed in gold gilt. But then she was taken down several flights of stairs and nothing was adorned in these hallways. She was afraid they intended to take her to some kind of dungeon, like solitary confinement on the ship, only darker, scarier.

She thought of using her magic, but then she decided against it. If they didn't know she had any, she might be able to get herself out of here more easily.

They took her to a wooden door and opened it. It was a small cell, like she was worried about, with one window high above and covered in sturdy metal ironwork.

She pondered whether she should mention to the whiskered, narrow-eyed guards that she might be a high elf too, or keep her secret that she might be one, so they wouldn't contain her magic somehow. She didn't know if they could, but she didn't want them to do that, if so.

"How long do I have to be in here?"

"For as long as the prince or his father and mother say. They are away at the moment. Enjoy your stay," the darker-haired man said, and locked the door.

She wished she could elevate herself to the window, but she couldn't. What if she could call Talom, the dragon? What if he could tell Viator that she'd been locked in a dungeon! From what she knew, the winged elves couldn't communicate with the dragons. She suspected Talom wouldn't come. It was her amulet that had called him and how would he see it when she was so far away from the window in the dark dungeon?

Still, she called out to the dragon, just to see what would happen.

He didn't come, naturally. But she wasn't giving up. The thing about her translator was it seemed to work with all kinds of creatures, and she thought maybe she could get word to him through one of the dragons staying at the castle, or visiting, or whatever they were doing here.

After an hour, she heard fluttering outside her window, but she couldn't see what it was. It sounded large, like a dragon. But what if it was one of those things that tried to kill her before? Or a griffin?

She called to Talom that she needed to be set free.

But whatever creature it was, it went away. She called out over and over again. Then she heard several more fluttering wings and it sounded like a whole swarm of dragons. Or, maybe something deadly.

Then a dragon poked its nose at the grate and peered into the window, looking down at her.

Her amulet glowed bright green, but the dragon wasn't Talom. She swore the dragon smiled, showing off lots of wicked teeth.

"Can you help me get out of here?"

The dragon made a funny sound, and then she understood its language. That's how the translator worked. The creature had to say some "words" and it began translating so she could speak to it.

"Talon isn't close by," the dragon said. "Why are you in here?"

"Prince Zorak doesn't want me to see a friend of mine, Persephonice, who now lives among the shadow elves."

The dragon shook her head. "Do you not remember me?"

Eloria shook her head. "I don't remember anything about being here before."

"We were nest mates. I'm Ilea. You have started quite a commotion. All of us are distressed to hear that Zorak has imprisoned you down here. The word is being passed along from dragon to dragon and to those who are carrying high elves who are on quests. They are returning them to the castle, offering no explanation. We won't have one of our own imprisoned without good cause. Even so, we deal with our own kind ourselves."

"But I'm not a dragon." Eloria had a hard time fathoming the new world she'd found herself in. She wasn't an outsider like she thought she was, but part of the primitive world. And it wasn't really so primitive at all. Except for when predators were trying to eat her or hide her away on an island covered in mists, or elves were trying to kill her, or she was being locked up by other elves, her own kind, it appeared, she loved it here. She wondered if the land held some kind of magic of its own, because she felt totally spellbound with the beauty of the world, and she loved Viator. Even Balen, Lord Balen. But especially Viator.

And Talom too. And Ilea. This was her home again. She might not remember it at all from her childhood, but she knew she'd never be able to leave. That was okay with her too.

"We have sent word to Talom. This is a joyous day. I'm returning to the courtyard to let the other dragons there know who you are. I'll be back." Ilea smiled again and then swooped off.

Feeling tension in every pore, Eloria hoped this all didn't backfire. She didn't want the dragons to battle the high elves, but she was eager to leave the dungeon. She realized she had accomplished the greatest inspiration of her life, rallying an army of dragons to aid her in her time of need.

22

W hen Viator saw Balen return to the ballroom, a place Viator didn't want to be, but his queenly mother insisted on it, he was dancing with Sendal. He hadn't wanted to do that either. But then he saw Balen and Ren return also, and he knew by Balen's expression that he was peeved that Ren would make sure he carried out the queen's wishes. Balen tilted his head to the left, indicating he needed a word with Viator. Viator wanted to release Sendal at once, but he finished the dance and abruptly left her standing in the middle of the floor. He joined Balen and said, "What news?"

"Eloria is a wonder. She saw what looked like the symbol of the coiled rope. It doesn't look like it from the ground, but from the air, it does. It's the green wizard's memorial."

Viator grabbed his arm and hauled him out of the great hall. "Why didn't we think of that!"

"Because you were right. This has to do with Eloria, and I think she's right in saying she needs to be with us to complete these quests."

Viator looked sharply at Balen.

Balen shrugged. "That's what she says, and I tend to agree with her. We've been on most of the missions together with her."

Once they were on the wall walk, they saw dragons from all over headed for the high elves' castle in the mountains, making it look like swarms of giant bees with leathery wings outstretched. They stared at the unusual sight. "What in the world is going on? I've never seen them massing like that before."

"Any coincidence that Eloria is over there and can call Talom to her?"

Viator shook his head. "I see even the ones our own people have claimed and tamed as companions. Paying homage to her?"

"What is going on?" the queen asked, coming up behind them, probably worried Viator was going to seek Eloria out.

Viator motioned to the dragons, some flying in a v-formation like geese traveling to the south for winter. Others in singles or pairs. They were landing on top of the wall walk and the castle towers, everywhere they could find a spot. They looked like black specks, but they turned the top edges of the castle walls from glistening white to black, though the dragons were all different colors, depending on birth and origin.

"Our dragons are joining them too?" the queen said, sounding as astounded as Viator felt.

"Should we leave well enough alone, or do you want us to see what's going on?" Viator asked, planning to whether his mother agreed or not.

"You will keep me informed."

"Aye, my lady mother." Viator felt a great victory and didn't wait for his mother to change her mind but spread his wings and flew off for the castle. Balen went with him.

Viator remembered his mission was to investigate the memorial in the river, but when one mission had to do with his quest and one had to do with Eloria, he was off to find her first.

Besides, she might be needed to help them find the other quests.

They passed over the memorial and he agreed with Eloria. It looked just like the coiled rope symbol. They ended up flying with a group of dragons and for the first time, he felt intimidated by them because there were so many of them. And he wasn't sure if they were in for a battle. Which meant the dragons were battling against the high elves, and the darkland elves needed to mind their own business. But he didn't worry one bit about any flying predator coming after them this time either.

He was determined to ensure that Eloria was okay and take her away from all this if she was in trouble.

When they reached the courtyard, they saw Prince Zorak, his arms folded across his chest, and he was talking to one of the dragons. "She's human." His face was red, and he was extremely agitated. His guards were standing by his side, but no one dared to unsheathe their weapons.

Zorak glanced up to see Viator and Balen and raised his brows.

They waited for a couple of dragons to move aside to give them room to settle on the stone pavement.

"Zorak," Viator said. "Eloria is one of you. Or half one of you. She came to see you about her heritage." He glanced around, surprised Eloria wasn't there. "Where is she?"

The dragon Zorak had been talking to growled at Zorak.

"In the dungeon. Bring her here," Zorak ordered one of his guards.

The guard looked relieved to be leaving the courtyard.

"No way is she one of us. She's human," Zorak said.

"And she has magic."

Zorak's eyes widened.

Viator's eyes narrowed. "Why did you lock her in the dungeon?" He couldn't imagine she had given him any trouble, not when he didn't even know she knew magic. It appeared she hadn't even been able to tell him that she was probably one of them.

Then Zorak frowned. "I've seen her use magic. But...not because she's a high elf. I don't know what it was. No high elf can do what she can do. She wants to return Persephonice home. I won't allow it."

"She only wants to talk to her about what Persephonice's father wants. She said she wouldn't try to make her return with her." Viator was totally exasperated with the high elf prince.

"I've destroyed the bracelets she had with her. So, no, she won't be returning Persephonice to her father."

"We think she was raised among dragons."

Zorak's mouth dropped open. Then he clamped his lips shut and looked around at all the dragons facing him, waiting for resolution.

"I suggest you don't lock her in the dungeon any further." Not that Viator believed he had to tell Zorak that, but he was irritated with the high elf prince for doing that to Eloria.

Then it seemed the hundred or so dragons looked up at the sky, making Viator and the other elves look that way. Viator squinted, trying to make out the dragon flying toward the castle. *It. Couldn't. Be.* The rogue dragon who would not be tamed. Talom.

Zorak cursed under his breath. The dragon he'd been talking to called out to Talom in greeting. Several other dragons did as well. "Go, get the girl, now!" Zorak told his other guard, when the first one didn't bring her up there quickly enough.

The second guard hurried inside the castle, looking relieved to be leaving the tension-filled courtyard.

"We think she has ties to the green wizard," Viator said. "At least, he seems to speak to her in dreams."

Zorak's jaw dropped again. "No."

"Aye. Do you know of her now?"

Zorak let out his breath. "One of our elves was a granddaughter of the green wizard. She'd found an injured human, a griffin about to make short work of him. She used her magic to kill the griffin and then called on a dragon to carry him to her lair. She was a protector of dragonlings, a dragon keeper, when they were hatched, and their parents were off hunting for food. She used her magic to ward off predators. It's a way for us to continue the bond between our kind and the dragons. She came from a long line of dragon keepers. No one is allowed in the dragons' caves but the dragons and the dragon keepers. But this time, they made an allowance for Nesta's human. She had lost her own mate two years earlier when he was trying to protect the dragonlings and was killed by a griffin. She fell in love with the human, George Cresthaven."

Viator shook his head. "She told me her last name was Cresthaven." Then he saw Eloria enter the courtyard with the guards, the one carrying her pack.

When she saw Viator and she rushed forward, Zorak quickly stepped out of her way as if he was afraid the dragons would take offense to his blocking her path to see the darkland prince.

Viator hurried to join her, belatedly hoping the dragon circling above them didn't incinerate him for trying to reach Eloria. She threw her arms around Viator with enthusiasm and kissed him.

Balen had quickly joined them, as if he didn't want to be associated with the elf who had put Eloria in the dungeon, but with the one who was hugging her. "Can I have a hug too?"

She looked at him, her expression troubled.

"So that the dragons know I'm on your side."

Then she smiled, released Viator, and gave Balen a hug too. "Does this mean I don't need to call you by your title any longer?"

Viator laughed.

Balen didn't answer. His title was all too important to him, and Viator was certain he was afraid if people heard a non-royal human calling him by his name and not his title, others would do so too.

Talom seemed to think everything was okay, circling, just waiting to see what would happen though.

Zorak quickly asked, "Will you dine with me?"

One of the guards handed Eloria's bag to her.

"We have other business to attend to," Viator said, not trying to give the prince the brush-off after what he'd pulled with Eloria, but he truly did want to accomplish his next quest. With Eloria.

"What are you going to tell your parents, if they learn you have disobeyed them again?" Balen asked Viator.

"That we settled the controversy with the dragons." Viator smiled, then wrapped his arms around Eloria. "See you later, Zorak."

Zorak didn't look happy in the least. He was a crown prince too and someday would rule his own people, but he really messed up this time.

The two winged elves flew off and the dragons began to disperse. Talom followed the winged elves, and Viator hoped that wasn't a bad sign.

"Thank you for coming to my aid," Eloria called out to the dragon.

He dipped his head, acknowledging her statement, but he continued to follow them.

They flew to the green wizard's memorial and Eloria said to Viator, "I'm glad I could go with you."

"I'm glad you could too, but you and Balen need to let me do this on my own, whatever it is I must do."

She agreed. "Of course. Balen can stay with me and watch over me and protect me while you're doing your duty."

Talom flew off as if he didn't need to be there any longer, as if he knew the two winged elves were her protection. Viator still didn't know what to think about that part of his quests. He was supposed to tame the dragon. It wasn't Eloria's duty to do so. The fact that the dragon wouldn't land in the courtyard proved he was still wary of people. He'd never offered to allow Eloria to ride on him either, which would have shown how much he wanted to be her companion. Still, Viator believed he would have to find another dragon to tame to become his companion. Talom and Eloria had some kind of bond that he wasn't about to try and break.

When he went to the door of the memorial, Balen took a seat on a bench there.

"Are you sure we shouldn't go inside with you? We won't do anything. But if this is a memorial to the green wizard, maybe he'll appear to me here," Eloria said.

Viator agreed. He really wanted to do whatever task needed to be done on his own, but he did want to keep her with him. He just felt that whenever she was out of his sight, she ended up in trouble. He glanced at Balen who was looking hopeful he wouldn't be left outside, contemplating how he'd turn his wings completely invisible.

"Come on, Balen. Keep Eloria company while I do whatever needs to be done."

He'd never been inside the memorial, and he had the thought that it might be sacrilegious to come in here, which had also made him believe that taking Eloria with them could be a good idea. Especially if she was related to the green wizard and he was continually keeping in touch with her. Viator again wondered what the gift was that the wizard had told Eloria about. He was thinking too about how Zorak had taken her bracelets from her that would be the only way she could communicate with her ship and return to her world. He hoped that Persephonice's father wouldn't send more people to try and locate his daughter and take her away from Dracolin.

Viator got the impression that her commander didn't care what happened to Eloria. But Viator did. What would it be like to be married to a powerful, half high elf who had the greatest dragon connections, and who seemed to care for him as much as he cared for her? His parents would have a fit. But they weren't marrying her. He was. If she'd agree.

But then he thought, as he lit the lanterns inside the memorial and peered at the symbols on the green marble walls, if they had a baby, would he or she nest with the dragonlings? Would Eloria herself be called upon or feel the calling to become a dragon keeper? Would he be relegated to the role of joining her in the dragon's caves? An honor, to be sure, but also a step down from his life in a castle.

"The symbols Eloria saw in her dreams, sire," Balen practically whispered.

Eloria was walking around looking at each of them—the ten that she had seen in her dreams, the last one not pictured here.

When she reached the symbol of the coiled rope, her amulet glowed and the symbol on the wall responded with the same kind of green glow.

"There's a button there. Maybe you have to push it in," Balen said, pointing at the round button that matched the wall but had a slight gold ring around it.

"Or it could be a disaster." Viator didn't want to cause them any trouble, but he suspected Balen was right. He glanced at Eloria to get her agreement and she nodded. He depressed the button, and nothing happened.

She continued to walk around the circle until her amulet flickered as she drew close to the symbol on the wall. Viator hurried around to where she was standing to push the button. She continued to circle around the room, locating the glowing symbols, and each time, Viator would push the corresponding button until he had pushed all ten. Nothing happened.

"The eleventh symbol must be here somewhere," Eloria said.

"Why wouldn't you have seen it? That's what I don't get," Viator said. "If they were important to you for some reason, like coming here and setting all this in motion, then why not show you all the key symbols? Wait, you said you have nightmares of falling. Could you have been blocking recalling the last symbol? Terrified of where it is?"

"Mist. Hidden in the mist? I fall into a pit. That's the night terror I have." She peered over the brass railing down into the dark below. "What is down there? The ladder curls down into the depths." She looked up at Viator and Balen. "Do you want to go see? Maybe the last button is down there."

Viator and Balen looked down below. They were both brave warriors and had fought many battles, so why was the lady more willing to go down there than they were?

"Yeah, sure. I'll go first." Viator started the climb down. "Wait for me to get to the bottom and then you can join me once I know it's safe." He used his light while Eloria cast an even longer light to penetrate the darkness.

He saw nothing down here, to his relief. Nothing that would eat him. No bones. "It appears safe. There are ten doors in a circle, all with a symbol on them."

"I'm coming down." Eloria began to make her way down the ladder.

When she reached the bottom, Balen headed down.

As soon as she stood before a door, the symbol of the green wizard glowed, but there were no buttons to push. Just a door-knob to turn.

"Walk around and see if we have to go in the same order as

we did up above or if it doesn't make any difference." Viator watched as she walked around the circle, but only the green wizard symbol on the one door lit up. "Okay, here goes." He opened the door and stepped into a living area, furnished with seating for several people. "This looks like a hideaway, rather than just a memorial."

They found a bedroom, a place to make food, and supplies.

"And the food is fresh." Eloria rubbed her arms and shivered.

"Someone lives here."

"The green wizard? He is supposed to be dead." Eloria left the living quarters and went around the circle of doors to find the next one that would open. The symbol that glowed next was of the dragon's lair.

Viator opened the door and stepped inside. A long, winding, dark tunnel snaked up and up like a winding river. They all used their lights in the tunnel that seemed to go on forever.

"Do we just keep following it?" Eloria asked.

"I think it leads up into the mountains. To a dragon's lair, don't you think?" Viator asked.

"Maybe," Eloria said.

Balen wasn't saying anything, just following them. Viator had never known him to be that quiet. "What are you thinking, Balen?"

"That the green wizard is alive. That the memorial is his home, and that the doors lead to places he needs to go without being seen."

"But why? He was revered by all the elf kind. Why would he have to go into hiding? Unless someone else lives here. Maybe a keeper of the memorial?" Viator said.

"No," Eloria said to Viator. "The wizard visits me in my dreams. How could he if he's dead? What...what is that sound up ahead?"

"Dragons. Dragonlings," Viator whispered. "I think it's a dragon's lair."

"We can't go there then," Balen said. "It's forbidden."

"So the green wizard would come up here?" Eloria asked.

Then they heard the awful screeching of an opinicus. Viator pulled out his sword and raced up the tunnel leading to what he believed was the dragon's lair, Balen right behind him.

"But we can't go in there," Balen said.

"I'm going with you." Eloria wasn't about to be left behind.

"Just stay behind us," Viator warned.

"Yeah," Balen added.

But she was thinking she had somewhat of an "in" with the dragons and Viator and Balen might need *her* protection from them!

Still, Viator burst into the cave where little dragonlings were squealing and he began slicing at one of those horribly, frightening opinicus, claws clawing at Viator, his beaked head angling to bite him.

Balen swung his sword at the great beast, trying to cut his leg, but the creatures wing struck him and sent him sailing across the cave where he hit the wall and collapsed.

Eloria yanked out her stun gun and blasted the opinicus with a bolt of blue light. It slammed into the opinicus, and he screamed out in pain, backing off. She surrounded the dragonlings with a golden light, a comforting spell and they calmed. But then she continued to fire her stun gun, knowing that once it ran out of power, it would be useless. On the ship, it was easily recharged. On the primitive planet? It wouldn't be worth a thing.

But Viator wasn't making much headway with the opinicus, and Balen was injured and unconscious. Viator cut the opinicus's leg and the creature screamed. She kept zapping him, the stun gun not knocking him out like it would lesser creatures. He was just too big. But he was slowing down, his head drooping a bit, his wings tilting down, the one lower still because of the cut to it. She wondered if he could even fly out of here.

She drew nearer to him, knowing the closer she was to him the more of an impact the stun gun would have. But it was more dangerous the closer she got to him too. He'd been concentrating more on Viator because he'd been closer to him, his sword's reach not long enough to keep a lot of distance. He was fleet of foot, and he used his wings to help him maneuver too. Because of his smaller size, he could outmaneuver the beast.

When she moved closer to the opinicus, he ignored Viator and turned his wrath on Eloria. His head twisted around to grab her with his beak. Viator took advantage of his distraction and flying above the opinicus, brought his sword down on the beast's neck, slicing his head from his body.

"Good!" she said, then raced to see to Balen. "Balen, are you okay?"

He had a bloodied head and a raised welt where he'd smacked the wall with his head. He looked up at her with glazed eyes and said, "*Lord* Balen."

She smiled and helped him to sit. Then she removed his sash from his waist and tied it around the wound on his head.

"We have more trouble coming." Viator sheathed his sword. "Dragons are headed this way in force."

"Let's go then. I'll remove my calming spell from the dragonlings, and we can take Balen down the mountain through the tunnel. The passage is too narrow for the dragons to manage."

Viator hurried to take hold of Balen's arms and pulled him to stand. "Come on, Balen, snap out of it."

"Lord Balen," Balen said.

Viator only cast him a sardonic smile, then helped his friend through the tunnel.

Eloria removed the calming spell from the dragonlings, but before she could rush off after her winged elf companions, the dragonlings surrounded her as if they had imprinted on her and she was now their mother. She was going to be cinders if she didn't get out of here now!

"Eloria!" Viator called from deeper in the tunnel.

She figured he had hurried further down into the tunnel to ensure that the dragon's flame wouldn't reach them, even if the dragon couldn't follow them. But she couldn't move, afraid she'd step on one of the little dragons that came up to her knees. They were flapping their little leathery wings, bouncing around on their toes, thrilled to be with her, as if they knew she had saved them, even if Viator had done the actual saving.

Then a couple of the little more aggressive dragonlings investigated the opinicus and began shooting tiny flames at it. She smiled and figured this was like training on how to take down a predator.

She kept trying to get around the dragonlings when she saw the mother dragon headed for the entrance of the cave. Viator suddenly popped his head out of the tunnel entrance, saw that Eloria was having trouble joining them, and he flew out of the tunnel to grab her.

Lifting her, he carried her into the tunnel, and ran her down to where he'd left Balen. Apparently, he was still too groggy to move. She cast her light down the tunnel as they heard the dragon mother and another dragon enter the cave above, all the little dragonlings excitedly squeaking at the adult dragons.

Before Viator helped Balen back up, he spread his wings and smiled. "They are a full credit more transparent."

"You must have gotten all the credit for killing the opinicus and saving the dragonlings," Eloria said, proud of him.

"But you and Balen helped."

"Right, but you actually accomplished the mission."

They continued down the passageway, hearing the sounds of the dragons for some time, then the noise all faded away.

"I hope we won't be in trouble for invading their lair," Viator said.

"How could we be?" Balen asked, still sounding like he was hurting and had to lean on Viator to get him down the tunnel. "We saved the little ones."

"I was afraid they had imprinted on me," Eloria said.

Both men stopped in their tracks and turned back to look at her.

She shrugged. "They were excited to greet me, and I don't know, they seemed to think I was their mother. Or guardian, or something."

Continuing to walk, Viator shook his head. "Dragon keeper. Here I want to ask your hand in marriage, and I've got to live with you in a cave to protect the dragons? I'm a prince, you know."

This time she stopped walking and stared at Viator.

He turned to smile at her. "What? You don't think I'd give you up after all you've put me through? You are mine to keep." He chuckled and walked off again.

The notion came to mind that she couldn't marry any man because he wouldn't like it if she could protect his back, if he were a warrior class, and if he was not, he could feel intimidated by her. With Viator, there was no problem in that. She was there to watch his back and vice versa. He didn't seem to have any difficulty with the roles she played.

"Your parents won't be happy," Balen said.

"They knew about the prophecy long before I did. Who's to say we can go against such a powerful mandate? It is written in our ancient scrolls." Viator shrugged. "So be it."

"Besides, he loves me dearly," Eloria said, because she didn't care one star galaxy if their prophecy stated that some girl would upend their kingdom. If he didn't love her, the whole deal was off.

"Because I love her dearly," Viator said.

"I will never hear the end of it from Sendal," Balen said.

"Did she know about the prophecy?" Viator asked

"Aye. Why do you think she's been trying to get you to marry her before another human from another world ended up in our lands?"

When they finally reached the circle of doors, they found the green wizard's door could be opened. "It appears that once we opened the door, we can return without activating it again with the amulet." Eloria helped Balen into the living area and Viator had him sit on the couch.

"We're going to check the next door. You sit here and recuperate. Are you going to be okay?" Viator asked his friend.

"Aye. Holler if you need me to help out."

"I will." Viator and Eloria left him then and headed back out to the circle of doors. A coiled-rope symbol glowed on the next door, and Eloria held her breath as she and Viator checked out the next passage.

23

Viator knew he should leave Eloria behind on these ventures, worried he was going to truly lose her one of these times. This time, they were walking through a tunnel that was level, no elevation whatsoever.

"You do want to marry me? My parents could be awful to live with," Viator said, taking Eloria's hand as they shone their lights into the tunnel.

"I have nowhere else to go. And yes, you would make the perfect lifemate for me."

Viator pulled her into a hug and kissed her. "Good, because I'm a prince and I wasn't taking no for an answer."

She laughed. "You're just lucky I fell in love with the elf who took me hostage."

"Look what happened when Zorak got ahold of you again. I'm still angry with him for locking you in the dungeon."

"But see what happened? We learned that I have some value. The dragons rallied around me."

"Yeah." He frowned at her. "That stun gun is powerful."

"But it only has enough power for a while. Then once it runs out, it will be useless."

"That's a shame. Then again, that's what makes our more primitive weapons so important. They are as good as we maintain them and can stay alive."

"You did great back there," Eloria said. "That was one hard beast to kill."

"You did too. If it wasn't for you shooting him over and over again, and then getting closer to distract him, I wouldn't have managed to eliminate him. What did you do to the dragonlings? They were making such a racket and so was the opinicus, it was hard to think straight."

"I calmed them with a spell. I couldn't think either while we were trying to terminate the opinicus and keep him from injuring or killing us. I wonder what the dragons will think when they see we'd killed the opinicus and then run off into the green wizard's tunnel."

Viator brought her to a stop at a railing around a pit. "They will know who was there. They'll smell our scents. Hopefully, they'll forgive us for trespassing in their den." He stared down into the abyss.

Eloria shone her longer ray of light into the darkness and took a sharp breath. "It looks like the pit where I fall in my dreams. Though I have actually been shoved into a pit before, which has fed my nightmares."

"And pushed off a cliff." Viator was frowning at her. "You need a protector."

She smiled, then shined her light on the walls of the cave. "Crystals! Green crystals."

"Why wouldn't this be the room featuring the symbol of the amulet?" Viator asked, wondering out loud.

"I think we need to get a crystal."

"What?" Viator didn't know why she thought she had to have another. She already had one. He glanced at her glowing amulet, then looked out at the walls of green crystals below.

"Why would you need another?"

"In my dreams, I'm the age I am now. If it was like my dad had said—that the amulet I wear was a gift from my mother, then maybe I'm supposed to obtain one that is my own."

"In the dreams, the wizard guided you to locate the green crystal."

"Right. I really believe I need to get a crystal."

"But *I* wasn't in the dream, was I?"

"No. But what if this is just a dream to guide me to what I have to do. You could be there, but not essential to the quest."

Viator raised a brow, his mouth curving up slightly.

She smiled at him. "You know what I mean. The wizard needed me to do this, but it didn't mean you weren't there. Maybe he didn't want to clutter the scene for me."

He chuckled. "I am now just clutter."

She laughed, her laughter echoing off the walls of the cavern.

In the center of the cavern of crystals, it appeared there was a pit filled with water.

"Does it matter which crystal we take?"

She shined her light down into the cavern, the crystals all sparkling in the glow of her light source. But then her amulet again came to life and Viator saw a crystal glowing even in the darkness.

"There." He figured it had to be the one that seemed to call to the other, if his guess had any merit.

She moved her light over the crystal, and it continued to glow brighter than any of the others touched by her light. "I have to get down there to get it."

"You stay here. I'll get it for you. I don't want you falling down there and making your nightmare come true."

"I don't die. I just scream and wake myself up."

"In the nightmare. But in real life? That could be another

story." Viator went around the whole railing that encircled the opening to the cavern. He suddenly spied a rope dangling next to the wall near where he was standing, maybe reaching about thirty feet. "There's a rope down there. It's knotted all along its length as if used for climbing. But I can fly over to the crystal. If you can shine your light on the crystal, I can have both hands free to try and pull it loose. Hopefully, I won't need a tool to pry it loose."

"Do you have one?"

"My dagger, but I'd rather not chip away at the crystal and ruin it or, who knows, cause it to react in some magical way if it doesn't like my treatment of it."

"Okay, true. I'm ready."

He pulled her into his arms and kissed her before he left. He realized that he was wanting to do that an awful lot. As if any misstep on his part, or hers, could spell their doom and he didn't want to leave her without showing her how much he cared about her. She seemed to appreciate it and kissed him back just as greedily.

He sighed. "I'm off." He flew toward the crystal across the chasm when he saw something dark moving against the walls in the darkness. He cast his light on one of the massive figures. "Trolls. Blasted." At least here, he had the advantage because he could fly and stay away from the trolls, except when he was trying to tug at the crystal. He thought about the similarity between this situation and the one with the mermaid where he had to land on the rock to tug at the fishing net. Only this time the trolls would be reaching for him while he tugged at the crystal.

He saw an opening in the cavern way down below that let in some light and he wondered where that led to. As soon as the trolls knew where he was heading to, they also scurried across the walls to reach his destination. He was certain they didn't care anything about the glowing crystal. Though he wondered why it wouldn't deter them when Eloria's had the last time. Wait, Eloria's crystal!

Trolls might look like hairy, dumb beasts, but they were clever enough to work in packs and they could calculate what an elf was up to before the elf could accomplish his quest. Viator knew he couldn't grab for the crystal without them grabbing for him. And he was certain he couldn't wear Eloria's amulet so that she could stay safely where she was.

What if he could carry her here, and she could ward off the trolls while he tried to remove the amulet? He turned to go back for her, but she was climbing down the rope into the cavern, and the trolls were scattering all over the walls, trying to stay as far away from her as they could.

No wonder her light hadn't been focused on the crystal, only his. He flew to her and wrapped his arms around her from behind, so she could still shine her light and show off the glow of the amulet. "I forgot how your amulet scared them away the last time. But why wouldn't the glowing crystal also?"

"I forgot how it scattered them too, until I saw they were staying well away from me. Maybe the crystal embedded in the wall with the rest of them can't scare them off. Maybe it has to do with me wearing the amulet. By itself, it doesn't have the power to keep them away. Of course, I'm just guessing here," she said.

"Okay, that could be. There's a narrow shelf near the crystal. If you can stand on it and hold on to the crystals jutting out from the wall while I try to tug on the one we need, you can scare off the trolls at the same time."

"Let's try that."

He carried her to the shelf and did worry about her falling off it, so he hovered next to her and the crystal. "Just grab ahold of me if you slip off."

"I will. Though I have the ability to slow my fall and cushion it somewhat. But then I would be leaving you without my protection."

"That's how you fell off the cliff without dying." He was tugging as hard as he could at the crystal, but it wouldn't budge. "It's not coming out at all. Maybe I need to use my dagger to help loosen it, but I'm afraid to damage it." He glanced down at Eloria to see what she thought.

Eloria was watching for the trolls, but they didn't grow close to their location. "Maybe *I* need to pull the stone free."

Viator had thought if he could do it, it might be one of his quests, but he guessed she might be right. If the wizard told her that she needed to get it, then she needed to be the one to pull it. He dropped down to lift her and then flew just a couple of feet higher so she could reach the crystal.

Holding her tight, he flapped his wings to hover in place while Eloria reached out to grab the crystal. Both her amulet and the crystal glowed even brighter, nearly blinding them. She pulled with so much force, he nearly lost hold of her, and she did lose her grip on the stone, not expecting it to come free so easily.

It fell. He dove for it, still holding tight to her and his sudden dive made her scream.

"Sorry."

"I never scream."

He smiled.

Her arms were outstretched, but he couldn't fly as fast as the crystal was falling. They heard it splash down below in the pool of dark water and she groaned. "What if it has gone too deep?" she asked.

"Then we're doomed as I cannot swim." He reached the dark water, but they could still see the green glow of the crystal.

"It looks like it's close."

"But water can be deceiving," he warned, hovering over the water.

"Let me go and I'll get it."

"What about the trolls?"

"They can't get you while you're flying, and they won't come near me while I'm wearing the amulet."

As much as it bothered him to release her into the water, worrying something might get her down there, other than trolls, he released her gently into the pool and watched as she disappeared beneath the surface. She was just like the sirens of the sea, able to swim and dive beneath the water, which seemed impossible to him.

Then he saw her finally swimming toward the surface with the crystal in hand. He smiled. She burst forth from the water and shouted, "Pull me out! Now!"

Panicked, he grabbed both her outstretched arms and she wrapped her legs around him and he carried her to the top off the railing as a mermaid broke the surface of the water.

He settled Eloria on the stone floor and they both looked down to see the mermaid floating in the water. She wasn't the same one that he'd pulled the fishnet out of the sea for.

"There must be an outlet to the sea down there. The crystal wasn't too far down, but just far enough to get me in trouble with the mermaid."

"Thank the goddess for that. We need to dry out your clothes and check on Balen," Viator said.

The mermaid talked away to them, but he had no idea what she was saying.

Eloria said something back to the mermaid in her own language.

Viator frowned at Eloria. "You can do what Persephonice can do. Talk to creatures that don't speak the elven language? The blue elves are the only ones who can actually speak with them."

"I can."

"And swim."

"But I can't fly."

He smiled. "I can take you wherever your heart desires. But I suspect you will be able to call any dragon to carry you wherever you want also."

They left the crystal chamber and returned to the living quarters were Balen was sound asleep on the couch. She pulled some clothes out of her pack and headed for the bedroom. "I'll be right back. I guess we can dry my things outside on the memorial in the breeze."

"What do we do—" Viator stopped speaking, mid-speech, when he saw Eloria staring at his wings. He spread them wider and glanced back at them, then smiled. "Well, I'll be. I didn't think I'd earn a whole credit, not even half a one, when you were the one who got the crystal."

"You took me there to retrieve it. I couldn't have done it myself. And then you helped me reach the water and escape the mermaid. If it's anything like what we think, it wasn't that you saved me, but you helped to save the crystal."

"Huh. Okay, so now what do we do with it?"

"Make it into an amulet? I can't imagine what else we could do with it."

"The green wizard never showed you what to do beyond just finding and securing it?"

"Right," Eloria said. "I'll be right back." She headed into the bedroom, and he was thinking they needed to eat. But he wasn't sure he wanted to take her back to his castle.

He did consider taking her to see the shadow elves, but what if they were worried that she was going to try and convince Persephonice to leave, and they wanted to eliminate her?

She came out of the room, dressed in more of the kind of clothes that she had worn when she first arrived at the cliffs.

"Okay, do you want to check out the next door?"

"I was thinking of eating."

"I don't believe the wizard will mind if we eat here."

Viator wasn't so sure.

"He will want us to continue with our mission." She went into what appeared to be the kitchen and began rummaging around for food. She motioned to the room. "Uh, unless you know how to cook, I'm afraid we'll all just starve."

"We have food in our packs. But I do know how to cook." Viator began boiling potatoes and spinach, then found dried pork and added it to a broth. "Your duties do not require you to cook?"

"Our technology is...different." Even so, she watched what he was doing and helped him to make the food. "I'm surprised that a prince would know how to cook."

He smiled. "I know how to do many things."

The aroma of the pork stew caught Balen's attention, and he came in to see them. "Oh, good, I was getting hungry." Then he said, "Oh! Your wings. What did you do?"

Eloria held up the crystal for Balen to see. "Viator saved it."

"Another crystal. Why would you need another crystal?"

Eloria explained what they had done. "Are you feeling all right?"

"Yeah." Balen had removed the bandage that she had made for him, and the area was still swollen and now bruised. "Where to next?"

"Another door. But we need to turn this into an amulet also."

"We have a jeweler at the castle," Balen said. "He can create anything you're interested in creating." He frowned. "Why would you need two necklaces?"

"I don't know."

Viator glanced at her and the amulet, that was shining brightly. Then Viator began serving up the stew. "This should keep us going for the rest of the day. I'd say we should return to the castle tonight, but I'm afraid my parents will still be reluctant for Eloria to stay there."

Balen eyed the crystal again before she tucked it back in her skirt pocket. Balen rubbed his forehead below his injury. "All the elf kingdoms have their own jewelers. I was thinking we could take it to either the high elves or the shadow elves and see if one of their jewelers could make it into a necklace."

"What if the shadow elves are afraid of the same thing as Prince Zorak? Even though the prince has changed his tune, I'm not sure that Eloria would be comfortable going back there." Viator sat down at the table with the others.

"After what happened with the dragons, we might just get the royal treatment. Also, I was thinking, what if the high elves' jeweler made this amulet? Then he would know how to create the perfect necklace for this one."

"The prince and I would be afforded royal treatment anyway," Balen reminded her.

She only smiled at him.

"I agree with Eloria. But should we continue to check out the doors?" Viator asked.

Eloria ate some of his stew and he paused to see if she liked it. She smiled. "This is fantastic. You don't even want to know what our food tasted like on the ship. I might just have to keep you around."

"You have no choice but to keep me around."

Balen snorted. "The prince does not make it a habit to cook meals for the general populace."

"What are you going to do if I marry the prince?" Eloria ate some more of the stew. She was almost done with her bowl and that pleased Viator.

He was also amused that she didn't take Balen seriously. She might not be a royal, but she certainly had royal qualities.

"The king and queen would not allow it." Then Balen smiled wickedly at her. "But I know, too, they will have no say in it."

"Did you have any other dreams that might aid us in our quest?" Viator asked.

"Only that I would receive a gift. I have no idea what it is. Or if it would help you in your quest."

Viator dished out more stew for everyone, glad they were finishing it up. Once they were done eating, Balen cleaned up the dishes, and then they packed their backpacks and left the living quarters to search for the next door.

Her crystal led them to the coiled-rope door. Viator opened it, and found they had another long, rock tunnel to traverse. Again, the tunnel wound its way up the mountain, and he suspected from the direction the other had taken to the dragon's lair, this one went to the high elves' castle. But he couldn't fathom what a coiled rope would have to do with anything.

"High elves' castle." Balen was walking behind Viator and Eloria.

"That's what I'm thinking," Viator said.

"Maybe we can stay there the night," Balen said, "if whatever the quest here takes us some time."

"We could." Viator was thinking Eloria was probably ready for a rest. He was feeling like he could settle down, visit with Prince Zorak, and then retire for the night, getting an early start the next morning.

When they did finally reach a doorway, they found they couldn't open it.

But then Eloria brought out the other crystal and both glowed brightly. The door opened as if by magic.

"It appears we couldn't have opened this door without the other crystal," Eloria said.

"Just like the doors with the symbols had to be opened in a

certain order." Viator glanced around at the place they were now. "It looks like we are in the dungeon."

There were no prisoners in any of the cells and they soon made their way to another wooden door. This one wasn't locked. Since no one was incarcerated in the cells, no one was guarding them either. They headed up a flight of stairs and finally reached the main part of the castle. As soon as a couple of guards saw them, their jaws dropped.

"Prince Viator, we didn't see you enter through the main doors. We'll send word to Prince Zorak you have returned." The guard gave Eloria an irritated look, as if she was the one who had caused all the trouble between the high elves and their dragons. The guard motioned to a page who quickly went to tell the prince that Viator and his companions were there.

24

T he page spoke with Prince Zorak while he was talking to his advisor and said, "The human Eloria has returned with Prince Viator and Lord Balen."

Immediately, Zorak thought there was going to be some real trouble. Why else would they return here after all the fuss Eloria had caused the first time?

"Send them in at once."

"Aye, Your Majesty." The page hurried out of the great hall.

Prince Zorak ran his hands through his hair and stood up from his chair. "Now what?" He still felt that Eloria was here to attempt to steal Persephonice away. Even if the bracelets she used to travel from here to her ship were now destroyed, he feared the ship that left her off could return for her, only this time with warriors who would battle the elves.

The page returned, escorting Prince Viator, Lord Balen, and Eloria.

He acknowledged both the prince and the duke but ignored Eloria. She smiled.

"To what do I owe the pleasure of you returning here so soon?" Zorak asked.

"Does the green wizard still exist?" Viator asked.

"No. Why would you ask? Everyone knows he is long gone." Zorak thought it was an odd question.

"In his memorial, he has living quarters and fresh food."

Zorak motioned to seats around a table and asked the page to bring them wine. "All right. He's dead, but our high minister arranges for a page to leave fresh food there weekly."

"How does he get into the room? It's locked. Does he have a special crystal to open it also?" Eloria asked.

"No. He says a special incantation and the door opens for him. How do you know about the door?" Zorak asked, frowning.

"It opens to her amulet. All the doors in his memorial do, in a specific order." Viator folded his arms. "We need to speak with your jeweler. Did he fashion the amulet that Eloria wears? He would know if he did, I'm sure."

The page brought them goblets of wine and Zorak motioned for the door. "Have Xeon come see us."

"Aye, Your Majesty." The page hurried out of the great hall.

"You're still trying to prove Eloria is a high elf."

"She knows the ancient symbols of the elves' dead language. And she dreams of the green wizard. She knows magic. She's able to open the doors to the various places we believe the green wizard must have traveled to. Why would he give her this knowledge if she was not one of us? So yes, I think she's a half high elf."

"What happened with the dragonlings?" Zorak had been told there'd been a great fight between Viator, Balen, and Eloria and an opinicus in one of the dragon's lairs. They'd killed the beast, protecting the dragonlings when the elves and Eloria weren't even allowed to be there. And yet Zorack's dragon companion had told him how glad he was that they'd come through the wizard's tunnel and saved the young ones. So Zorak couldn't find fault with Viator or the others.

"They needed protection," Eloria said. "We were there to help them out."

"Your wings are more transparent," Zorak said to Viator. "Yours too, Balen."

Viator smiled. "Yes. And it all has to do with Eloria and the green wizard."

The jeweler entered the great hall and Zorak said, "Did you create the necklace Eloria is wearing?"

"Can she remove it so that I may have a closer look at it?"

"Yes," Eloria said.

"No!" both Viator and Balen said.

"Sorry. When Lord Tal looked it over, her amulet called Talom," Viator said.

"The rogue dragon," Zorak said. "No one can tame him."

"Aye."

"I can just look at it from here." Xeon examined the necklace and smiled. "Aye, I created this amulet for the dragon keeper, Nesta. She saved a human, married him, and they had a baby. The human took the young girl away with him when the dragon keeper died."

"That was my mother's name," Eloria said.

"So you didn't make the amulet for Eloria." Viator wrapped his arm around Eloria's shoulders.

"No. I made it for her mother."

"Can you make another?" Eloria asked eagerly.

"Not without—"

She pulled the green crystal out of her pocket, and it glowed, making the amulet she was wearing glow also.

Zorak just stared at the crystals.

"I can do it. Come with me to my workshop." Xeon looked at Zorak to make sure it was all right with him.

"I'll go with you." Zorak was astounded at the sight of the glowing stones.

They soon reached the jeweler's office and there they found coiled chains of gold and silver that looked like coiled rope sitting in neat stacks on long tables, and jewels of every kind resting on black velvet fabrics. But none of them were the color of the green crystals Eloria had from the wizard's cave.

"What kind of chain do you want to use?" Xeon asked.

"Silver," Eloria said. "I didn't realize it until now, but the amulet I saw in my dreams had a silver chain. It shown in the sunlight, unlike the rose-gold chain of this amulet."

Xeon worked away at setting the stone in the chain, not cutting on it, but leaving the long, angular piece intact. Zorak was glad for that because it obviously had magical powers and he was afraid tampering with it could cause a drastic reaction.

When the jeweler was done, he marveled over his handiwork. Viator offered to pay for the work, but Zorak dismissed his offer. "It is a gift for helping to save our dragonlings when you are not even dragon keepers. A high honor. To be sure, you will always be welcome in the dragons' lairs."

"Thank you." Instead of Eloria placing the silver chain over her head, she placed it over Viator's.

His jaw dropped and Zorak and Balen were just as surprised.

Xeon nodded in approval. "As your mother offered her hand in friendship and marriage to your father through the same means, so you have done the same, formalizing your relationship with the prince. Many blessings upon you both."

"Your parents won't only want to disown you, they will want to banish me for not stopping this," Balen said, shaking his head.

Eloria and Viator kissed.

"You mean everything to me, Eloria." Viator turned to Zorak. "Thank you for witnessing this. I'm sure I'll have a lot of explaining to do when I return home, but we appreciate your help in this."

"If you need me to assist you in any of your quests, let me know. I know you're supposed to accomplish them yourself, but sometimes a helping hand is needed." Zorak glanced at Eloria and Balen, knowing the two of them were needed in the quest. In a way, he envied them and their adventures and would have eagerly joined them.

"We would appreciate that," Eloria said, before Viator could respond, and Zorak was glad she seemed to harbor no ill-will against him.

Though the issue of Persephonice and her father was still worrisome.

"About Persephonice—" Zorak said.

"I can't imagine that she wants to return to the ship, any more than I do. But if you're concerned others will follow, you're probably right. Maybe she and I can help to change their minds and get them to leave us alone," Eloria said.

Zorak inclined his head to her.

Before they left, Viator paused. "You said the page leaves food for the wizard. Is the food ever...consumed?"

"For a while it had been. For the past couple of weeks, no. We thought somehow someone else had found a way into the chamber and was living there unbeknownst to us. But then he vanished. The page dutifully replaces food that has been spoiled with fresh food anyway, just in case the green wizard is truly not dead and does return."

"Thanks again, Zorak," Viator said. "We have more quests to do and then must eat and sleep and start over again tomorrow."

"Return here for supper then," Zorak said. "Eat and then sleep here where it's safe."

Eloria raised her brows slightly.

"I can't apologize enough to you for locking you in the dungeon."

She nodded. "I understand why."

"You will have a comfortable bed. I can imagine if you stayed at the darkland elves' castle, Sendal may try to eliminate you. We'll see you tonight then." Zorak walked them through the castle to the courtyard where Viator was about to carry Eloria back to the memorial when three dragons alighted nearby.

"We will take you," the one said to Eloria.

"Thank you."

Zorak and all high elves understood the language of the dragons, and he realized that Eloria understand them too, just like Persephonice did, except Persephonice wasn't a high elf. "You can swim too, can't you?"

Eloria nodded.

Amazing. Zorak realized then he'd lost out on the chance of having the red-haired human, well, and high elf, as his own.

Then Viator helped her onto a dragon. Even though her mother had been a dragon keeper, Eloria hadn't been raised around them, once her father had taken her away from here. So she seemed apprehensive. But the dragon was patient with her and talked away, trying to calm her nervousness.

Then Viator climbed onto one of the dragons, and Balen, the other.

The winged elves normally didn't ride on a dragon alone, not until they had tamed their own.

They said they'd return for supper and waved goodbye as Eloria told the dragons to return them to the wizard's memorial.

Once they arrived at the memorial, Eloria thanked the dragons in their language and Viator and Balen thanked them in the elves' language. The dragons left them, and the three companions went into the memorial to find the next door they were to enter.

Once they reached the circle of doors, Eloria and Viator's crystals glowed in response to one of the symbols on the closest door. "The fishnet," Balen said.

When they went through the door, they were immediately standing on the shores of Neferon. The fishnet was no longer on the beach but on the rocks in the sea again. And a mermaid was frantically waving for help. The island of mists was gone.

"Okay, so we accomplished this mission before," Balen said. "Do you see anything wrong with this? You felt compelled to come here and remove the net before, so the mermaid wouldn't get caught up in it and drown. Now, with Eloria's clues, we have to do it all over again?"

"Like we did them out of order and have to do them in the right order?" Viator said. "That could be a problem because the river was poisoned, and we took care of that. Has Lars and his people poisoned it again?"

"I hope not. We might not get so lucky the next time to learn which poison they used," Balen said.

"It may not be so. The fishnet is again on the rocks and the mermaid is beseeching you to remove it so she can safely reach her rocks," Eloria said. "So what do we do?"

"We are not going to do this again, are we?" Balen folded his arms and watched the mermaid as she pleaded with them to help her.

"I was thinking once was enough. Though I have to admit it's tempting to do it again, only to see if it helps to make our wings more transparent." Viator studied the mermaid. "She is not singing. How much do you want to bet that if we did this again, as soon as we were busy trying to remove the fishnet, she would try to call on Eloria?"

"I agree, sire."

"But if you can earn another half credit and I stuff cotton in my ears to keep her from enticing me into the sea with her siren's song, wouldn't it be worth it to at least give it a try?" Eloria asked.

"I agree," Viator said.

"You do want me to come with you, don't you?" Balen asked.

"Aye. I'd like you to protect Eloria also, but I believe we need to see if anything happens differently, now that we're going in the green wizard's order of events. Be sure you can plug your ears with the cotton before we leave, Eloria." Viator glanced back at her when she didn't say anything.

"What? I can't hear you." Eloria pointed at her ears.

He kissed her mouth. "All right, Balen. Let's go." Viator no longer cared as much about earning the credits to make his wings transparent. He wanted to learn more about what all this meant, regarding Eloria, the green wizard, and the crystals. When they flew out to the rocks, the mermaid was under the surface of the water, floating around, looking up at them, acting as though she only wanted them to remove the net from her home, nothing more. He knew better.

It was a different mermaid this time, her fish scales pink and silver, her hair a strawberry blond. Viator wondered if the mermaids took turns soliciting the elves to help them with the deadly fishnet. This time as they flew closer to grab the net, watching the water and the mermaid, he and Balen worked together, tugging and struggling to pull the net free from the jagged rocks. They waved at each other when the water was about to splash them when a wave crashed into the rocks. But when the mermaid surfaced to grab Viator's ankle this time, his green amulet glowed. She looked shocked, her lips parted in surprise, and she quickly sank into the water and stayed there.

"Man, I need one of those. I wonder if yours could chase away the trolls too." Balen sounded in awe.

Viator felt the same way. He wished they could arm all his people with a crystal amulet. He did recall though that the opinicus was not afraid of it. Maybe not the griffin either.

Between the two of them, they freed the fishnet from the rocks and carried it back to shore.

"What happened? I didn't see the mermaid but once," Eloria said.

"Thankfully, the amulet kept her at bay. I imagine now if the one we had encountered before that had reached you when you were swimming in the water—if the creatures from the island of mist hadn't taken off with you and imprisoned you in their castle—your amulet would have chased her off." Viator lifted the fishnet off the sand again. "The same with the one in the cave of crystals. Let's return to the memorial and take this with us so the mermaids can't carry it back to the rocks again for the next unsuspecting elves."

"Viator, your wings are even more transparent," Eloria marveled.

"He is a prince," Balen reminded Eloria.

"My wings *are* more translucent." Viator examined his wings, surprised. "It was worth removing the net to protect others too. Yours are also, Balen."

"What if we drop the fishing net on the rocks again?" Balen asked. "Do you think we'd get more credits if we went after it again?"

"You can try, but I'm not going to test it," Viator said. "You carry the net and I'll take Eloria back to the memorial."

Balen agreed and they all flew off together, the sky hiding behind building clouds. "I think we might be in for some rainy weather."

Viator hoped not. They would be grounded until the rains let up.

When they finally reached the green wizard memorial, Viator figured they'd only have time enough to check out one more quest before they had to see Zorak and have dinner with him.

"We have accomplished something to do with the green wizard's symbol, the amulet, the coiled rope, and the fishing net," Balen said. "We have the dragon symbol, shadow, and mist left."

"Unless we've already dealt with the dragon when we rescued Eloria from the ledge below her window at our castle," Viator said.

"Maybe we did the mist one already also. I keep thinking that it has to do with the green isle of mist," Eloria said. "You freed the other elves and the mermaid. Now that the island has disappeared, you can't do that quest."

"We've had several quests dealing with water. Even finding the crystal that had plunged into the water," Viator said.

"And the poison in the water," Balen added. "But we haven't had any quest to do with fire. Which makes me think of a dragon's fire."

"The shadow symbol is glowing on this door," Eloria said.

If Balen was right about this having to do with the shadow elves, Viator hoped that they wouldn't try to lock Eloria up once they realized why she was there. They went through the door and on the other side, they were in woods that he recognized. "You were right. This is the shadow elves' territory."

The shadow elves could even be following them now, hidden in the trees, not showing themselves, sending word to the king to see what he wanted to do about the intrusion.

"Good. Then I can see Persephonice and finish *my* mission," she said.

"Somehow, I feel that all of this has been part of your mission. What if she wants to return to your world?" Viator asked. "We've only believed she wouldn't."

"She can't. Neither of us can. Zorak took away our ability to return to the ship or to contact them when they're within range."

"You're really all right about staying here with us?" Viator realized that might be some of the reason she was staying here. Not because of him but because she had no choice.

"I don't have a choice, but it doesn't matter. I doubt Perse-phonice will want to leave, and I would never have tried to force her to go back to the ship. Which means her father might have abandoned me here anyway for not doing what he wanted."

Balen shook his head. "We are glad you are here, even if you can't remember to include our titles when you address us or speak of us to others."

Eloria smiled. "I'm glad to be here with both you and the prince, even if the prince's parents are not happy about it."

"I will work on that," Viator reassured her.

They hadn't traveled far when they were suddenly surrounded by warrior elves, both male and female, dressed in clothes that blended in with the woods. One moment they weren't there and the next, they were. Viator wasn't surprised. Rumors said that's how they got their name.

"Prince Viator, Lord Balen, and...?" Prince Cronus asked, as the crown prince of the shadow elves. He eyed Eloria with intrigue. "You are like the other one."

"Persephonice? She is my best friend." Eloria smiled.

King Sar was Prince Cronus's father, and Dracolin's father, Lord Palmoran was the king's chief advisor. Viator hoped they wouldn't take offense to Eloria's being here.

"She is Eloria," Viator quickly said. "Truly a friend of Perse-phonice."

"From Persephonice's home world? Have you come to take her away from Dracolin and our people?" Cronus asked, looking ready to arrest Eloria and take her prisoner, sounding as though he didn't trust the human.

"No. I'm here to ensure she is happy and to renew our friendship."

"You must understand that I don't trust you, nor will my father or Dracolin's." Cronus and several of the warriors escorted them to their village.

Viator suspected the only way that they could convince the shadow elves that Eloria had come in peace was if she didn't steal Persephonice away from them, and Eloria instead returned with him to his own kingdom. Which remained a tenable situation with his own mother and father distrusting her.

When they finally reached the king's court, they discovered King Sar was actually conducting court business. But he dismissed all his courtiers upon seeing the red-haired girl with his son and Viator and the others. Lord Palmoran was also present.

"What do we have here?" the king asked, narrowing his eyes as he studied Eloria. "Another one like Persephonice?"

"Her friend," Cronus said. "So she says."

"Are we to welcome you, or imprison you?" the king asked, sitting back against his throne.

"You should welcome me," Eloria said, sounding sure of herself, before Viator could say the same. "Yes, Persephonice's father sent me to locate her and convince her to return to the ship. But Prince Zorak destroyed the means we have to either contact the commander or return to the ship. I have learned Persephonice is married to one of your men, and I'm fairly certain she is happy here and wouldn't want to leave anyway. I still have to see her for myself, and I'd love to renew our friendship."

"So you say that you are both stuck here, until her father sends others of your kind," the king said, sounding angry.

"It's possible, but he won't be returning for me. Just Persephonice."

The king raised his brows.

"I haven't done as he commanded me, and I'm sure if he sent more people, he would only take Persephonice back. Or at least try. I would be on my own."

"Eloria is staying with me," Viator quickly added, so that no one would get the idea that Eloria might be interested in joining the shadow elves. She was his.

"I thought you were betrothed to Sendal," Cronus said. "Eloria can stay with us, since her best friend resides with us."

Viator was amused that Cronus would say so, even though his father didn't appear to agree with them harboring any more of these humans. "Rumors only. Unfounded rumors."

Balen scoffed. "My sister will be a terror."

"And the king and queen?" King Sar asked. "Your mother and father? How do they view this...arrangement?"

"Eloria is the one destined to turn my kingdom upside down, according to our prophecy." Viator figured it didn't matter if the shadow elves knew the trouble she was for them. It was their prophecy after all.

King Sar's mouth gaped, his eyes widening. He looked as though he was horrified at the news, yet a small smile lifted the corner of his lips and he appeared glad that she wasn't staying here. Prince Cronus looked amused also.

"Is Persephonice here?" Eloria asked.

"She is still in the northern reaches." King Sar sat taller. "If you want to see her sooner than later, you'll have to go there and meet up with them. But you'll need warmer clothes than you now wear."

"We can loan you some clothes," Cronus said. "And if you're not prepared, we'll gather food supplies for you. We've been worried it's taking them too long."

"Thank you," Viator said. "Balen and I are good for clothes, but Eloria might need something warmer. And we really hadn't prepared to be gone for too long." He was thinking about how they were supposed to return to the high elves' castle for dinner. "If you wouldn't mind sending word to Prince Zorak that we might miss dinner with him, we would be grateful." He had considered returning to see him before they left, but he'd rather do this now, as eager as he knew Eloria was to meet up with her friend. He was just as eager to resolve this situation between the two women, finish his quests, and then deal with his parents' issue of taking Eloria in as their daughter-in-law.

"Thank you." Eloria sounded relieved that she was going to see her friend and Viator was glad to help her out in any way that he could.

"Make it happen." King Sar dismissed them then.

Cronus said to the three of them as they left the court, "Viator, you and Balen come with me to gather what you think you'll need in the line of food. Eloria, you can go with Helena. She will help you dress more warmly."

"Thank you," Eloria said, and then Helena led her to another abode.

Cronus led Viator and Balen to the main kitchen of the shadow elf castle and said to Viator, "If you find another one of these extraordinary humans, send word to me, won't you? I seem to always be too late to catch one of my own. Where did you capture her?"

"Sontran's Cliff."

Cronus's eyes widened. "The same place where Dracolin found Persephonice?"

"Aye, the very same place. Prince Zorak actually rescued her from the blue elves, and I took her hostage before he could do so."

Cronus smiled.

"But then the river elves threw her from the cliffs and Lars was fuming mad. He wanted her for his own."

Cronus shook his head. "Do you think she will bring trouble to all of us when Persephonice's father realizes neither woman is returning to him?"

"I do. We will either have to hide the women away or face our new foes."

"They have abilities none of us do," Cronus warned.

"And so do Eloria and Persephonice. They can teach us how to repel the invaders from our cliffs."

"You have no prophecy about that, I take it."

"No."

"The cooks will set aside whatever meals you need," Cronus said, half to Viator and half to the royal cooks. Then he said to Viator, "You will tell me if you find another one of these creatures, won't you?"

"You would have to both suit each other, and I doubt your father would agree to you marrying anyone other than another shadow elf."

Balen pointed out the food they would need and nodded. "Viator's father and mother don't agree with Viator's choice. They've banished Eloria from the castle."

"Yet you still intend to keep her for your own?" Cronus looked like maybe he had a chance with her yet.

"They seemed to be tied together no matter what." Balen pointed to rolls and nodded to the cook.

"I noticed your wings are nearly transparent. You are both coming of age."

"Just a couple of more quests." At least Viator was hopeful. "What is it that Persephonice and Dracolin are attempting to accomplish in the northern reaches?"

"They are trying to resolve issues between the snow giants and the ice dragons. I can't imagine anything more difficult than that."

"Maybe we can help them." Though Viator didn't know how they could.

Balen glanced at him, sharing the same view, that he didn't know how they could manage either.

"Can Eloria speak with other creatures like Persephonice can?" Cronus asked.

"Aye. She can talk to the dragons. She can call on the dragon who won't be tamed."

Cronus clamped his gaping mouth shut, shook his head, and folded his arms. "I want one of those."

"The dragon who cannot be tamed?"

"No, one of these land-bound mermaids. Eloria can swim?"

"Aye."

Cronus sighed. "I will be more vigilant, searching the cliffs daily, if not to look for another one of these remarkable women, to alert our people if warriors come to try and take Persephonice home. She thought that her father had given up on her."

"We will let her know that he hasn't and maybe she can tell us what we need to do to deal with more of them, should they show up." Viator just hoped it would never come to that.

25

Eloria selected clothes that she could wear so that she would be comfortable in the cold: winter boots, a warmer winter cloak, leg bindings, and a tunic lined with fur with a fur hood. The female elf warrior also gave her a backpack that, when Eloria filled it with her clothes and the warm weather gear, it was as if she was holding nothing at all.

"My gifts to you," Helena said.

Eloria gave her a hug, surprising the woman, but she smiled in return.

"I am a good friend to Persephonice. I would be the same for you. Dracolin's former girlfriend, Tslian, is still angry he would take an outsider to be his mate. But I enjoy Persephonice's company. She is a true friend in every way."

"I'm glad to be your friend as well."

"Viator will be your mate?"

"If all goes well, yes. Persephonice is happy with Dracolin?"

"Oh, yes. The two of them are inseparable. They couldn't be happier. I'm a warrior. What is your occupation?" the elf asked.

"A warrior also. But my job is to persuade others to do what is right without resorting to violence."

"Oh, that's what Persephonice does." Then Helena frowned. "Is that why her father sent you? To persuade her to return without resorting to violence?"

"Yes, and because I'm her best friend. But her father won't get *his* way this time."

"I would like to go with you, but my job is here, protecting the shadow elf realm. Good luck to you."

"Thanks."

A knock on the door sounded and Helena answered it. "She is ready. Good luck to you, my lords."

"Your wings will be all right in freezing weather?" Eloria asked Viator and Balen. She wasn't even sure they could call a dragon to their aid if they needed one.

"Aye. They withstand snow, just not rain." Viator took her hand.

"We have to be careful of ice though," Balen warned. "But our warm cloaks will protect our wings when we're not flying. Once they are fully transparent, they will be as if they don't exist and will withstand all weather conditions. Which is why it's imperative that we complete our quests."

"That will be good." Eloria noticed that Viator was no longer insisting that he do the quests first so that his wings would be transparent sooner, and she was glad that he and Balen could do this together. She was a bit apprehensive of going into the northern reaches and meeting enormous giants and trying to persuade them to not kill them outright though. She was proud of Persephonice for helping the creatures of this world find peace. Eloria could think of no greater vocation than that.

They said goodbye to Prince Cronus and Helena and several other warrior elves before they took to the sky while Viator carried Eloria on his back.

"Do you ever weary of carrying me?" Eloria asked.

"I am honored. I never thought I would have the opportunity

to share this kind of intimacy with a mate of mine, whom I thought would be a winged elf and flying on her own."

"What will we do if Persephonice's father sends a whole bunch of warriors to search for her?"

"We will prevail. We have for several millennia," Viator assured her.

But she wasn't reassured. Her people had vastly superior technology compared to the elves. She feared for them. But she would stand against her people to protect the elves the best she could.

"How will we even find Persephonice and Dracolin?" She hoped Viator had some clue. She could imagine them flying around until Viator and Balen were exhausted and not ever finding them.

"Prince Cronus gave us directions. There's only one place where the snow giants and ice dragons live in the same vicinity. As long as Persephonice and Dracolin are still there, we should find them."

They flew for about an hour and then spied snow-covered mountains dotted with caves. "Ice dragons'?" she asked.

"Possibly. I hope that your reputation with the dragons reaches this far north."

"Aww, but you and Balen also aided the dragonlings' rescue, so hopefully we'll all receive a good reception."

That's when they saw five dragons flying in their direction. They were almost impossible to see because of their silver, white, and pale blue scales against the snowy sky, a soft scattering of snowflakes falling about them. She'd seen snow before and loved it. She'd love it more once she was sure they'd all be safely done with this quest.

"Do they shoot ice?" Eloria supposed she should have asked that before.

"Fire. The creatures up here are well protected from snow

and ice, so the dragons have fire to heat things up. They're checking us out, making sure we're not here to harm them."

Balen glanced at Viator and Eloria. "Your crystals are both glowing, which could be a good sign or bad, depending if the green wizard was friends of these dragons."

The dragons hovered in the chilled air several hundred feet away.

Then one moved in their direction and called out, "You are like the other, but not."

"Persephonice? Is she here?" Eloria asked.

"She can speak with the dragons," Balen said, as if he'd forgotten that she could.

"I am Rollin, king of the ice dragons in this region. Merkle, king of the snow giants in this territory, has taken the overseer Persephonice and the warrior Dracolin hostage. We cannot free them. But we can tell you where they are, if you do not know. Can you help them? They were trying to aid us in finding peace with the giants. King Merkle is a hardheaded giant and I doubt we can resolve our issues."

Eloria told them who they were first. "What issues do you have between your dragons and the giants?" It was always important to learn what the problem was right up front.

"We ice fish for our dragonlings. Once they are old enough to hunt for food farther away from our lairs, we replenish our food that way. But until they can fly and hunt on their own, with us, of course, we have to fish in the rivers here. The dragonlings can only feed on sturgeon. It has always been our way. But the current snow giant king has declared the sturgeon are his. Persephonice has said that the reason the king has decided the fish are his is because an elf told him that they will make him more powerful than any other food or fish he can consume."

"What kind of elf?" Eloria had to learn which kind had caused all the trouble in the first place.

"A river elf."

Eloria explained to Viator and Balen what had happened.

"Come. I'm sorry. I should have offered you shelter while we talk." Rollin led them to one of the ice caves.

Eloria was expecting to see it full of ice and as cold as the weather outside, but deeper into the cave it was warm. She thought they'd see a bunch of dragonlings here, but it appeared to be the king's own cave full of treasure. A couple of female dragons, one that appeared to be his age, and another that was smaller, maybe a teen, were there, watching the newcomers.

"Another of them has come, my king?" the older female dragon asked, sniffing at them.

"Eloria, dragon keeper," the king said, waving his arm at her. "Prince Viator of the darkland elves and Lord Balen, also dragon keepers."

The other two dragons' eyes widened.

Eloria was surprised to hear him call them dragon keepers. The news must have been spread from the other dragons.

Then the older female frowned. "What are they to do about the giants when the others could do nothing? Before long, our dragonlings will die. They can only eat the sturgeon in the rivers, and they have had none for four days."

"Is there a way into the castle where the giants live?" At least Eloria thought they would live in a castle. What did she know? She felt pressed to do this as quickly as she could, hating to hear that the dragonlings were being starved.

"Aye," the king said.

The teen spoke up. "You are tiny enough that you can crawl into spaces that giants and dragons can't access. Maybe you could get inside and free the others. At least we believe they've been taken prisoner."

"That's a great idea!" Eloria said.

The girl smiled a little, her wicked teeth on display.

"You'll have to find it yourself. We have a map of the region and where everyone resides. But we can't accompany you. They would take our arrival as an act of war," King Rollin said.

"No, we'll go alone." Eloria figured they didn't have any choice.

"The sun will begin to go down soon. If you fly from the direction of the sun so that it is in their eyes and shine your lights at the same time, you might be able to reach their castle without detection."

"We'll try that," Eloria said.

"If you don't succeed, you could be imprisoned like the others."

Eloria turned to Viator and Balen. "Maybe only two of us should go. If we don't return, the person who stays behind can return home and tell the king and queen we didn't make it."

"You know I stay with you," Viator said.

"I wouldn't be able to save face if I went on a mission with you and left you both behind to your fates. I stay with the two of you." Balen folded his arms.

"All right. Are we ready to do this?" Eloria was trying to sound brave, but she was terrified. It was one thing to face her own death for what she believed in, yet another when she took others she cared about into danger.

Persephonice was her good friend and her companions, and she had to find a way to save them. Viator and Balen had heard of her, but they didn't know her like Eloria did. But they had to find a way to aid the dragonlings.

"Aye. Now that the sun is at the right place to help hide us," Viator said.

They headed out and she prayed that this part of the plan would work. Beyond that, she hoped they could find a way into the castle and a way to the dungeon without getting caught.

They didn't say anything as they flew in the direction of the giant's castle, not wanting to be heard, if the giants had exceptional hearing. They used their lights to help disguise themselves against the backdrop of the sun, though Eloria was trying to maintain her hold on Viator also.

Then they saw the snow-covered white stone towers of the castle looming tall in the distance. Everything was in giant proportions, and it didn't take them long to reach the huge castle.

She could see right away that gaps between the stones were big enough for them to squeeze in. But some of the gaps had been filled with mortar deeper inside, and they'd have to chip away at the mortar, or fly off and find a gap that wasn't blocked off with mortar. Because they were afraid that chipping away at the mortar might catch a giant's attention, they opted for flying close to the walls and searching for a place where the gap went all the way through to the inside wall of the castle. They finally found one after a dozen tries and they rested inside for a moment, before proceeding into the castle. Viator went first, shoving his amulet into his woolen tunic to hide the crystal in case it began to glow.

The building was huge and drafty. Though they were small, they were still big enough for a giant to see if one should come across them. She wished she could turn invisible.

Then they had a bit of luck. A white rat came out of a hole in an inner wall, spied them, and wrinkled its nose as he smelled them.

"Can you understand me?" Eloria whispered.

"Yes, though I can't believe you can. You look like the other one who is here, with the red hair and rounded ears," the rat said.

"Yes. Did she speak to you?"

"No, I only heard her speaking to the giant king and he had

them locked in the dungeon. I didn't know she could speak with other creatures, like me."

"Can you tell us where they are?"

"I could show you if you could follow the path I take, but you are too big."

"Is there another path?"

"What would you give me?"

"The dragons would be most grateful if you could help us change the giant king's mind about eating the sturgeon."

The rat smiled. Then he frowned. "I do have a way. But what would you do for me?"

"Take you away from here, if you wish."

"Agreed. To the warmer climes? Where I can forage for food in lush, green forests?"

"We can do that," Eloria said.

"All right. But it's a long and dangerous path to the dungeon. Come this way." The rat took them down one passage and then the next. Every time they felt the floor vibrating with a giant's footfalls, the rat showed them a place that was big enough for the elves and Eloria to hide. They watched as a giant stomped past them, and she couldn't help but break out in a sweat, despite how chilly the place was.

Viator wrapped his arms around her, warming her, before they had to rush out of their hiding place to follow the rat again.

They were going lower, until they had to traverse stairs that led down into the dungeon. Here, they didn't see any place to hide, but no one seemed to be about. When they finally reached the bottom floor, the rat ran ahead, but Eloria saw Persephonice and two shadow elves in a cell. Eloria and the others rushed to the iron grated door. She was afraid they'd have to find a set of keys for the cell door.

"Eloria," Persephonice whispered, rising from her bed. She pointed to a room ahead. "The guard is sleeping inside."

"We need to get you out of here."

"Stand back." Persephonice proceeded to melt the bars.

Eloria's mouth gaped. When had her friend learned to do that? And why hadn't they already escaped?

"Interesting." The rat whispered, "I will do the most odious thing I can do, uhm, leave some of my digested food mixed with the pounds of fish the giants have stored for their king. I can tell you he will be sicker than..., well, you can imagine. He will swear off the sturgeon. But do not leave me behind. I will meet you where I first saw you. Can you make it back without my aid?"

"Yes, thanks. We'll see you there." Eloria hugged Persephonice as soon as she was free, and they all hurried to vacate the dungeon. With more of them there, she was afraid it was going to be harder to leave undetected.

Not only that but a bell began to ring. Giants were pounding the halls with their huge footfalls and the elves and Eloria and her friend couldn't figure out if the giants were coming or going. Every time the footfalls faded away, they would hurry to the next safe place and work their way through the wall to another hall.

They heard a lot of noise and laughter somewhere off in the distance. It sounded like the giants were feasting. Eloria hoped that the rat had made it in time to add some seasoning to the fish the king would eat before he had his dinner. She wanted to know that their mission was successful before they left the castle, but she wasn't sure it would be possible. She never liked to have to wait on anything, preferring to get things done as quickly as she could.

They finally reached the place between the rocks that would afford them escape from the castle and introduced themselves to each other.

"Okay, how about Viator and Balen take Persephonice and either Dracolin or Balon. And then I'll wait here with whoever is left, since I can talk to the rat. Then the two of you can come back for the remainder of us and the rat."

"As much as I hate leaving you behind, we have to. It would be better to do so now while we have the chance." Viator held Eloria in the narrow space and kissed her.

"Take Balon. I'll stay with Eloria," Dracolin said.

"My thanks." Viator then left with Persephonice and Balen carried Balon to the ice dragon's lair.

Eloria knew it would take a while before Viator and Balen could return. She also assumed Dracolin would think she was the enemy, but they didn't talk while waiting to hear from the rat.

Then there was a roar in the great hall where the king must have been feasting with his people. The conversation was no longer cheerful in the giants' boisterous, loud and gruff manner, but concerned.

"It is fresh caught today, Your Majesty. It is from the same river we always fish from."

"The sturgeon will kill me!" the king roared, his angry voice shaking the walls all around them.

"It was the river elf who said it was good for you," another giant shouted.

"He is a dead man if any should set eyes upon him again."

Eloria wondered what a river elf would hope to gain by causing issues between the ice dragons and giants.

Suddenly, the rat jumped into the space between the walls, startling her. She clasped her hand over her mouth to silence her squeak.

"Will you love me and take care of me?" the rat asked Eloria.

She thought it was an odd question, but perhaps he needed friendship if he was to leave behind his fellow rats. "Yes, of course." She would do anything to make this right for the ice dragons. She realized she had a real affinity for them—for all dragons, it seemed.

"Good. You must seal our bargain with a kiss."

She frowned at him, thinking how awful that would be. "I'm good for my word."

"You kiss the prince, and you love him," the rat said.

She sighed. "All right." She would pretend the rat was like a puppy she once owned. She kissed the rat and to her shock, he grew and morphed into an elf.

She stared at him, but Dracolin pulled out his sword, ready to skewer the elf.

"I am a high elf, turned into a rat when I betrayed a fellow high elf. But I have learned my lesson well." He bowed his head to her. "You don't really have to love me now. You just had to show that you did while I was a rat to break the spell. You are my savior. I'm Reynaldo, by the way."

She couldn't believe she'd kissed a rat who turned out to be a high elf. She wanted to ask him about his betrayal, but she wanted to limit how much they talked while they could still be overheard by the giants, should any come this way.

It seemed to take Viator and Balen forever to reach them, but as soon as they made their way between the blocks of stones, both of them stared at the high elf like Dracolin and Eloria had done.

"The rat," Eloria said, taking hold of Viator. "Reynaldo. Let's get out of here while we can."

"I promise I'll return for you," Balen said, "once I've delivered Dracolin to the dragons' lair."

"I will wait for you to return for me," Dracolin said to Balen. "Since the high elf helped to show you the way to free us and to solve the issue between the giants and the dragons, we owe him much gratitude."

Reynaldo eyes misted. "My thanks to you. You don't know

how much I've wanted to escape this place. And...my former, furry form."

The sun had nearly set when they flew off, but a distant fire on a mountaintop lighted their way. They could not use their own lights to help them, so they were glad that the dragons had done so for them.

Eloria loved the freedom of leaving the castle behind as they flew in the direction of the dragon's lair. They were quiet until they were halfway to the cave and sure that the giants couldn't throw stones at them, if they could even make out the elf specks flying in the night.

She explained who the rat was, and that the king had become violently ill.

"But what if he believes it's just a one-time occurrence?" Viator asked.

"I have many rat friends. They promised to do the same with any sturgeon the giants fish out of the river. The dragons shouldn't have any more problem from them," Reynaldo said.

When they finally arrived at the dragon's lair, the king greeted them with wariness.

"It is done," Eloria said, thankful that they could help the dragons, but also that they could save her friend and the others. In the light of the cave, she realized Viator and Balen's wings were nearly transparent. "You know, I loved seeing your wings."

Viator smiled, looking pleased that she liked them. "No problem. Once they are completely invisible, I can make them fully visible anytime I want."

"And we would, whenever we're trying to catch a woman's attention," Balen said. "Or show another prospective male who is interested in a woman we want to court to bug off."

She chuckled, but then she turned serious and said to Reynaldo, "How did you betray a fellow high elf?"

"I'm returning for Dracolin," Balen said, and took off again.

"I was the apprentice to the green wizard," Reynaldo said. "He told me to get the ingredients for a particular potion. I'd always done everything he asked of me, no matter how dangerous. I...I wasn't worried. I thrived on danger. That was until I had to extract poison from a spider. One drop of the venom can kill an elf. I have to admit I'm terrified of spiders. I failed him. He told me if I didn't bring the poison back by the appointed time, I'd turn into a rat and one of the high elves would banish me to the giants' castle in the north. The only way I could ever return to my elf form was to make an elf fall in love with me. Which I knew would never happen because the elf would need to rescue me, profess her love, and kiss me. But Eloria isn't even an elf, so I don't know how come the spell was broken."

"She is a half high elf," Viator said, "and since she can speak and understand the various languages of other creatures, you got lucky."

Persephonice was staring at Eloria. "You're a high elf? You know magic?"

Eloria smiled. "Yes. But you know I had to keep my talents hidden from your father."

"My father. He sent you to return me to the ship, didn't he?" Persephonice asked Eloria.

"Yes, but I learned you and Dracolin were married. Prince Zorak destroyed my bracelet and the one I was to give to you. So we can't return even if we wanted to and neither of us do. I'm staying with Viator, though his parents may not approve of me returning to the castle. Why didn't you leave the cell when you had the ability to melt the bars?"

"We had no place to go. We couldn't fly away. And if we'd called out to the dragons to come take us from the castle, we could have started an all-out war. We only hoped that I could convince the giant king to free us." Persephonice smiled. "It's so good to see you. I didn't think I'd ever seen any of my kind here, nor that one of my kind was one of the elf kind too."

"I'm so glad to see you too." Then they caught up on what was going on with crewmembers on the ship.

"Same old thing. You suspected you couldn't convince me to return, and you knew what would happen to you," Persephonice said.

"Yeah, but I'm glad I'm here now with you and the others I've made friends with."

Balen returned with Dracolin, and the winged elf looked worn out, but his wings were also clearer!

"You can live with the shadow elves," Persephonice said to Eloria. "We would be happy to have you there and you can be an overseer like me."

Eloria smiled.

Viator laughed. "My parents will come around. I'm the only son they have."

Dracolin agreed. "It was the same with me marrying Persephonice to begin with."

"So you didn't know that the green wizard died?" Eloria asked Reynaldo.

Tears actually filled the apprentice's eyes. "No. If...if I could do it all over again, I would."

"Why didn't he obtain the poison from the spiders himself?" Eloria asked.

"He was as terrified of them as I was."

Everything they'd had to accomplish, seemed to correspond directly with the green wizard. What if the door with the symbol of poison on it referred to a poisonous spider and not the poison Lars men had put in the river? She mentioned it to Reynaldo and he sat back.

"Oh, no, no."

"You've been through all the doors of the wizard's memorial?" Eloria said.

"Aye, since I was the wizard's apprentice."

"The door with the symbol of the mist on it?"

"No. It never appeared."

"But you know of it."

"Aye. It's only supposed to appear when all other tasks were met. But, from what Sarazan said, they would be different quests for different people."

"You had to go into the cave with the poisonous spiders beyond the door that carries the symbol of poison, right?"

"Yes, but I can no longer open any of the doors. Sarazan took my amulet away from me, thereby removing my apprenticeship."

"Do you know what he was going to do with the poison?"

"Make a potion. You know he befriended all elves and many others, but I suspected the poison was meant for someone who he couldn't befriend. Someone who caused trouble for the elves."

"We can access the doors," Eloria said.

"You...you are the wizard's new apprentice?"

"Uh, sort of. If we can open the door to the spiders' cave, can you make the potion?"

"I can make the potion. I just can't extract the poison from one of the spiders."

"Okay, we'll do it, and you make the potion."

"But what good will it do? The wizard's already dead."

"That might be true. Or maybe not. What if we could learn who he was going to use the poison on? And we could finish his work?" Eloria asked.

"Maybe it was in his journal. I can help you get to it," Reynaldo said.

"We didn't see a journal," Eloria said. "I guess we weren't really looking for one either."

"He had it well-hidden. If it's still in the same place where he had tucked it away, I can find it."

"Can we help in any way?" Persephonice asked.

"No, thanks though," Viator said. "We were supposed to go to the high elf's castle tonight, but it's going to be too late."

"You can stay here," the dragon king said. "It sounds to me that you will have your work cut out for you when you leave here in the morning. We will provide a dragon escort for those who cannot fly."

"Thank you," Viator said. "We appreciate your generosity."

With that, the king had some of his dragons prepare beds of warm furs for the night and the elves and the langolars ate some of the food that the shadow elves had sent along with them. Afterward, they slept together in the great hall, contemplating all that they'd done and all that they still had to do.

26

The next morning, the dragon king said he'd received a message from the giant king. They could eat all the sturgeon they wanted.

The elves and Eloria and Persephonice cheered. The dragons smiled.

"If you ever need our help, let us know," the king said. "We would serve you morning meal, but I don't believe you'd relish what we eat."

"We appreciated the beds for the night. And we had food with us that we ate this morning. May all remain well with you." Viator bowed low to the king.

Everyone else did the same and the king planned to have four of his dragons carry some of them to the shadow elf realm and the high elf to the green wizard's memorial.

"You will come see us, won't you?" Persephonice asked Eloria before they parted ways and headed to their destinations.

"We will. As soon as we can complete our tasks. I just hope your father doesn't send anyone else to try and track you down."

"Oh, Jupiter, what if my father put tracking devices on your clothes or your backpack?" Persephonice asked.

"I'll get rid of my clothes." Eloria hated to leave her clothes behind—which made her an individual among the elves, if the rounded ears weren't enough. If the commander had ordered tracking devices tacked onto her clothes or backpack, when the ship returned, he could send trackers to locate her. Why hadn't she thought of it before?

"Maybe you could put them in the cave of spiders. No one would ever be able to get into the cave, but if they managed somehow, they'd never come out," Balen said.

"But then they would be near your kingdom, searching for me."

"True," Viator said.

She pulled the backpack off that Helena had given her while she held onto Viator's back with her legs and he held her legs with his arms to keep her nice and secure. She began pulling clothes out of her backpack and dropping them to the snow-covered forest while everyone hovered in place to wait on her. She truly was leaving her langolar life behind. She tossed her backpack last and then she pulled Helena's backpack back on her shoulders. "All done."

Persephonice sighed. "Are you all right?"

Eloria smiled. "Yeah. It's time to make a stand. This is my home now." She swore she heard Viator let out his breath in relief. "We will see you as soon as we can!"

"See you soon," Persephonice said.

Then they parted ways and Viator asked, "Are you sure you're all right?"

"Yes. I feel like I'm shedding the last of my life onboard the ship. It's something I knew I'd have to do, but it still feels like a big step." She hadn't been here long enough to feel like she was part of this world. Everything was so new and different, and there were so many creatures here she'd only read about in myths and legends that made it a fascinating place to explore.

Viator smiled. "It's a good thing for me. I will make sure you have all the clothes you ever need."

She laughed, thinking about her friend who lived for clothes. "On the ship, we have very little space for clothes. It just wasn't a priority for me."

"You will have room galore for your clothes and whatever else your heart desires."

She still couldn't believe that here among the elves, she was someone special, loved even, well, at least Viator loved her. His parents were a different story. And she wished she could cast a spell to make the river elves and blue elves peaceful, rather than so wicked.

"I'd say we could drop by my castle, but I'm afraid my parents wouldn't be happy," Viator said.

Reynaldo said, "The high elves may not be pleased to see me either, if we went there instead."

"We have plenty of food at the green wizard's memorial, if everyone wants to eat there," Balen suggested.

"All right, we'll go there." Viator headed in that direction and when they finally reached the memorial, they all landed.

Reynaldo leaped off the dragon's back and thanked him.

Eloria spoke to the dragon also, thanking him for helping them out.

"You saved our little ones from a certain death. Our thanks can never be enough." The ice dragon bowed his head and then took off for the northern reaches.

Reynaldo waited while Viator, Eloria, and Balen went into the memorial first, as if he felt he wasn't welcome.

"Come, Reynaldo. You know where the wizard's journal is. Maybe that can give us a clue as to what we must do next," Eloria said.

"I cooked all Sarazan's meals," Reynaldo said, still slow to join them.

"Good," Viator said. "We will assist you."

Before long, they were sitting down and eating wild boar and pickled greens. Eloria hadn't thought she'd like these fresh meals that were so different from what their food simulators produced. But it was great. Tasty, not bland. She did wonder if they were getting all the nutrients they needed. The food on the ship had all the required supplements designed specifically for each member.

She finished her food and then opened the journal that Reynaldo had found while they were waiting for the food to cook.

She was reading through the journal, mostly just near the end so she could see what had happened to him.

She read about the issues he'd had with his apprentice and sending him away.

"He wrote about me, didn't he?" Reynaldo asked, sounding dejected as he cleaned up the dishes.

"Some. He was disappointed, but more so in himself. He couldn't get the poison from the spider either. It doesn't say why he needed it though." She read through a few more pages. "Wait, here. He needed a potion."

"Right. I know how to create it if we can just get the poison." Reynaldo shook his head. "One bite from the spider and you're dead. There are all kinds of creatures, big and small, in the cave that have died because of the bite of the spider."

"Maybe I can talk to them."

Reynaldo looked at Eloria like she was crazy.

"She might be right," Viator said. "She can talk to creatures that we can't."

"Do you want to risk losing her?" Reynaldo looked upset that they would want to send her into the cave with the venomous spiders.

"I must do this. If it's important to aid the green wizard."

"If he's alive, Eloria. And if it truly is important," Viator said.

"It is. For the elves. He was trying to make peace with the creatures of the island of the mist, but they wouldn't agree, according to his journal. He had one alternative. Use the potion on their leaders to stop them from taking the elves hostage. We have to do it. We have to finish his work. I can do this." She hoped. "None of you can come with me."

"I don't want you to go in alone," Viator said.

"I should go. It was my mission," Reynaldo said.

"Together then with Reynaldo," Eloria said.

Viator drew her into his arms. "What if this doesn't work? What if you and Reynaldo die?"

"We have to do this. I'm sure of it."

They all left the wizard's quarters after that. Reynaldo had grabbed a flask to use to extract the spider's venom. They went straight to the door that had the poison symbol and it glowed, just like Eloria figured it would. "Just Reynaldo and me."

"Are you sure you want to do this without us?" Viator asked, kissing Eloria.

"Yeah. I can talk to them. Hopefully, I will be able to convince them we only need a little poison"—she glanced in Reynaldo's direction to see if he was agreeable, he nodded— "and then extract it. Since it's his duty to Sarazan, he should do the extraction."

Then she opened the door, but before she went into the light-filled cave, she began talking. "I've come on a quest to obtain a small amount of poison for the green wizard. He needs it for a potion to aid the elves. Would you be willing to give us some?"

"No one has ever entered our cave and asked for our poison," something said from the dark.

"Are you okay with it?"

"Why did the green wizard never come for some on his own?"

"Could he speak your language?"

"You are the first."

"Maybe that's why. Will you allow us to gather some of your poison? And is there anything we can do for you?"

"Now, this is another first. An elf offering to aid my kind."

She didn't tell him she wasn't all elf. If it helped to encourage goodwill between the elves and the spiders, she had done a good thing.

"Come into our cave. We will talk among ourselves about what you could do for us. I will give you the poison you need."

"Thank you. My friend, Reynaldo, was supposed to take the poison. Is it okay if he does that?" Eloria asked, not wanting Reynaldo to upset the balance, since they seemed to be getting somewhere.

"Can he not ask me himself?"

"No. I'm the only one, possibly a friend of mine also, who can speak with you."

"All right. But you will come with him and continue to talk to me?"

"Yes."

"Come in then."

Eloria and Reynaldo entered the cave and she kept looking around at the wet, mossy walls, searching for any sign of the spiders. She should have thought to ask Reynaldo if he knew how big they were. But then she saw a spider about six feet tall and just as wide, standing half-hidden in the shadows. She nearly had a heart attack.

"Are you the one I spoke to?" Eloria asked.

"Yes. How do you want to do this?"

"Reynaldo has a flask that we can carry the poison in."

"Then he will have to get closer."

"Come on, Reynaldo. You must do as the green wizard asked. We have to do this together."

Then he moved with her, looking as terrified as she felt.

"The other elves don't want to join us?" the spider asked.

"No. I asked them to stay behind."

The spider exposed his fangs.

Reynaldo held up the flask with shaking hands.

The spider said, "If he cannot do this, then you should."

"He can do this." Eloria knew Reynaldo had to, to prove to himself he could be a great wizard himself someday.

Reynaldo took a fang and milked the venom into the glass vial. "Thank you," Reynaldo said to the spider.

"Thanks. We'll return later and you can tell me what you want in exchange for aiding us."

The spider agreed and Eloria guided Reynaldo out of the cave. He was still shaking with fright, and her own heart was still pounding. When they left the cave, Viator shut the door and wrapped his arm around her waist.

"I think the spider took years off my life," Viator said.

"Mine too," Balen agreed.

"You weren't even as close as we were." Reynaldo headed into the green wizard's quarters. "I can make the potion now."

"Then what?" Viator asked.

"Fire," Balen said. "We haven't gone through the door with the fire symbol."

"But what do we do with the potion?" Eloria asked.

"Well, according to the journal, it has to do with the island of mist," Viator said.

"I have the potion." Reynaldo joined them, showing them the flask of blue misty liquid.

"Are you ready to check out the door with the symbol of fire?" Balen asked. "I think we need to complete one or two more quests and we'll have transparent wings."

"Yeah, let's do it." Viator glanced at Eloria to see if she was ready.

She agreed.

They headed for the fire symbol door, but it was gone. In its place was the door with the symbol of mist.

"The island of mist," Eloria whispered.

"I have really bad feelings about this," Balen said.

"But the island is gone. For years," Viator said.

"I suspect we can reach the island through that door." Reynaldo was still holding onto the flask.

"Okay, let's do it." Viator opened the door and they walked into a room. "This...this place looks familiar."

Eloria frowned and whispered, "No, it's...it's the castle on the isle of mist. How can it be?"

Balen said, "This is not good."

"What if we're supposed to rescue more people?" Eloria began looking for a trapdoor in the floor like the other room had but there wasn't one.

"I don't see another trap door." Viator looked out the window. "We're on the ground floor."

Balen looked in a closet and said, "Here. A passageway down."

They followed him into a tunnel that led downstairs. They were using dimmed elven lights, the men's swords ready when they came to a door.

They all stared at it for a moment, unsure as to what to do next. But then both Eloria's crystal and Viator's glowed lightly.

"Be ready," Viator whispered.

"Let me open it," Eloria said softly.

He allowed her to open the door and she gasped. An old man was sleeping on a bed, surrounded by a green misty light. It was the green wizard from Eloria's dreams, his nightshirt of green, his cloak and tall, pointed hat sitting at the foot of the bed, his hair and beard long and white. What was he doing here? On the island of mists?

"Sarazan," she whispered to him, knowing it was probably a bad idea. What if he had been the one to steal her away to this place earlier? And had her locked up?

But the old wizard turned to her, his green eyes widening. "Oh, Eloria. You and your companions have come to save me." He frowned at Reynaldo. "No longer a rat, eh? Someone must have shown you some love."

Reynaldo pulled out the flask. "The potion you requested I make."

The green wizard smiled.

27

Eloria couldn't believe that the wizard who had guided her throughout this venture had needed her to save him. If he was a powerful wizard, why wouldn't he be able to free himself?

"They've put a spell on me to keep me here. For now, the island is beneath the sea. I made it possible for Eloria to reach me through the crystal and the tunnel in the memorial, but I knew she'd need another to break their spell."

"What do we do?" Eloria asked.

"You see that vent on the wall? Pour the contents of the vial into the grate. The winged elf and Eloria have done the rest."

Reynaldo hurried to do it.

The crystals Eloria and Viator were wearing began glowing brightly and the green light surrounding the wizard was fading fast. Once it was gone, Sarazan said, "We must hurry. I can seal the tunnel from the memorial, but we must leave here before they catch us. They'll get rid of your amulets, and we'll be stuck here for the next sixty-six years."

He didn't need to say another word as they were hurrying through the tunnel to the room where they could reach the door to the memorial. The wizard seemed spry, despite how old he looked with his long white beard and hair.

"I may look decrepit," he said to Eloria, as if he could read her mind, "but I'm physically as young as you are."

When they reached the room, she expected alarms to go off, but nothing happened.

"They don't believe I could set all this in motion to facilitate my escape. Hurry, before they catch us at this though."

They went through the doorway and ended up in the room of doors. When the wizard shoved the door closed, it disappeared. "You see, it doesn't exist. They have no way to reach us."

"Why were you there?" Eloria asked.

"I went there with the notion of making peace with them. I'd heard for years they captured hostages to study while they were under the sea. I'm afraid even I, who have a reputation for making peace with all different kinds of elves, couldn't with these creatures. The potion was my chance at turning this around, but I couldn't get to it. I'd left a way out, if you ever returned to us."

"How long were you there?"

"Too long. Twelve years. I could only contact you through your dreams and hope that someday you would return to our people. I had word that the islanders had taken you hostage, but I couldn't get to you. They were furious when two winged elves saved you. I still hoped you would come back for me." Sarazan led them into his living quarters.

"We were supposed to do a fire quest, we thought," Eloria said.

"Aye, I saw the quests as you completed them with regard to freeing me. The winged elves started a fire to warm you after they saved you from the river and you were drenched and shivering, despite knowing the fire would alert other beasts who would attempt to kill you. Of course, you did it out of order, before you knew there was any order, but the end result is all that mattered."

"I am truly half a high elf?"

"Aye. You are one of us. You are my granddaughter."

Eloria stared at him in shock. Some had said she might be related to him in some way, which was how he had communicated with her. They were blood relations, but she still couldn't fathom that he was her own flesh and blood.

"Grandfather."

"Aye." Sarazan opened his arms to her, and she quickly closed the distance and gave him a hug.

She couldn't believe she'd freed the wizard, who all elves got along with, and who was her last living relative.

"I was surprised when Prince Zorak saved you from the blue elves. I must speak to them about such a matter. But then the winged elf stole you away." The green wizard chuckled.

"I wish to marry her," Viator quickly said, as if seeking permission now that she had a guardian of sorts.

"Is that what you wish, my princess?" Sarazan asked.

"Yes. We saved you together."

"And me," Balen said.

Reynaldo was quiet, though he offered a small smile and lifted the flask to say he helped too.

"All four of you, aye. And I thank you. It looks to me like I have an apprentice again," Sarazan said.

"Do you know anything about our prophecy?" Viator asked.

"Aye. That you would wed a half high elf, granddaughter of the ambassador to all elf kind. That's me. Your darkland elf parents are opposed to the notion, of course."

"What about the poisonous potion that I put in the air vent?" Reynaldo asked. "I thought you only made peace with other creatures."

"Ha! It's not poisonous to those creatures, but they now will believe all other creatures to be their allies. They will no longer take them hostage."

"Lars poisoned the river and some of his men threw Eloria off Sontrans Cliff," Viator said.

Sarazan waved his arm in a sweeping motion. "Aww, yes. I saw that as well. I will speak with him and his people. This won't happen again. But first, I must go with you to your castle, Prince Viator, and meet with the king and queen. Afterward, I will speak with my people to let them know I have returned, with your help, and that Eloria is indeed a high elf."

"What about me?" Reynaldo asked.

"You are my apprentice. You have lots of books to read up on for lost time."

Reynaldo only smiled at the notion, probably because anything was better than being a rat in the snow giants' castle.

"You knew Eloria would go into the cave with the spiders."

"I knew she could speak to all manner of creatures, even a high elf turned rat. I was certain she could convince the spider to give up his poison."

"For something in return," Eloria said. "He still wants something."

"What we all want, dear Eloria. To be understood. You will continue to be the spiders' liaison with others, when they need someone to speak for them."

They went outside and the wizard said, "I will meet you at the castle." And with a flick of his wrist, he was gone.

Eloria climbed onto Viator's back and he and Balen flew to their castle.

"He wasn't like anyone I ever expected to meet," Eloria said. "So much more real than my dreams of him."

"I like him. I suspect he'll have straightened my parents out before we even arrive home," Viator said.

"I like him too. Maybe he can straighten out my sister too."
Balen smiled.

When they finally arrived at the castle, they hadn't expected
any fanfare, but everyone cheered them when they landed in the
courtyard.

"Come," one of the guards said. "Everyone is waiting to feast
with you, Your Majesty."

Sure enough, when they walked into the great hall, the
wizard was smiling and speaking with the king and queen, the
courtiers all gathered for a feast.

Except this time, Eloria sat with Viator at the head table, and
so did the wizard. Balen was also among the dignitaries.

"You didn't say that Eloria was the granddaughter of the
green wizard," Viator's mother said, scolding him.

"Of course you can marry the girl," the king said.

Eloria smiled at Viator, and he kissed her. "When do we get
married?" she asked. "I want Persephonice, Dracolin, Helena,
and Balon to attend the wedding."

"And Prince Zorak," Viator said. "Because you are a high elf,
we will have to have his mother and father attend, along with
many other dignitaries."

"And Lars," Sarazan said, "so he knows just who you are,
Eloria."

Eloria was glad to have family here, when she thought she
would be a stranger in a strange new land. Her only concern was
that Persephonice's father would come back for her yet again,
only this time sending a force to search for her.

VIATOR COULDN'T BE MORE thrilled that he had taken Eloria
hostage, his wings nearly transparent, the only thing he didn't

understand, unless he was just supposed to help Eloria save the wizard. Balen had the same situation with his wings.

Then they saw the blue flame of the dragon Talom, shooting off in the night sky.

Viator remembered then that he and Balen hadn't tamed a dragon yet. Eloria left the table, without permission, to go to the window and peer out. Viator and Balen quickly followed her. They saw then three dragons headed their way, Talom in the lead.

When Talom landed on the wall walk, Eloria hurried out of the great hall to join him. The other two dragons landed on either side of him like they were his guards.

"The green wizard is back," Eloria said to Talom.

He bowed his head to her. "You have made it possible."

"And so did Viator and Balen, and the wizard's apprentice, Reynaldo."

"Which is why we have come to help the winged elves in their last quest. But there is no need to tame us," the one said. "We know you have helped the ice dragons in the northern reaches, and you've aided us with the killing of the opinicus. You will always be known as dragon keepers. Any dragon is yours to call whenever you need a lift or aid."

Eloria looked back at the castle and saw the green wizard standing at the window of the great hall, smiling, his white beard and hair and green silken garments flowing in the breeze.

"Can we take a ride tonight?" Viator asked.

Talom bowed his head.

Viator helped Eloria onto Talom's back because he knew the dragon would always protect her, then he and Balen climbed onto the other dragons, Lynx and Zoran.

Everyone cheered them as the three of them took flight, the last quest the winged elves needed, and Viator couldn't have been any more thrilled as they swooped down over the ocean where a merman called out to them.

"I am Eloria!" Eloria called out to him. "And I am home."

Then they saw the blue elves running along the beach, shaking their spears.

Viator wondered if the green wizard could ever convince the blue elves to be more peaceful with the other elves. But tonight, it didn't matter. All that mattered was that he was taking his first ride on a dragon he had "tamed," and the woman he loved was with him on the ride.

They swooped down over the shadow elf village where they were having a celebration of their own, and the dragons landed in the midst of all the revelry.

"We are getting married and you are all invited," Eloria said to her friend and the others who had aided them.

And then they partied with the shadow elves, telling of all their adventures. But when they were through, Persephonice and Dracolin and Balon told of all their missions.

"We will help you whenever we can," Viator said, though he shouldn't have spoken for Eloria and Balen too.

But both of them agreed. What would life be without a little adventure?

ALSO BY TERRY SPEAR

Heart of the Cougar Series:

Cougar's Mate, Book 1

Call of the Cougar, Book 2

Taming the Wild Cougar, Book 3

Covert Cougar Christmas (Novella)

Double Cougar Trouble, Book 4

Cougar Undercover, Book 5

Cougar Magic, Book 6

Cougar Halloween Mischief (Novella)

Falling for the Cougar, Book 7

Catch the Cougar (A Halloween Novella)

Cougar Christmas Calamity Book 8

You Had Me at Cougar, Book 9

Saving the White Cougar, Book 10

Heart of the Bear Series

Loving the White Bear, Book 1

Claiming the White Bear, Book 2

The Highlanders Series: Winning the Highlander's Heart, The Accidental Highland Hero, Highland Rake, Taming the Wild

Highlander, The Highlander, Her Highland Hero, The Viking's Highland Lass, His Wild Highland Lass (novella), Vexing the Highlander (novella), My Highlander

Other historical romances: Lady Caroline & the Egotistical Earl, A Ghost of a Chance at Love

Heart of the Wolf Series: Heart of the Wolf, Destiny of the Wolf, To Tempt the Wolf, Legend of the White Wolf, Seduced by the Wolf, Wolf Fever, Heart of the Highland Wolf, Dreaming of the Wolf, A SEAL in Wolf's Clothing, A Howl for a Highlander, A Highland Werewolf Wedding, A SEAL Wolf Christmas, Silence of the Wolf, Hero of a Highland Wolf, A Highland Wolf Christmas, A SEAL Wolf Hunting; A Silver Wolf Christmas, A SEAL Wolf in Too Deep, Alpha Wolf Need Not Apply, Billionaire in Wolf's Clothing, Between a Rock and a Hard Place, SEAL Wolf Undercover, Dreaming of a White Wolf Christmas, Flight of the White Wolf, All's Fair in Love and Wolf, A Billionaire Wolf for Christmas, SEAL Wolf Surrender (2019), Silver Town Wolf: Home for the Holidays (2019), Wolff Brothers: You Had Me at Wolf, Night of the Billionaire Wolf, Joy to the Wolves (Red Wolf), The Wolf Wore Plaid, Jingle Bell Wolf, Best of Both Wolves

SEAL Wolves: To Tempt the Wolf, A SEAL in Wolf's Clothing, A SEAL Wolf Christmas, A SEAL Wolf Hunting, A SEAL Wolf in Too Deep, SEAL Wolf Undercover, SEAL Wolf Surrender (2019)

Silver Bros Wolves: Destiny of the Wolf, Wolf Fever, Dreaming of the Wolf, Silence of the Wolf, A Silver Wolf Christmas, Alpha Wolf Need Not Apply, Between a Rock and a Hard Place, All's Fair in Love and Wolf, Silver Town Wolf: Home for the Holidays (2019)

Wolff Brothers of Silver Town

Billionaire Wolves: Billionaire in Wolf's Clothing, A Billionaire Wolf for Christmas, Night of the Billionaire Wolf

Highland Wolves: Heart of the Highland Wolf, A Howl for a

Highlander, A Highland Werewolf Wedding, Hero of a Highland Wolf, A Highland Wolf Christmas, Wolf Wore Plaid

Red Wolf Series: Seduced by the Wolf, Joy to the Wolves

~

Heart of the Jaguar Series: Savage Hunger, Jaguar Fever, Jaguar Hunt, Jaguar Pride, A Very Jaguar Christmas, You Had Me at Jaguar (2019)

Novella: The Witch and the Jaguar (2018)

~

Romantic Suspense: Deadly Fortunes, In the Dead of the Night, Relative Danger, Bound by Danger

~

Vampire romances: Killing the Bloodlust, Deadly Liaisons, Huntress for Hire, Forbidden Love, Vampire Redemption, Primal Desire

Vampire Novellas: Vampiric Calling, The Siren's Lure, Seducing the Huntress

~

Other Romance: Exchanging Grooms, Marriage, Las Vegas Style

~

Science Fiction Romance: Galaxy Warrior

Teen/Young Adult/Fantasy Books

The World of Fae:

The Dark Fae, Book 1

The Deadly Fae, Book 2

The Winged Fae, Book 3

The Ancient Fae, Book 4

Dragon Fae, Book 5

Hawk Fae, Book 6

Phantom Fae, Book 7

Golden Fae, Book 8

Falcon Fae, Book 9

Woodland Fae, Book 10

Angel Fae, Book 11 (TBD)

The World of Elf:
The Shadow Elf
Darkland Elf

Blood Moon Series:
Kiss of the Vampire
The Vampire...In My Dreams
Demon Guardian Series:
The Trouble with Demons
Demon Trouble, Too
Demon Hunter

Non-Series for Now:
Ghostly Liaisons
The Beast Within
Courtly Masquerade
Deidre's Secret

The Magic of Inherian:

The Scepter of Salvation

The Mage of Monrovia

Emerald Isle of Mists (TBA)

ACKNOWLEDGMENTS

Thanks so much to both Darla Taylor and Donna Fournier who were so kind to beta read the book for me and help to catch my bloopers!!!

AFTERWORD

To My Readers

I hope you love The World of Elves as much as I had fun writing about them. This comes from my love of mythology and space travel and the paranormal. Enjoy!!

ABOUT THE AUTHOR

Bestselling and award-winning author Terry Spear has written over eighty paranormal romance novels and four medieval Highland historical romances. Her first werewolf romance, *Heart of the Wolf*, was named a 2008 *Publishers Weekly*'s Best Book of the Year, and her subsequent titles have garnered high praise and hit the *USA Today* bestseller list. A retired officer of the U.S. Army Reserves, Terry lives in Spring, Texas, where she is working on her next wolf, jaguar, cougar, and bear shifter romances, continuing with her Highland medieval romances, and having fun with her young adult novels. When she's not writing, she's photographing everything that catches her eye, making teddy bears, and playing with her Havanese puppies and grand-baby. For more information, please visit www.terryspear.com, or follow her on Twitter, @TerrySpear. She is also on Facebook at http://www.facebook.com/terry.spear. And on Wordpress at: Terry Spear's Shifters http://terryspear.wordpress.com/